The music faded away and Jace twirled Vivian one more time...

Then he stepped in and caught her, dipping her slightly. When he set her back on her feet, she was laughing breathlessly, her mouth open. She looked at him and his own breath caught as every part of him said *this*. This was what he wanted. Vivian in his arms, smiling up at him. Vivian having fun with him.

Her eyes met his and her smile faded, replaced by a more serious gaze. She wanted to kiss him, he could tell, and no way could he resist because he wanted it, too. So he held her gaze and brushed his lips over hers.

Her arms were on his shoulders from the dance, which was pretty nice, but nothing compared to the feeling of her sliding them around his neck, going up on her tiptoes and kissing him back...

Dear Reader,

After the Rodeo just poured right out of my heart. Jace, a former bull rider, and Vivian, a wildlife biologist, are both realizing that life won't cooperate with their plans. But they discover friendship, love, community and new dreams. I hope you enjoy their journey to happily-ever-after!

Writing the Heroes of Shelter Creek series is such a joy, in part because I get to write about my beloved heartland, the northern California coast. It was fun to include California's native elk, the tule elk, in this book. My favorite encounter with them was a couple decades ago. My friend and I were riding our bicycles down a steep hill when a group of elk started to run alongside us. They stayed just yards away from us, leaping and galloping, for a very long time. I cherish that magical memory!

In this story I get to explore another thing I care deeply about—chronic illness. I hope this story reminds us that even in difficult circumstances we can find new possibilities for ourselves, and more compassion for each other.

Thank you for reading *After the Rodeo*. Please look for me on social media or at clairemcewen.com. I always love hearing from readers!

Claire McEwen

HEARTWARMING

After the Rodeo

———

Claire McEwen

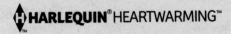

H HARLEQUIN® HEARTWARMING™

Recycling programs
for this product may
not exist in your area.

ISBN-13: 978-1-335-51081-5

After the Rodeo

HARLEQUIN®
www.Harlequin.com

Printed in U.S.A.

Claire McEwen writes stories about strong heroes and heroines who take big emotional journeys to find their happily-ever-afters. She lives by the ocean in Northern California with her family and a scruffy, mischievous terrier. When she's not writing, Claire enjoys gardening, reading and discovering flea-market treasures. She loves to hear from readers! You can find her on most social media and at clairemcewen.com.

Books by Claire McEwen

Harlequin Heartwarming

Heroes of Shelter Creek

Reunited with the Cowboy

Visit the Author Profile page
at Harlequin.com for more titles.

For Sally, who faced down a charging tule elk while I cowered in the bushes. It's been two decades since you scolded it into leaving us alone ("Bad elk! Go away!") and I'm still laughing.

And for Beth and Steve, who invited me to the Russian River Rodeo. That one fun day inspired many stories, including this one!

Acknowledgments

I owe a huge debt of gratitude to the Marin Agricultural Land Trust, the Lupus Foundation of America, the Point Reyes National Seashore, the California Department of Fish and Wildlife, the Center for Biological Diversity and the wonderful organization Wildcare in San Rafael, California. All mistakes and embellishments are my own.

No book is ever written alone. My brilliant editor, Adrienne Macintosh, helped me find the most important story in all of my ideas and tangents. My wonderful husband, Arik, helped me find time to write when time was scarce. I am so grateful to both of you for believing in my stories.

CHAPTER ONE

JACE HENDRICKS STOOD on the porch of his run-down farmhouse on his run-down ranch and listened to the social worker give him the run-down on everything he was doing wrong.

"Kids this age, and in this situation, need predictability," she was saying. *She* was Mrs. Roxanne Sherman, an older woman with stick-straight gray hair and dressed in a gray business suit, as if she was trying to blend in with the fog that had rolled in from the Pacific this morning.

Mrs. Sherman had been assigned to his case when Jace first brought his sister's scared, sad kids to his Northern California hometown of Shelter Creek to live with him. And she'd been on his case ever since. "Children need a schedule they can count on and a *parent* they can count on," she reminded him. "Someone steady and reliable."

That was pretty unfortunate, seeing as the kids' mom, Jace's sister, Brenda, and her boyfriend, Neil, had each been sentenced to almost twenty years in prison for various felonies.

Then it hit Jace like a dash of cold water. Mrs. Sherman was talking about him. *He* was the parent. *He* was the one who had to be steady and reliable. And if she thought those two words described him, she wouldn't be delivering this lecture.

"Right," Jace said carefully, because it seemed like she expected him to say something. "I am trying to be that kind of person."

He looked out at the kids, who he'd told to go play in the front yard. Though *yard* was an aspirational term. Right now it was just the raggedy stubble of weeds he'd mown, a few pieces of rusted-out farm equipment and the chopped-up trunk of a rotten oak he'd taken down yesterday.

Eight-year-old Amy, her red curls blowing in a wild halo around her head, was balancing on the stump of the oak. Six-year-old Alex, always so quiet and withdrawn, was perched on the seat of an ancient plow, reading a book. And Carly, fifteen and impossible to figure out, was leaning on the fence by the road, talking on the cell phone she'd conned Jace into buying her when she first arrived at the ranch back in June.

Who the teen was talking to, Jace had no idea. School had only started a month ago and the kids were new to Shelter Creek, but Carly's phone was already buzzing constantly with incoming texts and calls.

"Jace," Mrs. Sherman said sharply, sensing, perhaps, that his mind was drifting. "You have to take this seriously. These kids need a more child-friendly atmosphere than this."

That was one of Mrs. Sherman's favorite themes. And Jace got it. This ranch wasn't exactly kid friendly yet. But he wished she would cut him just a little slack. He'd bought the property just three months ago. It might need a lot of work, but it was the only ranch around here he could afford.

After over a decade on the road chasing rodeo glory, Jace hadn't owned a home of his own when he'd taken the call from Social Services, informing him that his sister was in jail and her three kids were headed for foster care.

Jace had been in a hotel room outside of San Antonio that night, celebrating his victory at the rodeo there with a bottle of bourbon and a blonde gal named Lovey. But once he'd put the phone down, he'd no longer been in the mood to celebrate. He had felt all of his dreams, dreams that had finally come together, sliding out of his grasp. Taking everything familiar right along with them.

He'd spent a long time making a living as a fairly good bull rider, knocking around the circuit for years. But then, somehow, just about a year ago, he'd started winning. And winning some more. After a decade of living out of his truck and paying his dues, somehow Jace's time had come. There wasn't a bull out there that he couldn't wring a ride from. He was a rising star, on the winning streak he'd almost given up hoping for.

And then one phone call changed everything. Jace couldn't let his nieces and nephew be raised by strangers. He wasn't going to let them endure any more uncertainty or abuse. They deserved a good childhood, not one that they merely tried to survive. Not a childhood like he and Brenda had endured. And not foster care, where, the social worker on the phone had warned him, the kids would probably be split up because the system was bursting at the seams and no one wanted to take in three older children.

Who knew where they'd have ended up? He might be the most unqualified parent on the planet, but he'd never hurt the kids. The memories of his own father's rage were etched too deep for that.

Plus he owed it to them. He owed it to Brenda. He'd known for a while that she was struggling. He'd known she had a problem with drugs. He should have checked on her and the kids more often. Should have tried to get her to rehab again. But he'd had his own goals to pursue, and maybe he'd been attracted to those rodeo lights and the thrill of riding those bulls as a way to deal with his demons, just like Brenda had been driven to drugs.

So right there, over the phone from San Antonio, Jace had agreed to take the kids. He'd tossed the bourbon in the trash, sent Lovey on her way, and called his agent and said goodbye to everything he'd worked so hard for. When dawn hit with its dim promise, Jace had been on the road to Los Angeles to get the kids. Each mile under his truck's wheels had pulled him further from everything he'd ever wanted and toward a life that was nothing but questions. Where to live? What to do for money? And how the hell was he going to raise a bunch of kids?

Jace barely caught Mrs. Sherman's next words. Something about clearing out the logs and setting up a play structure for Amy and Alex.

"Okay," he assured her. "I'll look into it." Gulping in a breath of misty air, Jace tried to cool the worry pressing hot on his chest. He didn't have the money to buy some fancy play structure right now. Most of his funds had gone to purchasing this ranch and fencing off some of the best grazing land on the property. The last of his money was set aside for the cattle he'd buy soon. The start of his herd.

Maybe he could nail some of this old junk together to make a structure, though he doubted that's what the social worker had in mind.

He turned to face Mrs. Sherman, wishing she'd go, because no matter what he did it wouldn't be adequate in her eyes. She'd wanted Jace to buy a house in town. Raise the kids in a safe, controlled setting. But walking away from rodeo had already felt a little like dying. If Jace moved to town, he might as well be buried, too. No way was he going to survive in some nine-to-five job, if he even qualified for one.

At least a ranch was something he could get excited about. He was planning to raise beef cattle for now, but maybe eventually he'd raise his own line of bucking bulls, so when the kids were older he could be a part of the rodeo again.

And even if Mrs. Sherman couldn't see it, growing up on this land would be good for the kids. On a ranch he could be around for them. He could provide them a healthy life with a lot of time out of doors. In fact, maybe once Mrs. Sherman left today, he'd take the kids down to the barn. He'd managed to find a couple docile horses—just older trail horses that had come cheap—and he was determined to get the kids riding. They all seemed happier around the horses.

Jace wanted to make them happy. He wanted to be happy, too. But most days they were all just getting by.

"It's not just a play area," Mrs. Sherman said. "This ranch isn't safe for kids. All of this old, rusty farm equipment should be disposed of, and the barbed wire fences lying on the ground have to be replaced or removed. Your porch is falling down. It has to be repaired, along with any outbuildings or structures that the children might get into."

What she was asking for was huge. The acres closest to the house were basically a junkyard of the previous owners' abandoned belongings. And just about every building on the property was falling apart. That's why this land had come so cheap.

He tried to explain. "All that is cosmetic. I need to focus on getting the barns and pastures ready so I can get cattle in here. Then I can start earning some income."

"These are safety issues." Mrs. Sherman's crossed arms and pursed lips allowed no argument. "Plus, cleaning up the property will increase the children's sense of order. It will improve their self-esteem and their feelings of security."

Jace bit back the words he wanted to say. That their sense of security would probably improve if he could earn an income. But he couldn't start an argument. He needed Mrs. Sherman on his side. He forced the frustration out of his voice. "I understand. But cleanup will take money. And I need the rest of my savings to get my herd started."

"You can always get a job." Mrs. Sherman's voice dripped with deceptive sweetness. Sugar on a toothache.

Even though she drove out to check on Jace from Santa Rosa, a city surrounded by ranches and vineyards, somehow Mrs. Sherman didn't think agriculture counted as real work. Jace was tempted to ask her if she knew where her food came from, but figured it wouldn't help their relationship much.

"Ranching will be my job." Jace forced his voice to stay calm. "I know you don't see it, but this property is starting to come together." He pointed west, toward the hills rolling parched and brown out toward the Pacific coast. "There's a valley just past that hill. Folks call it Long Valley and it's a part of my ranch. I finished repairing the fences there last week. That means I can bring my first cattle in. They'll graze there while I get everything else up and running. I'm on my way to making this ranch profitable. I hope you can be patient."

For a moment, something like regret shadowed Mrs. Sherman's impermeable expression. "I don't make the rules, Jace. You've said you want to legally adopt the kids. To do that, you need to show you can support them, long-term. I have to be able to write something on the forms where it asks for your income."

"Right." Jace forced the air past the tightness in his lungs. "And I *will* have income. Soon."

"*And* everything cleaned up and kid friendly."

"Yes," Jace managed. "That, too."

"I know you'll figure it out, if you want to create a comfortable home for the kids." Maybe Mrs. Sherman meant to be reassuring, but it sounded a lot like a threat.

"Just give me a little time." Jace pulled off his hat and ran a hand through his hair. Suddenly the damp morning felt sticky. His stomach seethed like he'd swallowed a rattler.

He'd been on the road for years, been his own man, accountable to no one but himself. Now he was being micromanaged by Social Services.

For about the millionth time in the past several months, he cursed his sister and her addictions and her drug-dealing boyfriend and her neglect of these poor kids. But that took him nowhere but down, so he tried to do what he did before a ride on a bull—pull in a deep breath and center himself for whatever came next.

Though sometimes Mrs. Sherman seemed more dangerous than the toughest bull. It wasn't just *his* life and *his* well-being at stake anymore.

"I'll do my best to implement all of your ideas." He had to push the words out through the cracks in his pride.

"That's good." Strange how she could keep her voice so brisk and to the point when he felt like he was being turned inside out. "Now. There's still something else we have to discuss. That citation a couple weeks ago."

And there it was. The thing Jace had been hoping she'd overlook. But of course she wouldn't. And she probably shouldn't, because even Jace could see that a guy who got arrested in a barroom brawl might not be the best foster dad.

"Yeah," he said slowly. "About that."

"The sheriff sent me a report. He said he had to detain you."

"Yes, ma'am." Jace's boyhood manners,

pounded into him by his dad's fists, emerged at times like this.

"You were drunk and disorderly."

"Well, more disorderly than drunk, actually." He'd been a few sips into his first beer when his best buddy, Caleb, heart all broken up over his girlfriend, had started a fight down at the bar. "I was defending a friend."

"A fight is a fight." Mrs. Sherman sighed, a breathy, long-suffering sound. "It's not your first arrest for this type of thing. When you agreed to take the children, the social worker in Los Angeles chose to overlook your history of…" she paused, as if she couldn't bring herself to say the words "…bar fights. Because you assured her that you didn't engage in that type of behavior anymore."

And Jace had meant it. As of that moment, he'd made a promise—no more drinking or late nights in bars. No more buckle bunnies like Lovey. "I don't fight, as a rule," Jace assured her. "My buddy, he'd had his heart broken. And he kind of lost it. He's a veteran and has a bit of a temper. I was trying to break up the fight, but then some other guys jumped in and it got out of hand."

"I see." The social worker nodded, but her

pinched expression made it clear that she didn't. "And this friend of yours, the veteran with the temper, he has access to the children?"

Access? Where was she going with this?

Jace had a sudden image of Caleb trying to coax Alex up onto his big gentle horse, Newt. His buddy was sweet with the kids, something Jace wouldn't have guessed from a tough, ornery ex-marine.

"He's a good guy." Jace tried to make his voice sound confident. Dad-like. "I've known him since we were both younger than Alex. He doesn't show his temper around the kids. In fact, he's helped me out with them a couple times."

At Mrs. Sherman's sharp look, Jace rushed to reassure her. "Not with babysitting. I don't leave them with him—or with anyone, actually, yet. But he let me bring the kids by his ranch to ride his horse before we got horses of our own. And since he got back together with Maya—she's his fiancée now—he doesn't really have much of a temper at all."

"You can't make excuses when you have children, Jace. You just have to do the right thing."

"Yes, ma'am."

"I could remove the children for this."

Jace's heart stopped beating. Just froze solid in his chest with an icy kind of pain.

"But I won't," Mrs. Sherman went on, as if she hadn't just about killed him with her previous words. "I am going to give you a warning instead. No more bars or fighting. No more sticking up for your buddies. If you want to be a father, act like one."

Jace nodded, his heart starting to beat again, relief making him mute. He knew he could do better. He had to. No way was he going to let his nieces and nephew go live with strangers. What if they ended up with someone abusive? He'd never forgive himself. He might not have a clue what to do with Amy, Alex and Carly, but he was family. And he was trying.

"I think we understand each other," Mrs. Sherman said. "Let's give this all six weeks. That should be plenty of time for you to make repairs and start earning a profit from those cattle you keep telling me about. Then we can revisit this discussion." She delivered her verdict in the same false-friendly tone she used for everything. Like it was no big deal. Like she hadn't just boxed him into an impossible corner.

"Six weeks." The words were heavy on his tongue. "That's not enough time."

"I think it should be plenty."

Mrs. Sherman *didn't* think. That was her problem. She just demanded, with no understanding of reality. Jace couldn't afford to hire help, which meant he'd have to do the repairs she wanted all on his own. And cattle didn't just magically multiply. There was this thing called breeding. Gestation. He opened his mouth to explain, but the social worker flashed him a brittle smile and shifted her big handbag on her shoulder.

"Now, I've got to get going. You have my card. Call me if you need anything. And make sure you keep out of trouble."

Mrs. Sherman waved to the kids as she headed toward her bland white government-issue sedan.

Jace watched her as she backed out of the driveway. The morning fog usually felt refreshing, but right now the air felt thick, like it was pushing in on him, trapping him. It got a little lighter as the social worker started down the lane toward the main road, though.

Once she was out of sight, maybe he'd be able to breathe again. But just as the road started to curve around the first sharp corner, she stopped. Reversed. And leaned on her horn.

What the...? Was there an elk in the drive? The local tule elk seemed to have a special love of this property, wandering through at all hours of the day and night. But most people would just sit back and enjoy the sight of them. Not lean on their horn to scare them.

Of course, Mrs. Sherman had already made it clear she didn't have much appreciation of this type of landscape or this type of lifestyle. So maybe elk didn't do much for her, either.

The little kids had climbed up on the rusted frame of an old tractor and were craning their necks to see what was up. Jace went to join them.

"What's going on?" Carly was interested enough to put her phone in her pocket.

"I'm not sure." Jace squinted. "Elk maybe?"

As they watched, the social worker reversed farther up the driveway.

"Do you think she's scared of them?" Amy asked. "Even Alex isn't that scared of them."

Alex glared at her from behind his dusty glasses.

"Amy, not cool," Carly said. She might be a grumpy teenager but she was good with her siblings and protected Alex most of all. He'd had the hardest time with all the changes and seemed to miss his mom more than the other two did.

Jace automatically reached for Alex's glasses, cleaned them off and set them back on the little boy's nose. "There you go, buddy. Now you can see all the action."

Alex regarded him solemnly and Jace wished, as he did every day, for a smile. For some excitement. Hell, he'd even take misbehavior. Anything but the fear and worry that seemed to have taken up permanent residence inside Alex's heart. Though maybe it wasn't fear. Jace had no way of knowing because Alex almost never spoke.

The social worker honked again and Jace sighed. "I'd better go find out what's wrong with Mrs. Sherman. Will you three stay here? Carly, will you watch them?"

When his oldest niece nodded, Jace jogged across the field, jumped over the downed wire at the end of it, crossed a weed-filled drainage ditch and came out on the lane behind Mrs. Sherman's car. And then he stopped.

A group of people were coming around the corner of his driveway, carrying signs. Jace read *I speak for the animals! Save the Elk!* and *Wildlife Matters!*

The meaning slowly sank in. Protesters. Almost two dozen of them. But what were they doing *here*?

Jace recognized Bunny Chadwick, local octogenarian firecracker, who constantly wrote letters to the editor of the *Shelter Creek Sentinel* when Jace was in high school. And there was Ed Portman who'd run the Boy Scout troop and made them go on grueling ten-mile hikes during the one year Jace had tried scouting. And Mrs. Sutcliffe, Jace's seventh grade teacher. Was activism the newest hobby for Shelter Creek retirees?

When Bunny spotted Jace, she raised her hand high in the air. It must have been some kind of cue because the entire group halted. And then they broke into an enthusiastic rendition of the old protest song, "We Shall Overcome."

Jace's boots seemed to grow roots.

Mrs. Sherman stepped out of her car and glared at Jace across the sedan roof, her penciled eyebrows touching her hairline.

His heart iced over again. Whatever this situation was, it wasn't going to help his case with the social worker. Not one bit.

The song ended on a wavering note and the group broke into cheers. Like they were proud of themselves.

How could they be happy when they were probably ruining Jace's chances of keeping his family together?

Of course, they couldn't know that. It was just more of his bad luck that they'd showed up here while Mrs. Sherman was on one of her visits.

And what was all this about elk and habitats anyway? When animals crossed his property, he just let them be.

Bunny stepped forward, a big manila envelope in her hand. "Jace Hendricks," she yelled out as she crossed the distance between them. "We, the members of Habitat Heroes, have been trying to reach you."

Jace somehow got his legs moving again and took a few steps to meet her. "You have?"

"We have." She shook a finger at him. "You should be more organized, young man."

Young. Ha. He was past thirty and had been feeling about ninety lately.

"You've got no phone line on this ranch and no one around town knows your cell phone number. What if there was a wildfire? How would anyone reach you to give you a warning?"

Fires were a real danger around here, but Jace had never thought about giving his phone number to anyone aside from Caleb. He glanced at Mrs. Sherman, stomach clenching when he saw that her lips were pressed into a thin line. She probably hadn't thought about that, either, but thanks to Bunny she sure was thinking about it now.

"We sent you three different letters in the mail. Did you even get them? Did you even open them?"

Guilt tugged on Jace's conscience. Come to think of it, there had been some mail, but he'd been letting it pile up. He was too tired by the time he got the squabbling kids into bed to do more than crack a beer and drink it slumped in a chair on the rickety porch before falling asleep himself.

Everyone seemed to be waiting for him to say something. He glanced at Mrs. Sherman again. She looked more disappointed in him than ever. "I didn't see the letters. No."

Mrs. Sherman reached for her phone and started typing something on it. Probably a note, to remind herself to take the kids away from Jace as soon as possible.

Bunny nodded sagely. "I suspected as much. Well, in this envelope I have a petition. We've collected over a hundred signatures, which is about a tenth of the population of Shelter Creek."

"Signatures? What for?"

"Because you built a fence right across prime tule elk habitat. Your land, Long Valley, is a big part of their range and now they can't access it."

"Save the elk!" Someone shouted from the crowd.

"Save the elk! Save the elk!" Others took up the chant.

Bunny turned around and beamed at her disciples and then handed the envelope to Jace. "Here you go. A photocopy of our petition. We'll be presenting it at the town council meeting Wednesday evening. That's the day after tomorrow. I suspect you'll want to be there."

And with that, she spun on her heel and rejoined her gang of protesters. They turned away, Mrs. Sutcliffe waving and smiling at Jace like she hadn't just destroyed his hopes.

Jace watched them march off down his driveway, Ed leading them in a rousing chant. *What do we want? Habitat! When do we want it? Now!* The chant faded as the group made their way down the lane to where their cars were probably parked along the main road.

As the usual country quiet settled back in, Jace glanced at the kids, still standing on top of the old tractor. Safe. At least, for now.

Mrs. Sherman cleared her throat. "You don't check your mail?"

"Not often enough, clearly." The words were dry as dust in Jace's mouth.

"Well…" Her voice was careful, brittle, like it might just fragment from her complete disillusionment. "Why don't you start?" With one last disappointed glance, she got in her sedan and drove away.

CHAPTER TWO

VIVIAN REED TURNED around in her front-row seat in the Shelter Creek town hall and swallowed hard. The place was packed. There had to be at least seventy people in the historic clapboard hall. It had probably been built before there were this many people even living in Shelter Creek.

The air pressed close. Everyone was seated elbow to elbow in their metal folding chairs, except for a group of older folks standing in the back. They were waving signs that said We Speak for the Elk and chatting among themselves while they waited for the meeting to start.

Rubbing the ache that had settled in her neck, Vivian faced the front again. This was going to be a strange night. She was here representing the Shelter Creek Wildlife Center, but it was only her second day on the job. And only her third day living in the small Northern California town of Shelter Creek.

Vivian's boss, Maya Burton, should be here with her, but she'd had to leave town to trap and collar a mountain lion up in Mendocino County. So, at Maya's request, Vivian had come to this meeting to help resolve a conflict between a rancher named—Vivian glanced down at her notes—Jace Hendricks, and a bunch of locals who felt he was harming local tule elk.

Vivian had never heard of tule elk until yesterday. She tried to recall the facts she'd looked up. *Tule elk. A subspecies of elk found only in California. Preferred diet is grass. Calves born with spotted coats.* That was all she could remember. She'd been so tired when she was researching last night, she'd drifted off right at her computer. And now she was unprepared. She hated feeling unprepared. Wasn't used to it. She'd worked for the same field office in New Hampshire for years, doing the same kind of work, with the same people.

Unfortunately, one of those people had also been Colin, her fiancé, which was one of the reasons Vivian had moved three thousand miles away to work at the wildlife center here.

But she wasn't going to think of Colin. Not tonight when she needed all the self-confidence she could muster. Tonight was not the time to remember that spring morning when she'd stood on the steps of the church with all of their wedding guests inside. With everyone there…except the groom.

He'd sent a note with a friend, apologizing for not ending things earlier. Saying that he couldn't attach himself to someone with her kind of health issues.

It still hurt, in a dull, achy, down-to-the-bones way. Or maybe that was the lupus. It was kind of hard to know sometimes.

Vivian pushed her fist into her thigh, the pressure bringing her back to the present. Colin was in the past. Something to learn from and let go of. She had new goals now, thanks to him. She'd moved out here to California to become strong and independent. To toughen up, so she could fight this illness that threatened to steal so much from her. And to make sure she'd never feel as weak and lost as she'd felt standing outside the church that day.

She glanced around at the hall full of

strangers. Maybe she could look at this meeting as a good opportunity to practice those qualities. It should be pretty simple. Maya had suggested that Vivian offer to study the elk situation. Easing conflict between ranchers and wildlife was one of the main purposes of the brand-new Shelter Creek Wildlife Center.

It had sounded pretty simple in the comfort of their office, which was really a trailer on the construction site of the barely begun wildlife center. But now, scanning the crowd, including the protesters waving signs, Vivian wanted to sneak out a side door.

Buck up, she admonished her cowardly self. *You preserved hardwood forests in Vermont. You defused conflicts over wetlands in New Hampshire. You can handle some elk protesters out here in California.*

But listening to the noises in the hall around her, the hum of conversation, punctuated by the occasional save-the-elk chant from the folks in the back, Vivian wished she'd prepared herself a little more. She hadn't thought enough about what this move to California would really be like. She certainly hadn't expected to be thrown into a town conflict her second day on the job.

She'd just been so desperate to get away, to put the entire continent between herself and Colin's rejection. And put that same vast distance between herself and her mother.

Ever since Vivian's diagnosis eight months ago, Mom had taken to coming up to New Hampshire from New York City every weekend. She'd arrive on Vivian's doorstep, her face twisted into an expression of dread, as if she expected to find her daughter dead every time. Vivian had tried to explain to her mom, over and over, that lupus wasn't a terminal illness. But no matter what Vivian said, or how many websites she directed her mom to look at, Tori Reed just could not accept that her daughter didn't need her constant help.

Vivian couldn't live with her mom's tear-filled eyes and overly solicitous care every single weekend. It made her feel like she really was about to die.

So when Colin had ended their relationship and Mom had started talking about a permanent move to New Hampshire, Vivian began looking for a way out. She'd seen the ad online for this job and sent her résumé on pure impulse. She'd had no idea where Shelter Creek, California, even was.

It turned out to be a tiny town out in the sun-browned coastal hills of Northern California, a few hours' drive north of San Francisco. At this time of year, early fall, it was foggy in the mornings, hot in the afternoons and so dry by evening that even the air felt baked and brittle. It was beautiful, but its beauty was the exact opposite of what Vivian was used to. Instead of hardwood forests, sparse oaks stood in lonely relief on the hot, dry hills. Instead of the full, flowing waterways of New England, the creek that gave the town its name had almost completely dried up. Apparently it dried up every single year.

But the barren hills allowed for big empty skies, and all that space eased something in Vivian's heart that had been crunched up in an anxious ball ever since her diagnosis. As if the big sky had room to absorb even her greatest fears.

"You look lost in thought."

Vivian glanced up and saw that the woman next to her, an older woman wearing a Western-style dress shirt, was smiling at her. "You wouldn't be Vivian, would you?"

"Yes, I am." Vivian studied her, confused. "How do you know my name?"

"I'm Annie Brooks. I've got a ranch south of town. Maya told me to look out for you."

"Oh, is this Vivian?" Another woman peered around from where she sat on the other side of Annie. She had wavy white hair and a warm smile. "Hello. I'm Lillian. Maya's grandmother."

"So nice to meet you!" Vivian wondered if Maya had sent these ladies to make sure Vivian didn't mess things up too much. Then she noticed Lillian's T-shirt. It was bright blue, with the words Cougars for Cougars splashed across it in white print. She bit her lip to keep from laughing out loud. "I like your shirt."

Lillian's lined face broke into a proud smile. "Thank you. It's from this summer. Maya was just starting up her mountain lion advocacy work around here and the ladies in my book club felt she needed our support."

Vivian motioned toward the back of the room where the protesters were still congregating. "This town seems to have a lot of activists."

"Well, we have a lot of wildlife," Lillian said. "And we all care about the natural beauty around town. It brings in a lot of tourists and the town relies on the money they spend. But I don't always agree with Bunny Chadwick's tactics."

"Bunny Chadwick?"

"Bunny is the leader of that group back there. Habitat Heroes," Annie explained. "They're very confrontational. Lots of protesting and things."

"Oh." Vivian tried not to smile but it was funny to think that there were rival environmental groups in this tiny town, each similarly made up of older people. "And Annie, are you a part of Cougars for Cougars, too?"

"Well, I mainly enjoy reading the books, but I'll put my Cougars T-shirt on if need be."

"Cougars and books," Vivian mused. "I like it."

"You should come to our next book club meeting," Lillian told her. "Maya usually comes, and her friend Trisha has started attending, as well, so you won't be the only youngster. It's a week from today. At five. Here." She pulled out a small notepad and quickly scribbled down the information, including her address, and handed it to Vivian.

"The Book Biddies," Vivian read. "It's very kind of you to invite me. I'd love to come." She folded the paper carefully and tucked it into the outer pocket of her tote bag. She shifted uneasily in her seat. She might not go anywhere but back to New Hampshire if she couldn't make herself useful at this meeting tonight. "Can you tell me what you know about this conflict?"

"Jace Hendricks is a good man." Annie answered. "He's a rodeo cowboy, a former star bull rider, who just moved back here a few months ago."

A rodeo cowboy? Did they really still have those? Vivian had never given rodeo, or cowboys, much thought, but Annie made it sound totally normal.

"Jace is a nice young man, dealing with a tough situation," Lillian added.

Vivian suddenly remembered Lillian's connection to him. "And Jace is good friends with Maya's fiancé, right? Maya mentioned that to me."

Lillian's expression warmed with emotion. "Yes. Caleb, that's Maya's fiancé, has been friends with Jace since they were children."

The room quieted as the members of the town council made their way onto a raised platform in the front of the room and took their seats behind a long table. Vivian counted five council members—three women and two men. Most of them were middle-aged or

older, except for a younger woman seated at
the center of the table. She rapped her gavel,
calling the town council to order.

"That's Rhianna Lang, the mayor. She's
just a few years older than Maya," Annie
whispered. "But she's a tough cookie."

Rhianna ran a sardonic gaze over the
crowded hall. "Where are you all when we're
discussing exciting things like parking fees
or repairing the water mains?"

A low rumble of laughter went through the
crowd, defusing the tension a bit. Wow. She
was good.

"Okay, let's address the most popular
agenda item first. The council calls Bunny
Chadwick on behalf of Habitat Heroes." Rhianna looked toward the back of the room.
"Bunny, apparently you have a petition?"

"Yes." A small, sprightly woman in a bright
yellow tracksuit and pink sneakers marched
up the aisle. She tapped the microphone. "Is
this thing on?" Her voice was shrill and tense.

"Yes, Bunny, it's on." The weary tone of
the young man seated alongside the council,
a laptop open in front of him, made Vivian
think that Bunny's visits to the microphone
were probably fairly frequent.

"Okay then. As the mayor noted, Habitat Heroes has collected a long list of signatures." Bunny passed the envelope to the weary young man, who passed it over to Rhianna. "We are concerned that Jace Hendricks's purchase of North Sky Ranch poses a threat to one of our area's most vulnerable species, the tule elk." Bunny pulled out a page of notes and Vivian was sure she could hear a collective sigh in the room. Clearly this was a bad sign.

Unperturbed, Bunny set a pair of reading glasses on her nose and continued. "As I'm sure you know, by the 1870s elk had been hunted to near extinction in California. Their survival is entirely due to one rancher, Henry Miller, who lived down near Bakersfield. He found a small band of tule elk on his land and had the foresight to protect and preserve them."

"We love you Henry!" someone yelled, as if they were a groupie at a rock concert, and the room erupted in laughter.

Bunny put her hand in the air in a thumbs-up to acknowledge her supporters and continued. "In the 1970s, conservationists, including my late father, advocated for establishing new herds of elk around the state, including the famous herd at Point Reyes National Seashore. We are incredibly fortunate to have free ranging herds around Shelter Creek."

Annie stifled a yawn and grinned when she caught Vivian's eye. "Never did do well with lectures," she whispered with a wink.

Vivian pressed her lips together to hide her smile. She liked Annie and Lillian. She was going to their book club, no matter how tired she was that evening. Lupus wouldn't keep her from making friends in her new town.

Bunny was still speaking. "Many of our local elk obtain food and water from a portion of Jace's ranch called Long Valley. Jace recently built a fence around Long Valley, thus blocking the elks' access to this important segment of their habitat. So we, Habitat Heroes, started the petition you have before you, to make him take down that fence."

"I see." Rhianna pulled the pages out of the envelope and leafed through them briefly.

"And furthermore," Bunny continued, "after consultation with many other conservation associations, the Habitat Heroes believe that Jace should permanently preserve Long Valley as the important wildlife corridor that it is."

There was silence in the room, and even

cool Rhianna Lang seemed at a loss for words. Finally she spoke. "You're talking about a few hundred acres, right? Probably a significant portion of Jace's ranch?"

"Yes." Bunny nodded vigorously. "It's the right thing to do."

Rhianna scanned the crowd. "Jace, are you here tonight? Can you please come tell us how you feel about this?" She turned toward Bunny. "Thank you, Bunny. You may sit down now."

Bunny huffed a little, clearly not thrilled about relinquishing the microphone, but she rejoined her group at the back of the room. Vivian craned her neck to see what would happen next.

A tall man stepped out into the aisle, tipping his cowboy hat to Bunny as she went by. It was a gesture that managed to be respectful and totally insolent at the same time. Then he casually made his way toward the podium.

Born and raised on the East Coast, Vivian had never seen anyone quite like him. Big and broad shouldered, he was dressed exactly as one would expect a cowboy to dress when he was out in town, in dark jeans and dark brown cowboy boots. He had on a neatly pressed, tan button-up shirt with Western trim and a big silver buckle on his belt. On many people his clothing might look silly. But this man had a weathered quality to him, a tall, rangy confidence that made his outfit look just right.

When he reached the microphone and pulled his hat off, Vivian noticed that his hair was dark brown. She wished, suddenly, that she could see his eyes, but even with her front row seat, she'd have to make do with a view of his clean-shaven jaw, prominent cheekbones and a nose that even from here she could tell had been broken at some point.

Vivian reached into her tote bag for her notebook. She shouldn't be ogling cowboys, no matter how interesting they were. She should be taking notes about what each side wanted in this situation.

"Jace," Rhianna asked. "Were you aware of this petition?"

"Yes, ma'am." Jace glared at the group of protesters. "They were considerate enough to hand deliver it to me this past Monday." His full mouth pressed into a thin line, as if something tasted rotten.

Vivian scribbled *Monday, petition* in her notebook and wondered how, exactly, that had happened. Clearly just the memory of it made Jace furious.

"And did you recently fence off the portion of your ranch known as Long Valley?"

"I repaired the previously existing fence that had been knocked down at some point." The cowboy paused for a moment as if considering what to say next. "The former owner had that valley fenced off for a reason. It's the best acreage on the property."

"And you plan to use it for cattle." Rhianna was taking notes, too.

"I do."

"And were you aware that in the years that your property had been abandoned, Long Valley had become tule elk habitat?"

"Well, I've certainly spotted them around. But this land was a ranch for a long time. I assume the elk moved in pretty recently. And I don't see why they can't just move back out again."

"Okay." Rhianna shifted the papers in her hands and regarded Jace with pursed lips. "Is there anything else you'd like to say to the council tonight?"

"Just that I bought North Sky Ranch to be my place of business as well as a home for my family. So in response to Bunny's suggestion…" He turned and cast a sarcastic look toward the back of the hall. "Not all of us have the means to donate hundreds of acres to wildlife."

He faced the council again and his voice was firm. "I mean to turn North Sky back into the working cattle ranch it used to be. And I'm truly sorry if that disappoints some folks in this room or any of you running this town."

"Amen," whispered Annie, and when Vivian glanced her way, the older woman added, "Jace is something, isn't he?"

He sure was. Handsome and furious and another quality Vivian couldn't quite pinpoint. Sad, maybe? Resigned? She watched as Jace made his way back to his seat, slow and casual, like he was used to being in the public eye. Which he probably was, if he'd competed in rodeo.

It all felt a little surreal, being in a place with cowboys, rodeo and elk. Like Vivian had stepped into the pages of a Western novel.

"Is there a representative from the Shelter Creek Wildlife Center here tonight?" Rhianna asked. "And for those of you who aren't aware, the wildlife center is a new organization in our town that will work to educate the public about local wildlife and also help resolve human and wildlife conflicts such as this one."

Vivian froze. This was it. Her first real work at her brand-new job. But, unlike Jace, she wasn't used to being in the spotlight. She'd always worked alongside Colin, and he'd always insisted on doing any public speaking that came their way.

Her heart hammered against her chest, every beat a reminder of her various inadequacies. She didn't know the people in this room. She didn't know enough about the local plant and animal species, ranching or Shelter Creek. She'd never even seen an elk in person and she certainly hadn't thought of a way to fix this conflict.

"That's you," Annie whispered. "Go on up there!"

Lillian reached around Annie and patted Vivian's knee. "You've got this, honey."

Vivian glanced down at the tattoo she'd gotten the day after Colin dumped her. A songbird in flight and the words *Courage to fly* scripted on the inside of her right wrist where she could see it always. She sucked in whatever air her paralyzed lungs would allow and stood. "I'm from the wildlife center," she said in the loudest, firmest voice she could find. Which, unfortunately, due to her current lack of oxygen, wasn't much more than a squeak.

Her cheeks flamed and she straightened her spine. She could do this. She *had* to do this. Forcing her reluctant feet forward, she made it to the podium and leaned into the microphone. "How…" The word boomed out over the room, making her jump back in shock and the audience gasp.

Knees trembling, she moved farther away and tried again. "How can I help you? I'm Vivian Reed, wildlife biologist."

CHAPTER THREE

JACE LEANED FORWARD in his seat and tried to get a better look at the woman Maya had promised would find a solution to his current dilemma. He'd wanted Maya here. Strong, confident Maya, who would know exactly what to do about the elk. Maya, who would have the right words to put Bunny in her place.

But unfortunately for Jace, some mountain lion up north had decided to go after a couple of sheep. Maya had to track it down, and she'd had no idea how long she'd be gone.

Maya had called Jace and tried to reassure him. "Vivian is new, but she'll be great. I have total confidence in her," she'd said on the phone.

But watching Vivian blast the crowd with the microphone, Jace had no idea why Maya felt that way. He listened to the brand-new biologist fumble her words while his hopes sank to the floor below his uncomfortable metal seat. This mousy woman couldn't even speak clearly. She'd be no match for Bunny and her Habitat Heroes.

She didn't even look the part. Shouldn't people who spent their lives studying wild animals be a little more rugged? Tough? Maya sure was. But this woman, Vivian, was dressed in simple black pants and a beige sweater, her long brown hair falling loose down her back. As Jace watched, she pushed black-rimmed glasses up her nose and waited meekly for Rhianna to give her the go-ahead to continue.

Jace's disgust with this entire situation grew exponentially.

"I propose that the wildlife center do an assessment of Long Valley." Vivian's voice gained a little strength as she went on, affording Jace a shred of relief. But her next words took it away again. "We'll identify the various plant and wildlife species living there, and then determine if a mitigation plan is necessary to ensure the preservation of sensitive habitat."

"Mitigation? What does that even mean?" Jace whispered to Caleb. His buddy had come with him tonight for moral support. Also, as Maya's fiancé, Caleb had learned a few things about wildlife biology. But he also hated events like this. It was a sign of true friendship when someone as restless as Caleb agreed to sit in a meeting.

"It means that if they find sensitive habitat on your property, you'll have to make some changes to protect the wildlife there," Caleb murmured.

"You've got to be kidding me." Frustration propelled Jace up out of his seat, his chair sliding back with a shriek.

"Dude, sit down," Caleb commanded.

But anger obliterated Jace's manners. He had a social worker scrutinizing every move he made with the kids. Now he had some nerdy scientist making plans for his land. "It's *my* ranch," he yelled out. "I have the right to run cattle on my own ranch!"

Bunny turned toward him, glee in her eyes, relishing a battle. "You have a responsibility to protect local wildlife," she called out.

"Habitat!" shouted the Heroes clustered around her. "Habitat! Habitat!"

"Order!" Rhianna brought down her gavel, hushing the shouts.

Jace directed his remarks toward Rhianna and the council as he started down the aisle. "I'm not going to let some scientist tell me what to do on my own land."

Vivian the Mouse went even paler and took a step back from the microphone.

Good, let her worry. It was easy for her to insist on a study, she got a paycheck out of it. But for him, for the kids, it could ruin everything. He had six weeks to repair his ranch and pull his business together. He didn't have time for her study, or for *mitigation* or any of this. Jace stopped where the aisle ended and the dais holding the council members began.

Rhianna's voice was filled with an authority that was hard to deny. "Jace, please calm down and try to understand. Tourists come to our town to see the wildlife. Those tourists support our businesses and grow our economy. The town of Shelter Creek has a stake in making sure that wildlife is preserved."

Jace shoved his hands in his pockets and tried to breathe, tried not to lose it entirely in front of half the town. He walked to the microphone and the biologist retreated to her seat.

"Tourists aren't the only thing that benefit

the local economy," Jace reminded Rhianna and the council. "I'll purchase feed and supplies locally. Eventually I'll hire people to work on the ranch and they'll spend their income in Shelter Creek."

"We understand that, and appreciate it, but we also have an obligation to protect our natural resources." Rhianna drummed restless fingers on the table, as if she were irritated. Ready to move on to the next agenda item. But Jace's life, his nieces and nephew, and his livelihood were a lot more than just an agenda item.

"I'm just trying to make a living here." His voice came out louder and huskier than he'd like. "I'm trying to build a business and raise my kids." *My kids*. He hadn't thought of them as his before. The idea felt strange, like boots that didn't fit quite right.

"Amen," someone in the crowd shouted. "Let Jace run his cattle."

Jace glanced back in time to see Juan Alvaro take his seat again. He tipped his hat toward the older rancher in gratitude and Juan gave him a thumbs-up.

"It's a free country," a man in a baseball

cap, sitting next to Juan, called out. "He bought that old ranch fair and square."

"We speak for the elk!" Bunny raised her arms like a conductor as she called out, and the rest of her group joined in. "We speak for the elk! We speak for the elk!" The Habitat Heroes must have rehearsed, they were so in sync. And so darn loud.

"That's enough!" Rhianna hammered her gavel and fixed the crowd with a stern expression. "You all need to keep it civil. If you want to speak, fill out a card up here by the microphone and wait your turn. Anyone who doesn't follow protocol will have to leave the meeting."

Then her gaze honed in on Jace. "I know you want to get your ranch up and running. But Habitat Heroes is right about one thing. The land you purchased *has* been abandoned for many years and wildlife *has* moved in. In light of that, I think we have an obligation to do this assessment."

Jace liked wildlife as much as the next person. He'd seen the elk roaming his land, and thought they were pretty. But the image of Mrs. Sherman, her disapproval etched in her scowl, loomed larger in his mind than any picturesque elk ever would.

The social worker had been clear. Jace had six weeks to create a steady home. To prove that he could support the kids. Fear clamped vise-like hands around his ribcage.

"We?" Jace just about spat the word. "There's no *we* here. You have no idea what you're costing me."

"We're just asking you to allow the wildlife center to do the study. And that you consider their suggestions."

Rhianna was trying to make this better, but she couldn't. This assessment would take too much time. It might even take away his chance to prove that he could give the kids what they needed. But he couldn't say all that here. Not in public. As a foster parent, he was required to keep the specifics of the kids' situation confidential. Mrs. Sherman had drilled that into him over and over.

"I want it all in writing." Jace pointed to the guy taking notes. "That you caused delays for me."

"We can do that." Rhianna scribbled something on a notepad in front of her. "I'll have legal counsel draw something up."

"And I'd like it noted, for the record, that this land is zoned for agriculture. I bought it with the understanding that I'd be using it for that purpose. It's a ranch. Not a wildlife park."

"Excuse me." Mousy scientist Vivian stood up. "I'd like to say something now."

Jace glared at her, but stepped back and motioned toward the microphone with a flourish. "Be my guest." He knew he was being a jerk but he was too furious and too worried to care. Making things work with the kids had been hard, but with this new obstacle, things were quickly veering toward impossible.

Vivian walked toward him, back straight, chin up, and Jace noted with surprise that she looked different up close. Her brown hair was streaked with gold, her eyes behind her glasses were dark brown and currently regarding him as one might a bug that had shown up on a dinner plate. When she tilted the microphone down to her level, he saw that she had big silver rings on a few of her fingers and a tattoo on her wrist, words Jace couldn't read from where he stood.

The scientist didn't seem quite so mousy, after all.

"I'd also like it noted, for the record," she glanced at him, deliberately mimicking his words, "that the Shelter Creek Wildlife Center is committed to helping community members find a way to coexist with local wildlife. We are not trying to put anyone out of business or prevent local agriculture from taking place. We look forward to working with Mr. Hendricks to find solutions that work for him, for wildlife and for the community."

Jace felt foolish that he'd come on so strong when she was being so calm and professional. But of course she could be calm. She had nothing at stake, while he had pretty much everything on the line here.

"Thank you," Rhianna said. "Jace, do you have anything else you'd like to add? Or can we move on?"

"I've got one more thing." He glanced around the room, letting his eyes rest briefly on the Habitat Heroes before he spoke. "My ranch is private property and no one is welcome to come around protesting or causing trouble. If you have something to tell me, then call me. Write me a letter. Send me an email. Don't show up on my property making some big scene."

"We only did that because you don't check your mail," Bunny called from the back of the room.

Jace rolled his eyes. "Trust me when I say that I'll be checking it more carefully in the future."

Vivian, still standing next to him, bit her lip as if she was trying not to laugh. At least the scientist with his fate in her hands had a sense of humor.

Not that Jace felt like laughing. More like punching something. Because this stupid meeting tonight was just one more complication. His sister's kids needed a home. He was the one who should be providing it. Not some stranger. Not someone who might yell at them or tell them they were a charity case or far worse. Yet Social Services threw up an obstacle a minute, and now this town, his own hometown, was getting in his way, as well.

Rhianna turned toward her fellow council members. "Can someone please make a motion to fund this study?"

An older man Jace didn't recognize made the motion and the council voted for the study.

Jace turned away and headed back up the

aisle, but he couldn't bring himself to sit down. He needed air, needed to shake this feeling that he'd crashed into yet another dead end. He ignored the Habitat Heroes as he passed them, pushed through the door and out into the night.

He made it to his truck and leaned on the cool, solid metal.

"You okay, man?" Caleb had followed him out. The ex-marine would never leave a man behind—or alone out in the dark after a miserable town council meeting.

"Yeah, I guess."

Caleb leaned on the truck next to him, both of them gazing out over the dark hills that surrounded Shelter Creek. The fog had stayed away so far tonight, and the stars were hanging, cool and bright and impossibly distant, overhead.

"I'll talk to Maya," Caleb said. "I'll make sure she knows that you need this study to go quickly."

"Thanks." Jace stared out into the dark, frustration simmering under his skin. "I miss it. Especially on nights like tonight. I really miss it."

"Rodeo?" Caleb glanced his way, his dark eyes even darker in the night.

"Not just the rodeo, though, yeah, it's hard to let that go. But I miss the freedom the most, you know? I miss the road, the motels, even sleeping rough in my truck. I miss not having to worry about rules and town councils and my crazy fellow citizens. When you're on the road, you never spend enough time in one place to let things get under your skin."

Caleb nodded. "It's weird what you can end up missing. When I first got out of the Marines I missed the mess hall, the schedule, all the stuff that I'd gotten so sick of. But I think what I really missed was how simple life was. How few decisions I had to make. Here, running a ranch, there are hundreds of choices every day. I can imagine, with kids, there are hundreds more than that."

"Yeah, and most of the time whatever choice I make ends up being all wrong." Jace's words came out heavy with the worry he sometimes thought might actually crush him. Just leave him flat on the ground buried under all the burned meals, the school supplies he didn't know he was supposed to buy, the reassuring words he had no idea how to give.

"Don't be hard on yourself," Caleb said. "Most people get to become a parent slowly, one kid at a time. And when they start, their kid doesn't know anything about the world except them. You inherited kids who were already shaped by someone else. And you've never been a dad before. So cut yourself some slack."

Jace didn't have time for slack. He had six weeks to get this right. But he didn't want to burden Caleb with more than he already had.

"Yeah, I'm sure you're right," he said. "Thanks for the talk. And for coming to the meeting tonight."

"Anytime," Caleb said. "How about if I bring some barbecue supplies over tomorrow night? Maya's gone and it would be fun to have some dinner with those crazy kids of yours."

Jace remembered Mrs. Sherman's words. About Caleb and his anger and not being appropriate, and for a moment he was tempted to say no. To play it safe in case the social worker decided to pay one of her drop-in visits.

But that was ridiculous. Caleb had bonded

with Amy and Alex, and even got a smile out
of Carly sometimes. It was surprising, because Caleb's tough demeanor could scare off
pretty much anyone. But the kids saw right
past that to his soft insides. Plus they treated
him like their own personal climbing gym,
a giant they could cling to.

Then Jace remembered. "I can't. It's Parent Night at the school."

"What's that?"

"I dunno. We already had Back-to-School
Night but this is more about what the kids are
actually learning or something."

Caleb shook his head. "Times have
changed, my friend. It's hard to believe you're
turning down my special-recipe smoked ribs
for a school event."

"I can't believe it, either," Jace said grimly.
"Everything is different now. But I'll take a
rain check on the barbecue. Maybe this weekend or something?"

"Not a problem. Just say the word."

Jace knew his friend was trying to find his
own clumsy way of helping, and the kindness threatened to get him all emotional. He
straightened and clapped Caleb on the shoulder. "Thanks, buddy. I'll see you soon."

Caleb walked to his own truck and drove off into the night. The meeting wasn't done yet, so the parking lot was quiet and Jace stayed where he was. Breathing in the stars a little longer. Relishing the rare moment when no one needed anything from him. For this one instant, it was just him and his truck, the way it had always been. The way he wished sometimes, deep down, that it still could be.

JACE SET HIS keys on the table in the hall and tried to leave the stress of the town hall meeting behind him. So what if a biologist was coming to study his ranch? It was just another hurdle in a life that had become a series of hurdles he'd never expected to deal with. He wouldn't show his stress to the kids.

Ever since they'd come to live with him, he'd done his best to make this home a peaceful one. Sure the kids fought and squabbled, but he wouldn't be one more out of control, upset adult in their lives. They'd had plenty of that and far worse.

He didn't know much about their life with his sister and Neil, but little details had seeped out of the kids. The day Amy argued she didn't need a bath because there'd been times they'd lived without water for months. The time Carly froze and went sheet white when an older guy in his twenties said hello to her at the feed store. Jace wondered if she'd been hassled by any of Neil's druggy friends. The way Alex barely spoke, like he was afraid of the consequences if he ever asked for anything he wanted.

So no matter what turmoil was inside him, what worries or fears or regrets he harbored, he tried to stay really calm around the kids. It was the one thing he felt like he was doing well so far and he wasn't going to let Bunny and her Habitat Heroes change that.

The house was quiet, which was a hopeful sign. Carly was supposed to have put Alex and Amy to bed and then finished her homework. But when he stepped into the living room, Alex and Amy were lying on the floor doing a puzzle, Carly nowhere in sight.

He forced his frustration down. Carly rarely did anything he asked, so why he'd even thought she might comply tonight just showed what a useless parent he was. Not that he needed any more evidence.

"What's going on?" He tried to imagine

what a real parent might say. "Are you guys okay? Where's Carly?"

Two heads, one red and curly, one blond and tousled, popped up from the puzzle. "Upstairs talking on the phone." Amy reached for the piece Alex was holding. "That's an edge piece. Put it right over there."

"Your bedtime was half an hour ago."

"It's okay," Amy assured him. "We're not sleepy, are we, Alex?"

Alex shook his head, but the yawn that overtook the little guy told Jace otherwise. And the kids would sure as heck be sleepy in the morning when he had to wake them up for school.

"Did Carly give you your dinner?" He'd left burgers and fries from the diner in town. Not the healthiest choice but easy to reheat, and he hadn't had time to cook anything.

"Yeah. She tried to eat all of my fries!" Amy folded her arms and lips in a dramatic pout.

"Not *all* of them." That was from Carly who came through the living room door with her phone still in her hand. For the thousandth time Jace regretted giving it to her. It seemed permanently attached to her, like a shiny, high-tech growth.

"Carly, what's going on? Didn't we talk about the kids being in bed by now?"

Carly shrugged. "I had to do some homework." Her gray eyes were hard as pebbles, shiny and daring him to challenge her. "Oh…" She pulled a piece of paper out of her back pocket. "And this is for you. You have to sign it."

Jace unfolded the white half sheet. "You got a *detention*?" Yeah, he'd had a few in high school, too, but nothing had prepared him for being on the receiving end of one of these slips. "What happened?"

"I guess I talked too much in class. And passed notes." She paused, as if wondering how much to actually tell him. "And I gave someone the answers on a test."

"Why would you do that?" It was just a detention, thirty minutes after school for poor choices, but Jace knew Mrs. Sherman wouldn't view it favorably. For the social worker, this paper would be one more red flag warning her that Jace wasn't good parent material. That she should start looking for some real foster parents who knew how to keep teenagers from getting detention.

Carly, oblivious to his panic, just shrugged again. "He asked."

"He? Who's *he*?" Jace knew he sounded like some protective dad from a bygone era, but the idea that Carly felt the need to give a boy answers needled him.

"His name's Diego. And I only did it because he barely speaks English and it was stupid of the teacher to make the poor kid take the test in the first place."

"Oh." Jace felt all the wind go out of him. Carly's sense of justice struck a chord. "Still, it's not your job to fix that for him."

She glared at him. "Maybe. But if I don't, who will? No one fixed anything for the three of us for years. Maybe it makes me a little more sensitive to the kids who are having a hard time."

The words smacked him across the face. He suddenly remembered the card she'd sent to his PO box in Missoula. It must have been three years ago now. She'd only been twelve or so then. Asking how he was. Asking if he was going to come visit anytime soon. Complaining, or so it had seemed to him, that her mom was in a rough patch.

But the truth was clear to him now. She hadn't been complaining. She'd been asking for help and he'd sent back some lame postcard with a bull wearing a cowboy hat, telling her he'd see her soon.

But he hadn't. He hadn't made it out to California. Not until just a few months ago when her family had already broken apart for good.

"Okay," Jace said heavily. "I get why you did it. But please don't do it again." He went into the kitchen for a pen, signed the detention slip and gave it back to her. "You'll stay after school tomorrow?"

"Yeah." She looked relieved, like she'd been expecting him to go off on her.

"Okay. I'll pick up Amy and Alex, then we'll wait for you." He tried to make his voice firm even though part of him was kind of proud of her for sticking up for that poor kid. Why would the teacher make the kid take a test when he didn't even speak the language yet? But it wasn't his problem. His problems were sitting right in front of him, and two of them should already be asleep. "But Carly, even if you've had a bad day, I need you to follow through on what you promised. You said you'd get these two to bed on time."

"Well, it's not like you're paying me or anything."

Jace stared at her defiant stance, jaw set and arms crossed, and realized that on some level she was right. She'd been expected to jump in and parent her siblings for way too long. No wonder she wasn't approaching the task with any enthusiasm. This was something he could change. Broke as he was, he had to be able to afford a teenager's babysitting wages. "We'll talk about a salary tomorrow, if you show me tonight that you can follow through on what you promised."

Something softened slightly in her hard eyes, like water pooling in the rocks down by the coast. "Fine. Come on, you two, let's get your teeth brushed."

"I'll come help in a minute," Jace assured her. "I just need a glass of water or a bite of food. Or something." Something to ease the anxiety. Of the meeting. Of parenting. Of not understanding how to reach Carly. Or Alex.

He'd only been in charge of these kids for

a few months, but his mistakes littered the road behind him like the car parts in that old insurance commercial where the car just fell apart as it drove. He was that car, bits of bad decisions strewn in his wake.

"But I don't want to go to bed," Amy whined. She was the type to wring every last drop from the day.

"Well, that's too bad," Carly said. "Because you're going."

"Am not."

"Are too."

"Amy." Jace's voice was sharper than he wanted. "We're all tired. Go get ready for bed now."

She glared at him with tired tears in her eyes. "I don't have to listen to you. You're not my daddy. I don't have a daddy."

This again. She'd said it several times a week when she first came here, but lately he hadn't heard it as much. He'd hoped it was because she was accepting that this was her home now. A cranky eight-year-old's words shouldn't cut deep, but they did tonight, maybe because he was tired. And he felt for her. Because she should have had a daddy, but Brenda never stayed in touch with the kids' fathers.

Jace steadied his voice and softened his tone. "You're right. I'm not your daddy. I'm your Uncle Jace and I get to take care of you now. And part of that is making sure you get enough sleep, even when you don't feel like going to bed."

"Uncle Jace is right." Carly's voice was softer now, as if Amy's words had reached inside of her and melted some of her brittle resentment. "He is here to help us, and we need to go to sleep."

"I'm thirsty."

Ah. She'd moved on to stalling. Things were getting back to normal. "Go brush your teeth," Jace told her. "And I'll bring you all some water. Do you want ice, m'lady? Or just plain?"

His formal waiter voice deepened the dimples on her cheeks. "Ice, please, sir."

"Very good. I'll bring it along in a moment."

"Why thank you."

"You're welcome, m'lady."

"Come along, then." Carly, bless her, played along with her own fake British accent. She took the two younger kids by the hands and led them upstairs, and Jace could hear them chatting about the weather and what a lovely night it was in their silly accents as they climbed the stairs.

He sagged against the counter in exhausted relief. His first detention managed. A bedtime meltdown resolved without too much craziness. He didn't know much about raising kids, but he'd realized recently that a funny accent could stave off a lot of problems.

But Alex's silence through the entire negotiation worried him. Was he scared? Did he have some kind of speech problem? Alex's teacher had said they'd wait and see, give Alex a chance to adjust before any *formal evaluation* took place. Whatever that meant.

Jace remembered what it was like to be too scared to open his mouth. He'd felt the same way, sometimes, around his own dad, and from what he could tell, Brenda's boyfriend, Neil, was a whole lot scarier than Jace's father had ever been.

If that was the case, who could blame Alex for keeping quiet and trying to stay out of the way? Jace just had to find a way to convince

Alex that everything was okay now. That he was safe to say what was on his mind.

Jace downed a glass of water for himself and then placed three full glasses on the tray he'd picked up at a garage sale a couple of weeks ago. He started upstairs, trying not to slosh. Hoping not to upset anyone else tonight. Hoping to get them all into bed as soon as possible so he could crash himself. It had been a long day.

Tomorrow he'd deal with it all—the ranch, the elk, the biologist. For a moment he saw her, Vivian, at the microphone, her silver rings, her tattoo, her hair gold-streaked and shiny, and something in his chest fluttered and woke. Curiosity, maybe, because she'd seemed so scared, but she'd gotten stronger right before his eyes. Or attraction, because once he'd really looked at her, he'd seen her full pink mouth and porcelain skin and that waterfall of shiny hair. But it couldn't be that. She wasn't his type at all. It was probably fear, because she held the future of his ranch in her hands.

Jace paused on the landing to gather his tired thoughts. He'd call Maya once the kids were in bed and tell her he needed this study

CHAPTER FOUR

Vivian's old SUV made it up the last turn of Jace's steep driveway with a cough and a gasp. The long drive across the country hadn't agreed with her old Ford, and it had been huffing and puffing ever since she'd gotten to Shelter Creek. Maybe with her first paycheck she'd have enough to get it looked at, though paying the deposit on the tiny cottage she was renting had taken a chunk out of her budget.

"Good job, Rusty." Vivian gave the dashboard a pat as she switched the truck off, trying to ignore the way the engine shuddered once, then settled.

And then she saw the house. "Oh, wow."

The old Victorian-era ranch house was gorgeous, with fanciful, carved wooden trim, gable windows and a turret. But further inspection revealed how neglected it was. The long porch sagged, the roof was missing shingles and the white paint had disappeared in many spots, giving the building a silvery tinge, as if it was carved from driftwood.

Vivian climbed out of Rusty, scooped up the notebook where she'd scrawled some basic information about Jace's property and walked toward the house. It rose from a yard delineated by a broken picket fence so overgrown with blackberry brambles that it was almost invisible. The area was littered with old farm equipment, tires and pieces of a tree. What a mess. On the phone last night, Maya had mentioned that Jace had recently taken over caring for his sister's kids, so maybe he hadn't had much time to clean up.

But Vivian could see that this place would eventually be worth the work. The house was perched on the crest of the tallest hill for miles. Hills the color of bleached straw went on and on when Vivian looked east. A band of redwood forest broke up the view when she gazed to the west, the low sun behind them promising a gorgeous sunset. To the south, the rooftops of Shelter Creek were barely visible.

It was a spectacular piece of property, and for a moment Vivian felt a stab of envy. What would it be like to know that all of this land was yours? That you could live here, work here, fix it up and be a part of something so grand?

She'd grown up in a rent-controlled apartment in Brooklyn with her mom and their two cats. They'd all crammed into two tiny bedrooms, a postage-stamp kitchen and a living room not much bigger than that. Maybe that's why Vivian had always craved wild places and empty lands. And why she'd chosen a career guaranteed to take her away from the city.

Two kids came flying around the corner of the house, interrupting Vivian's musings. A little girl was first, a head full of orange curls flying in the wind. She was holding a book and being chased by a pale little boy, his face scrunched in anger as he yelled, "Give it back, Amy! Give me back my book!"

The front door burst open and Jace appeared, a dish towel over his shoulder. "Alex! Amy! Come on inside and eat your snack."

The kids completely ignored him, disappearing around the far corner of the house.

Even from here, Vivian could see the weary expression on Jace's features as he stared after them. His shoulders slumped and he scrubbed a hand across his eyes. Then he spotted Vivian.

She wanted to sink into the ground when she saw his mouth press into a grim line of distaste. "Oh. It's you."

Not the warmest words of welcome, but she hadn't expected warmth. He'd made it clear at the meeting last night that he didn't want this study.

But however he felt, this was her job and she was going to do it well.

Forcing her voice into a professional tone she walked a few steps closer. "Good afternoon. I was hoping for a few minutes with you to go over my plans for the wildlife survey."

He glanced around as if hoping the children would materialize. They didn't, so he shifted his focus back to her. "This isn't a great time."

His eyes were such a vivid shade of blue, they were almost unreal, and rimmed with lashes so thick that any woman would covet them. No one had a right to be this handsome. And she had no reason to notice. Yet his image had stayed with her last night after he'd stalked out of the meeting, so irate and determined. He was so much more masculine than any man she'd ever met. Which sounded weird. *Masculine.* She'd never describe Colin or any of the other guys she'd known with that word. But Jace was like someone out of another era. Tough, strong, rough. And then his eyes…

Enough. Her inexplicable attraction to him, her lack of sleep, the headache growing in her temples, the anxiety because he'd called her boss to complain before she'd even done anything wrong, all gelled into irritation. Vivian stalked closer to his porch and stood on the creaky lower step. "You called Maya last night and told her that you wanted to get this done quickly. So she called me. I've been up since 5:00 a.m., trying to oblige."

His eyes narrowed. "Good. I want this study over with right away."

Maybe she was naive but she'd been expecting a thank-you. Though maybe it was good that he was rude. A reminder that she shouldn't spend one more second noticing his cowboy good looks. "Okay, then. If you want to get this 'over with,' I need a few moments of your time. Now."

His eyes widened just a fraction and his lips parted slightly, and she thought for a moment that he might smile. She wondered what that would be like. What changes it would bring to his brooding face. From here she could see that he was probably a few years older than she was. There was the faintest touch of gray at his temples and in the stubble covering his jaw.

Stop! She wasn't here in Shelter Creek to check out guys She'd put so much of her life on hold for Colin. This was her chance to see what she could do on her own, without worrying about a man.

Jace pulled the dish towel off his shoulder and wiped his hands in a nervous gesture that seemed out of place. He looked like he should be tossing around bales of hay, fixing trucks, riding the range or whatever it was cowboys like him did. Not fidgeting with a red-checkered cloth.

His eyes shifted to the sudden quiet in the backyard.

"Do you want to go check on the children? I can wait."

He relented, the reluctance clear in his eyes.

"Let me round up the kids and talk their big sister into watching them."

"Can we meet in your valley?" Vivian glanced down at the notes in her hand. "Long Valley? That seems to be the area the Habitat Heroes are most concerned about."

For a moment exasperation tightened his expression and she thought he'd say no. But he seemed to get control of whatever inner rebellion was boiling in his veins. "Yes." He pointed west to where the land sloped away. "If you turn right at the main road and drive about a quarter mile, you'll see a turnout with an old wooden gate. Park there and you can walk into the valley. I'll meet you along that path, by the first pond, in about half an hour."

"Okay." That was perfect. It would give her a few minutes to look around on her own. To start recording the types of vegetation on the map she'd printed out. And to examine the fence that had Bunny and her group so riled up.

"Amy, stop!" The little boy's voice came from somewhere behind the house and was edged with impending tears. Vivian felt her own heartstrings tug, wanting to make it right for him.

"I'd better go." Jace jogged away, the dish towel flapping from his shoulder like a shred of superhero cape. Except he wasn't *her* superhero. Far from it. He was more like the villain—angry with her, when all she was trying to do was her job.

She'd better keep that in mind when he was doing the bumbling dad thing. Who knew that tough cowboys chasing after little kids could be so disarming?

But she'd promised herself that if she ever got into another relationship, it would be with a man who put her first, who appreciated her, who never took her for granted. Jace didn't even *like* her. So whether he was handsome or not, whether he looked at her with piercing blue eyes or not, didn't matter. Not one bit.

Vivian climbed back into Rusty, who started up with an unsettling growl, and headed down the driveway to Long Valley.

FORTY MINUTES LATER, Vivian was sitting on a log by the first of three spring-fed ponds in Long Valley. It was beautiful here. The water made the grass in the valley green, a startling contrast to the brown hills rising above. There were wildflowers and a wide variety of birds and insects, too. Vivian had her note-book open and was noting down different varieties of wildflowers on her hand-drawn map. Squinting at the closest specimens, Vivian recognized blue-eyed grass and clarkia, but this miniature pink flower, so close to the ground, was new to her.

She studied the tiny perfect petals. Maybe if she took a photo, she could look it up when she got back to the office.

"Hey." Jace's deep voice jolted her from her thoughts. She squeaked her surprise at the big brown horse that loomed over her and fell backward off her log. Butt in the dirt, legs in the air, she wasn't sure whether to laugh or cry.

"Are you okay?" Jace jumped off the horse and jogged toward her as she struggled to get up from her undignified pose.

"I'm fine," she lied. Her face on fire, she retrieved her notebook and scrambled to stand up.

His eyes were dark with what seemed like real concern, but Vivian thought she saw a smile trying to form on his mouth. "I'm sorry if we startled you."

"I'm fine," she said again, refusing to let

him know how many of her body parts hurt. She'd landed on a rock, so her tailbone stung, and her shoulder ached. Though it had been aching for days, whether from the cross-country drive in Rusty's sagging seats or because of her lupus, she wasn't sure.

Wanting to change the subject, she gestured to the horse, which was eyeing her warily, probably wondering about this crazy creature rolling on the ground. "We?"

"This is Tioga." Jace looked at her skeptically. "Do you like horses?"

"From a distance," she answered.

"So let me guess. You're here to make decisions about my ranch but you're from the city. Am I right?"

She wasn't going to let him discredit her. "Just because I wasn't raised around horses doesn't mean I don't know wildlife."

"But you don't know *ranching*."

"Do you?" It was a cheap tactic, evading his question with one of her own.

"Yes." He flushed a little. "I worked on some ranches, in between rodeo seasons."

Aha. So maybe Jace wasn't quite the expert that he pretended to be. She'd file that away in case he kept trying to make her feel unqualified for this job.

Wisely, he let it go. "So, what are your first impressions?" He raised his arm, opened it to encompass the valley around them. "Can I put my cattle here?"

"You have a beautiful ranch. But I can't answer that question yet."

He put his free hand to his hip. "You've seen the valley. The kinds of wildlife here. What more do you need?"

She wanted to laugh. They were talking about tens of acres, and that was just on the valley floor. There were acres and acres of surrounding hills. "I'll need quite a bit of time to really study the area. To inventory the wildlife."

"How fast can you get it done?"

There it was again, that urgency she didn't quite understand. "It's hard to say. A month to six weeks, if all goes really smoothly."

His brows crunched down and Vivian was suddenly aware of how tense he was, and how alone they were out here. She could almost see the headline: Geeky Biologist Found Dead in Pond. Angry Rancher Suspected.

But he made no physical threat. The tension was all in his voice. "You need to be faster than that."

Her temper flared. "Earlier you told me to come back another day. Now you're telling me to go faster. *You* need to make up your mind."

He looked a little surprised, like maybe he wasn't used to people standing up to him. Well, he'd better get used to it because biological studies didn't happen overnight and she wouldn't compromise the integrity of her work. "Of course I'll do my best to work quickly. But a study of this scope is like putting together a big puzzle—it can't be rushed."

"But your study is keeping me from getting this ranch running. I need to bring cattle in. Soon."

Then he wasn't going to like what she had to say. "Can you walk with me? Back toward the road? I want to show you something."

He took Tioga's reins. "Sure."

Vivian put her notebook back in her bag and they walked side by side along the track. She searched her mind for something to fill the awkward silence between them. "Why did you decide to buy this ranch?"

"It was the only property I could afford."

His blunt honesty startled her. "Oh. Well, why Shelter Creek?"

"I grew up here. And when I found out I'd be taking my sister's kids, I didn't have much time to think. Some social worker down in LA asked me where I'd be living and I just kind of blurted out my hometown. It was the first thing that came to mind."

"Are you glad you chose it?"

"Not right now, I'm not."

Vivian glanced at him, but his face was shadowed under the brim of his cowboy hat. He gazed ahead, stoic, the big horse he led keeping a docile pace behind him. He was from another world, where people said exactly what they meant and nothing more.

"What about you?" He glanced at her, his expression almost awkward. "Why did you choose biology?"

"I love science and nature. I like understanding how it all fits together—the Earth, the plants, the wildlife, their habitat. There is still so much we have to learn. Did you know, for example, that scientists have recently proven that trees communicate with each other?"

The look he gave her was priceless in its disbelief. "Come on."

"Look it up. It's through their roots, and these sort of root hairs that travel underground. They use chemical signals to communicate."

"What do they talk about?"

"Danger, mostly, I think. If one of them is ill, sometimes they'll send nutrients to their sick buddy."

He stopped in his tracks and looked down at her suspiciously. "Are you just messing with me? The brainy scientist winding up the dumb cowboy?"

"No! It's true. You asked me why I liked biology and I'm trying to show you what it is that drives me. How much wonder there is in the natural world. How much we still have to discover."

"But why here? Why aren't you in a lab somewhere?"

"You were right about me being from the city. I didn't grow up in places like this. Once I finally got to spend time in beautiful places, I wanted to help protect them." Vivian gave herself a mental kick. Why did she say all that? She just gave him ammunition to call her a city girl *and* a tree hugger.

"That's kind of a luxury, don't you think? To look around good pasture like this and just see it for its beauty? I never had much time to sit around admiring the view. I've been too busy just trying to get by."

He shook his head and started walking again. Vivian followed, wishing she'd kept her mouth shut. She got so exhilarated, thinking about science, she forgot how geeky and strange it sounded to a lot of people. She definitely wasn't making the greatest impression on Jace.

They reached the gate, and Vivian pulled in a deep breath for courage and straightened her spine. If he was so into honesty, she'd just tell it like it was. "Okay, this is what I wanted to show you. See these hoofprints?" She pointed over the old wooden gate, spotted with pale green lichen.

"Elk, right?"

"Yes. And I can tell from the tracks, that they've got juveniles with them. They've been trying to get in."

"Well, yeah." Jace looked mystified, as if he couldn't quite believe how dumb she was. "That's why I built the fence."

"They need water, Jace." Vivian tried to

remain patient. "Shelter Creek is almost completely dry this time of year. So are all the other rain-fed streams. Your valley has springs in it. Do you have any idea how rare that is?"

"How do you know what's rare? Didn't you just arrive here the other day? From somewhere on the East Coast?"

Vivian bit her lip to hold her frustration in. "You called Maya and asked me to get started. So I did. And the first thing I researched was water sources for wildlife in this area. And guess what? You have the only springs. That's why the elk are trying to get in."

Jace pushed back his hat and glared at her. "So you're working for Bunny now?"

"No! I'm not working for anyone but the wildlife center and the town council." This was the tricky part. She had no real authority over him. Couldn't make him do anything. But she had to find a way to convince him. "The elk are thirsty. The juveniles especially, and they could die without water. Just open this valley to them for the next month or so. Until the rain starts and the creeks run again."

"A *month*? What about my cattle?"

"Can you put off purchasing them? Or put them somewhere else? According to the climate charts I consulted, it will only be another few weeks until it rains."

He snorted. "I don't know what charts you're looking at. This is California in October. We might not get rain until December or January."

"Just open this gate for them, Jace. Let the elk drink from your springs. They need the water and they are a protected species."

Jace leaned his forearms on the gate and the weary expression she'd noticed up at his house cut deep lines into his face. "And why is it my job to protect them?" His voice was quiet. Discouraged. "I have to run a business. I have to put cattle in here. Now."

Negotiate, Vivian reminded herself. The wildlife center's mandate was to negotiate between wildlife and ranchers. "Can you fence off half the pasture? Maybe let the elk have the first pond and your cattle can have the other two?"

Jace put a hand to his hat, pressing down as if he was literally keeping a lid on his temper. "I just built *this* fence," he said heavily. "And it was expensive."

"What if you moved the fence? You could rebuild it farther up the valley."

"You're talking about weeks of work." Jace's eyes narrowed and he skewered her with a skeptical glare. "Look, I might not be some educated scientist like you. But I know how things go. If I move this fence, then that pond and the whole lower section of my valley will belong to the elk. Permanently."

"That's not what I'm saying. I just want the elk to be able to drink for now."

"Well, yeah, but the council, the wildlife center, Bunny and her followers, they'll all see it as a happy solution. So forgive me if I'm not ready to give away a whole chunk of my property."

Vivian tried to find a way to reassure him. "Jace, no one's talking about a permanent solution yet. We just want the elk to have access to water so they don't die."

He blew out an audible breath. "Fine. I'll open this gate. For now. But I'm not moving any fences. And the elk can't stay. I need this land for cattle. Soon."

He looked so upset that Vivian tried to reassure him. "It's the right thing to do."

"For the elk, sure. For me? Not so much."

Jace pulled a bunch of keys out of his pocket and unlocked the gate. He shoved it open, and chained it to the adjacent fence.

"Thank you." Relief made her voice oddly breathy. She'd convinced him. And probably saved the local elk in the process.

Jace ignored her gratitude, swinging up on his horse instead. He looked down at her from the saddle. "I have work to do, and I'm sure you do, too. I'll see you around."

He touched the brim of his hat and turned Tioga away.

The big horse broke into a run along the valley floor, Jace completely at ease in the saddle. Vivian might not like his attitude, but as she walked back to the pond she couldn't help admiring the image he made, horse and rider, like something out of a book or a movie, disappearing into that gorgeous landscape.

But he wasn't some romantic movie cowboy. He was a hard, angry man who didn't care much for nature and wanted to make some money off cattle as soon as possible. She may have won the battle of the fence just now, but she had a feeling her conflicts with Jace were only just beginning.

But now that the elk had some water, her

job wasn't to engage with Jace, it was to study his land. Gather data and report her findings. She was a scientist. She knew the rules. Don't get emotional. Focus on the facts.

Though it was hard not to get emotional when she looked around the beautiful valley. Red-winged blackbirds zipped over the blue surface of the pond. The hills rose barren and stark, punctuated by the silver trunks of graceful oaks. She could be detached and scientific when it came to Jace. His rudeness should make that fairly easy. But this natural beauty? It would be harder to observe it with a strictly scientific eye. It was difficult to understand why Jace couldn't seem to see it, too.

A fox had crossed her path when she'd first walked in today. Sassy and adorable, it had stopped in front of her and sniffed the air, its black nose twitching. Vivian's heart was already caught up in the wonder around her. As much as she was supposed to remain neutral, she wished Long Valley could stay as pristine as it was now.

A movement in the distance caught her attention. Jace, leaning forward on his horse as they made their way up the hill, out of the valley, zigging and zagging up the steep slope. Heading home to the family he'd only recently acquired. He might be upset with her, but he'd taken in those three kids, so he couldn't be all bad.

Don't get involved. Nothing about Jace's life was any of her business. Science was her business.

Vivian picked up her pencil and the map she'd been working on earlier, and plunked back down on the log. She wouldn't get anything done by staring after Jace until he was just a speck nearing the top of the hill. Until he was at the top. Until he was gone.

She forced her eyes away, returning to the wildflowers, the shrubs, the reeds encircling the pond. She had work to do. Work was why she'd come here, to this tiny town across the continent. To work hard and prove she could take care of herself on her own, despite her illness. She had a focus, her reasons, her purpose. And none of that was going to get derailed by grumpy ranchers like Jace Hendricks.

CHAPTER FIVE

JACE STARED DUBIOUSLY at the tiny blue plastic chair. It didn't look like it could hold his weight, but all the other parents attending Parent Education Night were already perched in them, so he'd have to take his chances. He lowered himself carefully, wincing when the miniature seat creaked under his weight. Were first graders really so small that they required doll-sized furniture?

Pulling his hat off, he raked a hand through his hair and pulled in a deep breath. He'd been running all evening. Getting the kids fed and ready to come back to school so he could attend this Parent Night had been harder than pretty much anything he'd ever done. Amy was a picky eater, Alex wanted to stay home and Carly was telling them all to hurry up so she could go to her friend's house to study for a test.

Plus he didn't feel great about the way he'd

treated Vivian earlier today. He'd been pretty rude. Taking his stress and frustration out on her when she'd rushed to get started at his own request. And then down by the gate he'd been rude again.

But she'd put him in a tough situation. She hadn't been wearing her glasses, so he could see the plea in her pretty brown eyes while she told him about the elk, and their desperate need for water. But he was desperate, too. He needed that pasture for his cattle in order to show Mrs. Sherman that he could make his ranch a success.

But Mrs. Sherman and Vivian were a battle for another day. Right now he had to face a first grade teacher. Jace glanced around the room, nodding at a few parents who looked his way. Most people were chatting quietly with each other, waiting for the teacher to arrive.

Not much had changed since he'd been a first grader in this room, and Jace had the strangest sense of time warping, like none of the years since he'd been that young had ever happened. Here were the same green linoleum floors, the same old cracked ceiling tiles, the same smell of dusty paper and paste.

There were some changes, though. The blackboard had been replaced by a whiteboard. And his being here, trying to pretend like he fit in with all of these respectable-looking parents, well, that was also new.

He straightened his spine as best he could in his cramped seat and noticed the woman sitting next to him was watching him with wide eyes, like she'd never seen a guy in a cowboy hat before. Though that made no sense, considering this was a ranching town. Maybe she could just sense that he was green. That he had no idea how to do this parent thing. But he'd shown up, that was a start, and what Mrs. Sherman kept saying to him. *Just show up, Jace.*

He took his hat off and nodded at his neighbor. "Howdy."

She started a tiny bit, like she was embarrassed to be caught staring. Then she smiled. "Hi." She was pretty, in a cultivated way, with carefully curled blond hair, lots of makeup and round blue eyes. "I'm Wendy. My son is Terrence."

"I'm Jace. My kid is Alex."

Her smile faded. "Oh, yes. Terrence mentioned him."

Uh-oh. Jace had received a call from the teacher last week because Alex had gotten into a conflict with another boy. Had it been Terrence?

"We're new in town. He's still adjusting to school and...well...pretty much everything." Jace hoped that covered his bases, if an apology was required. The other boy had taken a book from Alex and refused to return it. Alex had gotten into some kind of book tug-of-war and the other kid had fallen down and bumped his head. Alex was like a stray dog with a dropped burger when it came to his books.

Wendy nodded curtly. Fortunately, at that moment, the teacher walked into the room and started handing out folders to all the parents. She was the youngest teacher Jace had ever seen; she couldn't have been more than twenty-five, despite the fact that she'd dressed up in a fancy pantsuit for the occasion. How could she possibly know what she was doing?

Then it hit him, how old he sounded, even in his own head. Here he was, feeling prejudged for his lack of parenting experience, and the first thing he'd done was judge the teacher. Maybe she was some kind of teaching prodigy or something. Or maybe, now that he'd reached the ripe old age of thirty-one, with way too many aches and pains from riding bulls, everyone else was starting to seem younger than they really were.

He accepted the folder the teacher handed him and returned her shy smile with what he hoped was a reassuring one.

She held out her hand. "Welcome to Parent Night. I'm Sarah Franklin."

"Jace Hendricks. Alex's uncle."

Her smile thinned to a tense line. "Great to meet you. I'd love to sit down with you soon to chat about Alex."

Of course she would. "Sure," he told her. "Give me a call and we'll set up a time."

Ms. Franklin nodded and continued down the row, handing out folders and greeting parents. Jace noticed she didn't ask to meet with any of *them* for a chat. She started her presentation and Jace tried to pay attention while she went on about first grade math and something called number sense, and then discussed reading development.

Maybe it was more evidence of his terrible parent potential that his mind drifted, that her words blurred together, but man, he was tired. Alex had woken up from a bad dream last night and hadn't gone back to sleep for a couple of hours, and just when Jace was able to tiptoe out of his room at five in the morning, Amy popped awake and Jace's chances for a little more sleep melted away in the light of her wide-awake smile.

He wondered how they were doing. Carly had wanted to study with a friend tonight, so he'd dropped her off on the way here and put Amy and Alex in the childcare center provided by the school. Hopefully they were playing, happy to have their normal routine shaken up a bit.

"So," the teacher said, her voice taking on a militant level of cheeriness. "The next order of business is to find volunteers for the annual Shelter Creek Fall Festival. To let you know a bit more about it, please welcome our room parent, Wendy Corman."

The blonde woman next to Jace stood up and walked to the front of the room. Facing the other parents, she flashed a taut smile. "As you know, every year, the school puts on a fall festival with fun games and activities for the kids. The event raises money for our art and music programs. We have many booths sponsored by community members, and each class provides one activity booth. Let's go around the room and share our ideas for the class booth." She pointed to the mom sitting closest to the door. "Arielle?"

"Um, how about scarecrow building?"

Ms. Franklin wrote the idea down on the whiteboard. Jace wondered if this was a good time to leave. He wanted to try to get over to Amy's classroom for the second half of its hour-long program. Thankfully, Carly's Parent Night had been last week. Carly hadn't wanted him to go, saying she was too old to have a parent coming to the school to check on her. But Jace went anyway and left with his head spinning with graduation requirements and credits and AP versus regular classes, each topic a reminder that his high school days were a long time ago and everything had been a whole lot simpler back then.

Or maybe he just hadn't paid much attention, seeing as his only life goal had been to get out of Shelter Creek as fast as possible.

As more parents shared their ideas, Jace stood and made his way toward the door. But Wendy's voice caught up with him just before he made it out of the classroom. "What about you, Jace?"

He turned to face her and the rest of the parents shifted their attention to him, waiting expectantly. He realized they were all moms.

"Do you have an idea for a fall picnic activity?"

Suddenly he really was that schoolkid again, called on by the teacher, never knowing the correct answer, dreading his classmates' snickering as he faltered. A fall picnic? He'd never been to one, not even as a kid. Either this was a new school tradition or his parents hadn't taken him and Brenda when they were kids. His parents hadn't been exactly the type to willingly attend community events.

He frantically scanned his memory for fall type activities. "Um...bobbing for apples?"

Ms. Franklin's hand froze over the whiteboard. Wendy's lips parted and she looked a little horrified. The thick silence in the room told him he'd gotten the answer wrong. *Just like old times.*

"Um..." Wendy put a hand to her heart as if she were physically recovering from his words. "It's just that bobbing for apples is... well..." Her voice trailed off.

"The children's mouths and all," Ms. Franklin chimed in, clearly trying to help. "We don't really want them exchanging germs."

"Oh, right, germs." Bobbing for apples was taboo now? Just more evidence that he didn't have a parenting clue. "I'll tell you what. Whatever you decide, I can provide a few bales of straw. For ambiance."

That brightened the mood. Wendy nodded, the moms all let out a collective breath of relief that the awkward moment had passed and Ms. Franklin put a note on the board. Jace clapped his hat back on his head and walked outside.

Amy's class was in one of the school's portable classrooms, and Jace crossed the dark schoolyard wondering how many ways he'd make a fool of himself in the next thirty minutes.

Fortunately, Amy's teacher, Mrs. McPherson, wasn't talking about the Fall Festival, though Jace figured he should probably offer her some straw bales, as well. Instead she was handing out multiplication tables and discussing the importance of math facts. This Jace could get behind. He was pretty sure Mrs. McPherson had used this handout when he was in her class so long ago. This was simple memorization, no hidden rules about what was considered acceptable in modern parenting.

He relaxed, thumbing through the folder Mrs. McPherson handed him with a welcoming smile, listening as she finished up her presentation covering the ins and outs of third grade. Her voice hadn't changed much, and he remembered how much he'd enjoyed third grade with her.

Everything had been clear in this class. A little boring maybe, very much by the book, but this quiet classroom had been an oasis of calm after the chaos of home. His dad would get back from a long haul across country, grumpy as heck after all those days driving an 18-wheeler. His mom was constantly hovering, shushing them, trying not to set Pa off.

Or maybe he was more relaxed in this classroom tonight because Amy hadn't gotten into trouble like Alex had. She loved school, greeted each day with the same enthusiasm she brought to pretty much everything. She had two speeds as far as Jace could see: full tilt and asleep. It seemed as if her experiences with Brenda hadn't affected her as much as the other kids. Jace knew enough about the emotional legacy parents left their children to be grateful for that.

When Mrs. McPherson thanked them for coming and bade them good-night, Jace got up to leave. But his former teacher called out, "Jace, a moment please?"

He had a feeling he was going to start to hate those three words. When he turned, the teacher's face had softened into concern.

"May I speak with you?"

His stomach dropped a few degrees south. That was how Mrs. Sherman always started her phone calls. But he kept his voice neutral. "Of course." He glanced around, worried that someone might hear their personal conversation, but the room had emptied quickly. Maybe the other parents were experienced enough to get out fast, to avoid little chats like this one.

"First of all, it's nice to see you. It's always a thrill to have a former student walk through my door again. Congratulations on all your success."

Heat seeped over Jace's skin. It had never occurred to him that his childhood teacher would follow his career. "Thank you very much."

"Now, I don't know Amy very well yet, but she has seemed, well, a little stressed since she started school."

"Stressed?" Jace tried and failed to remember a time Amy had ever seemed upset.

"She's very moody," Mrs. McPherson said carefully. "And I feel like she doesn't really relax. She often has trouble being...well, flexible."

Her attempt at diplomacy had Jace laughing outright. "You mean she's bossy."

The teacher's stern features relaxed into a smile. "Yes. She can be." Her kind eyes behind her blue plastic spectacles grew serious. "I read her student file. Her behavior makes a lot of sense, considering what she's been through."

"Maybe that's her personality," Jace suggested, an ache starting in his neck and spreading to his shoulders.

"She seems anxious," Mrs. McPherson said quietly. "And maybe a little scared."

That got him. When he took the kids, he'd promised himself that, no matter what, they wouldn't have another reason to be scared.

That he'd never be someone they feared, as he'd feared his own father. "Scared of what?"

"I don't know. Change? Living without her mom?" The teacher sighed. "The thing is, with a full class of kids, I don't really have a way to find out. That's why I want to suggest that she attend counseling. We can provide it, right here at the school."

"You mean, like a psychiatrist?" Everything in Jace rebelled. Counseling sounded so heavy for such a little kid. And yet, if it could help Amy...

"We'd start with the school's counselor. She's highly trained in how to talk to kids as well as how to help them handle the big things that happen to them. And Amy has been through something very big."

"Would this person be all alone with Amy? Or is it some kind of group thing?"

"It could be either, depending on what the counselor recommends for Amy. I just fill out a referral form."

"I'd like to talk to Amy about it first. I'll call you and let you know."

"That's fine." Mrs. McPherson reached out and patted his forearm in a grandmotherly way. "I know you've taken on a lot, Jace. And given up a lot, too."

His throat thickened and he swallowed hard. "Thanks."

"I hope to hear from you soon."

Jace nodded and told her good-night, grateful to step outside into the cool, damp air. The fog settled on his skin, filled his lungs with clean ocean mist. It soothed. It always had.

As Jace approached the cafeteria building where he'd left the kids, he was startled to hear a child crying. Stepping through the door, he saw that the room was empty except for Alex and Amy, huddled together on a bench, a teacher kneeling down in front of them, speaking softly.

Alex spotted him first. "Uncle Jace!" The little boy flung himself off the bench and hurtled toward Jace, grabbing him by the legs and hanging on tight.

"Uncle Jace!" Amy crashed into his side, her arms like barnacles attached to his waist, her tear-stained face peering up at him as if they hadn't seen each other in years, rather than just over an hour.

"Hey, you two, what's going on?" Alex was crying softly, snuffling against Jace's jeans.

Jace gently pulled Amy's arms away and knelt down to better see their faces. "What has you so upset?"

Amy's hands went to her face, covering it as a sob shook her tiny shoulders under her pink sweatshirt. Alex just grabbed Jace by the arm and held on tight. Tears had stained his glasses and Jace carefully removed them and cleaned them on his shirt. "What happened?" he asked the approaching teacher. She wore jeans and a school sweatshirt, and her dark hair was pulled back in a ponytail.

"I'm Peggy. I run the daycare program. I think that, when the other kids left with their parents, these two got worried that you weren't coming."

Guilt twisted Jace's stomach. "I was talking to Amy's teacher for a few minutes. I'm sorry they got upset."

Peggy shook her head. "It's no problem. I'm here to help. I tried to tell them that you'd be here any moment."

Jace reached for Amy. She took her hands from her heated, damp face and he saw the reproach and worry in her green eyes.

"Hey," he said, trying to think of the words that might soothe her and her brother. "I will try to be on time when I pick you guys up from things. Occasionally I might be a little bit late, but that doesn't mean that I'm not coming. I will always come to pick you up. I promise."

Alex loosened his grip on Jace's arm and glared at him with eyes dark with doubt. But, as usual, he didn't express his thoughts out loud.

Amy was the voice for both of them. "That's what our mommy said, but then she'd be really, really late. A couple times the school had to call the police because they were closing for the night and there was no one to take us home. And then one day Mommy didn't come home at all, because she went to jail."

Jace had never been one to believe that hearts could break. But he was pretty sure a piece of his shattered at Amy's plaintive words. "That won't happen with me. If I'm late, it's just traffic or something small, like tonight when your teacher wanted an extra word with me." He made a silent promise that he'd try to be early from now on. "So come on, now." He took his bandanna from his coat pocket and used it to wipe the tears from Amy's cheeks. "You two ready to turn off the waterworks and head home?"

Peggy bit her lip to stop her smile and even Amy's mouth curled up a tiny bit. "Yeah," she said, and reached for her brother's hand. "You ready, Alex?"

Alex nodded.

Jace took Alex's free hand and nodded to Peggy. "Thank you very much for looking after them. Sorry for any trouble."

"It's no trouble at all." She smiled down at Alex and Amy. "I'm here with my staff before and after school every day. If your uncle is busy working, you are welcome to come here anytime."

Jace wished Peggy a good-night and walked the kids back to his truck. They were quiet as they clambered into their seats with none of their usual squabbling over who sat where or Amy teasing Alex because he still had to ride in a booster seat. Instead they just seemed worn out by their worries and emotions.

As he started up the engine, Jace realized Mrs. McPherson was right. The kids had been more affected by what had happened to them than they let on. He'd call the school in the morning and let them know that both the kids could use a little extra help. And then he'd call Mrs. Sherman. Hopefully she'd view his decision to start them in counseling as evidence that he was trying hard to give the kids everything they needed. Because seeing their frailty tonight made him more determined than ever to take care of them, to be a parent they could count on and to chase their fears of abandonment away forever.

And if that meant he had to push back a little harder against nature-loving Vivian and her elk, then so be it. Mrs. Sherman had demanded he prove his ranch was a viable business before she granted him permanent custody of these kids. So he'd make sure his ranch became a business very soon. And if it meant kicking the elk off, and Vivian along with them, then so be it. These kids needed him. They were the most important priority he had right now.

CHAPTER SIX

THERE WAS NOTHING like lying on her stomach in the grass on a hot autumn afternoon to make Vivian sleepy. Fatigue was something she fought constantly, her life's companion since long before she'd finally gotten her diagnosis. But she suspected the main reason she was sleepy was because, after over a week of living alone in Shelter Creek, she was really relaxed.

There were no anxiety-inducing visits from Mom, with her constant litany of all that could go wrong. There were no awkward encounters with Colin or with well-meaning colleagues who tried so hard not to mention him or the wedding.

Vivian might be a little lonely in Shelter Creek, but she felt like she could breathe again. Smile again. Just be herself again. She felt more like the woman she'd been before she was defined as sick. Before she was defined as jilted.

That relaxation, combined with the sunshine, had her bones melting into the soft ground. But she couldn't sleep now. She was on the job in Long Valley, and she was waiting for a salamander to show up.

Vivian peered again at the reeds near the pond. She was almost certain she'd seen a California tiger salamander head for cover there as she'd walked along the shore just now. And they were on the list of the area's endangered species. Once the salamander decided the coast was clear, it might venture toward the water. And if it did, she was going to get a photo.

No sign of the little critter yet. She glanced around the valley to make sure the elk were still a safe distance away. Now that the gate was open, Vivian was both relieved and saddened to see that she'd been right, the elk *had* been congregating by the fence because they were thirsty. This valley *was* an important water source for them at this dry time of year.

The majestic animals were all over the valley now, the males in full autumn regalia, strutting around with their crowns of antlers on display. Vivian had to be careful; they'd charge if they felt threatened or if they were in the mood to show off. But they were absolutely beautiful. She could watch them for hours. She'd come here to watch them today, in fact. But then the salamander had shown up.

The thud of hooves on packed earth had her scrambling to sit upright, heart beating a little faster. But it wasn't tule elk heading her way. It was Jace on that big horse, with a boy sitting in the saddle in front of him. The same boy Vivian had seen so upset, chasing his sister, the other day.

But the boy didn't seem upset today. A huge grin lit up his little face, his eyes creased to happy half-moons behind his glasses. He looked so proud to be up on Jace's horse and Vivian understood why. Wasn't it every kid's dream to ride a horse with a cowboy?

Come to think of it, didn't a lot of people dream of sharing a saddle with a guy like Jace? Once again she was struck by his complete grace, and the quiet, confident way he held the reins and gave the horse direction.

He was watching her with those piercing blue eyes, his expression a little wary. Of course he must think her crazy for lying on the ground just now.

Vivian stood up hastily and tried to brush some of the mud and grass off her jeans and shirt. "Hi."

Jace stopped the horse and dismounted smoothly, then carefully lifted the boy down, too. "Hi, Vivian. This is my nephew, Alex."

"Nice to meet you, Alex."

Alex nodded and clung to Jace's hand.

"Do you like riding that big horse with your uncle?" she asked him. "Did you ride here all the way from the barn?"

He nodded again. What a cute little guy. Vivian had babysat her way through high school and college, and had spent a few summers working as a camp counselor. It had been a while since she'd been around kids, but something about Alex was so sweet, she wanted to engage him.

"Do you want to know what I was doing, lying on the ground?"

Alex nodded solemnly.

"I was searching for a salamander. Would you like to help me look?"

Jace spoke. "We don't want to disturb you. I just came by to see what's going on here in the valley, now that the gate is open." He glanced around with a wary expression on his handsome face. "I guess I've got myself a herd of tule elk."

While a petty part of her wanted to point out that she'd been right, Vivian's heart thawed a little at the anxiety in Jace's eyes. The guy just wanted to get his ranch started, and here she was, piling on elk and complications. "It looks that way. They really depend on this water right now."

"I need them to leave," Jace said, his voice firm. "They've had their drink. Now they have to go. Their thirst can be someone else's problem. Maybe Bunny can build a big trough for them."

Vivian stared. She'd been sure she'd gotten through to him the other day. He'd opened the gate, no matter that he'd been reluctant.

"They can't just change their habits, Jace. This ranch was abandoned for over twenty years. That's several generations of elk who are used to using this area. They won't know where else to go. They'll die." Just then a piercing screech ripped through the air followed by a grunt.

"What the...?" Jace grabbed Alex by the hand.

"They're bugling," Vivian assured them. "It's rutting season. They're competing for the females. That's how they call to them. Look." She pointed across the valley where a male was trotting, his antlers held high. He raised his nose and let out another high-pitched shriek, ending in another guttural sound.

"That's how they attract the ladies?" Jace let go of Alex and clapped a hand to his forehead. "These are weird animals."

"There have been clashes between the males all day. Keep your eye out and you might see a couple of them face off." Vivian clasped her hands together. "It's October, which is late for this type of behavior. I suspect their lack of water delayed the rut. Yet another reason we can't move them now, Jace."

"You're telling me the elk have to stay so they can—" Jace glanced down at Alex. "So they can hang out together?"

Vivian couldn't suppress her smile at his euphemism. "Yes, they need their hang out time."

"That's ridiculous. They can do that somewhere else."

"We can bring in state biologists. They'll

have to determine where to move the elk if
you want them gone. And you'll have a fight
on your hands with the Habitat Heroes."

Jace tugged the brim of his cowboy hat
down and walked a few paces away. He
stopped, watching the elk.

A small hand tugged at Vivian's sleeve. She
glanced down into Alex's big eyes, gray and
serious behind his glasses. He put a finger to
his lips to ask for her silence and pointed at
the edge of the pond.

There it was! The salamander was deep
brown, spotted in pale yellow. This was a big
one, stocky and about five inches long, tra-
versing the mud at the edge of the pond with
its awkward, almost robotic gait.

Vivian raised her camera and forced her
shaking hands to steady, though she wanted
to jump up and down in excitement. These
little critters were practically extinct, yet here
one was, strolling along the shore, happy as
could be. She snapped a few photos, zoomed
in and snapped a few more.

Ideally, she'd catch it, weigh it, try to determine its age, gender and overall health.
But she didn't have the right equipment with
her. She'd come here today to observe the

elk. She hadn't been prepared for endangered salamanders.

Her excitement faded. She might be excited about the salamander, but its presence would make Jace's life even more difficult. And, lucky girl that she was, she got to be the one to tell him.

She took a few more photos, noticing the way Alex stayed close to her the entire time, his eyes never leaving the salamander. "Do you like it?" she whispered. "You did a great job spotting it."

"It's really cool," he whispered back, and Vivian froze, realizing it was the first time he'd spoken to her.

"It's called a California tiger salamander," she said quietly. "They're very, very rare. It's special that you have them here on your uncle's ranch."

Alex ran to his uncle and pulled on his sleeve, his face lit with a true scientist's excitement. "Did you hear that, Uncle Jace? We have a *really* special salamander."

Jace's eyes widened, like he was as surprised as Vivian that Alex had spoken. "That's great, buddy." He ruffled his nephew's hair gently. Then he looked at Vivian with an expression so sharp she was tempted to glance away. "How special, exactly, is this salamander?"

She motioned for Jace to move away from the salamander. She wanted Alex to have as much time as possible to watch it, since it seemed to make him happy, and she had a sense that he wasn't often happy.

When they were a few yards away from Alex, Jace stepped close to speak quietly. "Do I have another problem here?"

Being close to Jace meant being more aware of how tall he was, how broad his shoulders were and the way they stretched the flannel of his shirt. His sleeves were rolled up to expose the strong sinews of his forearms. It was as if Vivian had fallen into his orbit and could feel the pull of his gravity. Vivian swallowed and forced herself to ignore that tug and meet his eyes. *Courage.* "Yes. It's an endangered species."

The muscles at the back of his jaw tightened as he stared down at the salamander, which was now climbing awkwardly over a stick. Vivian watched Alex, the boy's obvious delight in the small creature smoothing over some of the emotional turmoil in her chest.

She felt for Jace. For this man who was trying to start a new life on this beautiful property. Who just wanted a ranch to provide for these kids.

Finally he spoke, though his voice was strained, like he was forcing the words out through clenched teeth. "Do you ever bring good news?"

"Don't make this about me. I didn't buy this property, you did." Oops, that wasn't very diplomatic of her. But even if it was rude, it did seem to get Jace back on track.

"So what do I do next?"

"I'll need to speak with Maya, but I suspect we're going to call in another biologist to advise us. Someone from the Sacramento office who is more familiar with this species. We'll assess your population, and we'll need to see if they are living in the other two ponds up the valley and anywhere else around Shelter Creek. If they are, that may influence the outcome here."

"So, if there are a bunch of other salamanders down the road, I can still graze my cattle here?"

Vivian took a breath before she gave him the word he wouldn't want to hear. "Well, there's also the elk."

"This is my land!" Jace's hands clenched at his sides, like he wanted to take on the world of environmental regulation with his fists.

"And you bought some really sensitive habitat," she told him. "Look, I don't want to say anything further until we know more. We have to consult with the state."

He glanced around at the elk, then back down at the salamander, who was relaxing in the shallow water at the edge of the pond. "That's all well and good for the animals but what about my ability to feed my family?"

"I think," Vivian said as gently as she could, "that you should concentrate on fencing off some other areas of your ranch. Or renting out some other pasture. I wouldn't count on running cattle in this valley for a while."

JACE STARED DOWN at Vivian as her meaning sank in, each word burning like a nettle's sting. How could such bad news come from someone so pretty? When he'd first ridden up and seen her lying on the ground, his heart had slammed into his ribs. He'd thought something was wrong with her.

But then she'd sat up, her face flushed from

the sun, her clothes speckled with dirt and grass.

And he'd realized in that moment that she was truly beautiful. Her long straight hair was loose and tousled and flowing over her shoulders. Her lips had parted slightly and he hadn't been quite sure if that was because she was surprised to see him or if she was laughing at herself for being caught in such an odd position.

But that was the thing about her that sparked his attention the most. She'd been lying on the ground. Flat out on her stomach, her camera in front of her, staring at a bush. She'd been a hundred percent engaged in her work, completely committed even if it meant she was covered in dirt head to toe.

It reminded him a little of bull riding. The way you had to commit completely to the ride, to the life, to the crazy of it all. She had the same streak in her, only her passion was science, and she didn't care what it cost her. She threw herself into this work completely.

And for a moment he'd felt lucky to have her there. Maybe she'd solve this dilemma with the elk. Maybe she'd make it right.

Which made the news about the salamander feel like a betrayal. It made her dedication to her work dangerous instead of admirable. Because she wasn't going to do this work halfway. She'd crawl over every inch of this valley until she'd found every darn salamander personally. And who knew what other "special" animals she might find along the way.

And he had less than five weeks left to get this ranch going or Mrs. Sherman might follow through on her ultimatum.

"Are you sure?" Jace asked her, knowing he sounded desperate—a thrown bull rider still hoping for a good score when he was already airborne and about to hit the dirt. But he had to try. "Are you sure you haven't made a mistake?"

Vivian shook her head. "There is no other salamander in the state that looks like this one."

He'd hit the dirt and the landing was painful. He sucked in a deep breath, trying to think, trying to regroup. He needed to make other plans.

"I'm sorry, Jace. I know you really wanted

to graze this valley soon, but there's a lot we'll have to figure out first."

He glanced around at his new fence posts, new wire. He'd dumped most of his money into fencing this area first because it was the best for the cattle. But there wouldn't be any cattle here now.

Maybe he could buy enough hose to run water from the house all the way down to the troughs at the barn. But he hadn't repaired those upper fences yet because he'd been repairing these.

Vivian's gaze on him felt like a weight, like judgment, like pity. He didn't need this, didn't need this cool, composed girl who seemed so educated, who'd probably never experienced any real hardship in her entire life, standing here watching as his plans crumbled around him. But he'd been rude to her last time and he'd regretted it. He'd better just get out of here before he was rude again.

"Alex, time to go." Jace tried to keep his voice low so as not to worry the little guy. After seeing the kids so scared at Parent Education Night, he'd been extra gentle with them, trying hard not to let his frustration show.

When Alex didn't move, he went to kneel beside his nephew. Alex was so engrossed in the salamander's progress that he didn't even flinch when Jace put a hand on his shoulder, though normally he shied away from being touched.

"Look, Uncle Jace," Alex breathed in wonder. "Isn't it cool? Aren't those spots awesome? And see how it walks? It's so jerky." Alex looked up at Vivian, who had come to join them. "Does it eat bugs?"

Jace let his nephew's words roll over him like the miracles they were. Alex almost never spoke. When he did, it was usually single syllables, as if he was trying to have as little contact with the people around him as possible.

"They eat bugs, worms, all kinds of good stuff," Vivian answered. "I think this little guy's out walking because it rained a tiny bit this morning. Usually they like to stay underground as much as possible, but sometimes when it rains, they'll come out. We're pretty lucky we got to see him." Vivian knelt down on the other side of the boy and started pointing out the salamander's eyes and the way the tail was flat on the sides to help it swim in the pond.

Jace watched his nephew listen to her with a relaxed, wide smile on his normally tense face and repressed a flash of envy. He'd been trying to get through to Alex for weeks and had never made much progress. But here was Vivian chatting away, making the kid so totally happy. And making it all look so easy.

He walked a few paces away. Maybe he was grateful that the salamander and the scientist had finally gotten Alex talking, but that didn't mean Jace wanted to sit there admiring the slimy little thing while it destroyed his hopes just by existing. Instead, Jace glared at a bull elk with a massive rack of antlers who was eyeing him from across the pond while savoring an enormous mouthful of grass. The same grass Jace had planned to use to fatten his future cattle. Jace could swear the elk looked smug.

"Fine, you win," he told the elk. "Munch away. Enjoy yourself. Just be careful not to step on any endangered salamanders while you're lapping up my nice clean spring water."

"Are you okay?" Vivian was standing at his elbow, a concerned expression on her face.

Great. Now she'd heard him talking to an elk. Just another episode in the bad reality show that was his life. The Downfall of Jace Hendricks. Tune in tomorrow, folks, to see Jace try to build fences out of thin air.

He really was losing it. It was a gorgeous fall afternoon, the air was fresh and clear, but it took effort to locate any oxygen. He had to get out of here, away from her soft pity and her hard science.

"I'm fine. Never been better." His words were sharper than he'd planned.

"Can't you use another part of your ranch for the cattle?" She gestured to the pond. "I know there's water here but it's not your only source."

He didn't want to tell her his problems. "Don't worry about it. Just stay here in my valley and play with your animal friends."

"Is that what you think I'm doing here? Playing? This is my *work*, Jace."

"Well, it's mine, too. Or it was. Now I don't know what the hell it is."

"I understand you're upset." She was looking up at him again with her deep brown eyes that he'd come to think of as velvet because her gaze was so soft.

Anger—at her, at her findings, at this life he was trying to build that just wouldn't get built—boiled over. "You don't understand any of it. You just sit here and pass decrees about my land. The elk get to come in. The salamanders are in charge. Do you really think these animals are more important than people?"

Her hands went to her hips. "No, of course not. But there are plenty of people out there advocating for people. There are just a handful of biologists trying to do something to preserve animals that are in danger of dying off forever."

Another bugle squealed through the air between them.

"They sure as heck don't seem to be in any danger of dying off. Why don't I give Maya a call and see what she says?" It was a cheap shot, threatening to call her boss. But Maya was also a friend.

Vivian nodded gravely. "I think that's a good idea."

Which meant that Maya was probably going to tell him the same things as Vivian. A grim and brittle determination had Jace squaring his shoulders. He was on his own. He'd have to figure out a different solution. Maybe he could rent some pasture. Maybe he could get a loan to pay for the repairs he needed. But all of that would take time he didn't have.

He went back to Alex. "Okay, buddy, let's head home."

"I want to keep watching the salamander, Uncle Jace. Can't I stay here and help Vivian?"

"No, we need to get back. I have chores to take care of up at the house and Carly and Amy will worry if we're gone much longer."

"But I want to watch the salamander!" Tears pooled in Alex's eyes and Jace glanced skyward, wondering if God was laughing. Maybe he'd given Jace these kids and this situation just to make sure he was properly humbled every single day.

"Alex," Vivian said. "I'm going to do a scientific study of the salamanders over the next few weeks. Maybe, if it's okay with your uncle, you could help me find them sometimes? That way you'll get a chance to see this guy, or others like him, again."

She was trying to save him. Throwing him and Alex a line. And Jace wanted to be grateful but instead he was resentful. He didn't want her help. Didn't want to owe anything to the woman whose science was destroying the foundation he was trying to build for himself and these kids.

"Can I help out, Uncle Jace?" Alex's eyes held a plea. "Please?"

"We'll see. We don't want to bother Vivian. She needs to get her work done."

"I wouldn't have asked if it was trouble," Vivian said. "The truth is, I could use a fellow scientist around here."

Alex just about glowed with pride at her words and Jace couldn't say no after that. But he could apply leverage.

"If you do your best in school, Alex, and do your chores, you can come help Vivian. *If* she has time for you."

Alex stood up, casting one last look of regret at the salamander.

Jace figured he'd better get the kid out of here while he could. And get himself gone, too, because sitting here panicking wasn't going to help anything. It was only going to make him appear more incompetent and lost, and he was tired of looking that way in front of calm, composed, beautiful, ranch-ruining Vivian.

"I'll see you around," he said gruffly. He set Alex up on Tioga and swung himself up, too.

"Goodbye, Vivian," Alex called, startling Jace. The only time he'd heard the kid speak so loudly was when he was yelling at Amy for swiping one of his books.

"Goodbye, Alex, hope to see you soon," Vivian called back.

She didn't say goodbye to him and Jace only gave her a quick nod. Because they both knew what Alex didn't. That this small, spotted salamander had derailed his plans for the ranch more efficiently than an entire herd of tule elk ever could.

Jace and Alex were both quiet on the ride home. Alex retreated to his usual silence now that he didn't have Vivian and whatever kid magic she'd used to bring him out of his shell. Jace was quiet because he was trying to let it all sink in. That he might never be able to graze livestock in that valley. That he was flat broke now. And that he was all tangled up in a mess of frustration and attraction when it came to Vivian Reed.

CHAPTER SEVEN

VIVIAN WAS STANDING on the porch of the church where she was supposed to be married. It was spring again in New Hampshire, and the air smelled of rich, damp earth and millions of trees. The church door was locked, so she knocked, once, twice, again, wondering where everyone was.

Glancing down she saw that the full skirt of her wedding dress had stains on it, all kinds of mud and dirt, like she'd been wearing it during fieldwork. She tried to brush it off, but the dirt smeared so she gave up and knocked again and again and again.

Slowly other sensations trickled in. Blankets, tickling her chin. The dusty afternoon scent of sunlight through a window. She wasn't on a porch or in a wedding dress. She was in her bed in the cute little cottage she'd rented in Shelter Creek. As the dream faded, she realized the knocking was coming from her front door.

She opened her sticky eyes, so glad to be here, not there, jilted, in a dirty dress. But who was knocking?

"Hang on," Vivian croaked and scrambled out of bed. Her clock read 6:00 p.m.—the sunlight was the last of the day. She scrubbed her palms across her eyes and glanced down at her T-shirt and sweats. She remembered pulling them on this afternoon, after a quick shower to make sure she hadn't brought any ticks or other unwanted visitors back from Jace's ranch. Then she'd crawled into bed and been asleep in moments.

Pieces of the present fell into place. She'd left work early, flattened by a bone-deep fatigue that she couldn't ignore any longer. It could be the lupus—fatigue could be a warning sign that she'd pushed herself too hard.

She'd worked long hours for the past two days, ever since finding Jace's endangered salamander. She was determined to finish surveying the perimeter of the pond by the weekend, creating a grid on her laptop to document what she found in every square meter. She'd located only one more salamander, which was about what she'd expected. Most of them would be underground until the first big winter rainstorm.

Maybe Vivian had worked too many hours, because this afternoon her joints had ached, her shoulders and knees threatening to freeze up, as they had when she'd experienced her first, horrible lupus flare-up. The pain, combined with the fatigue, had finally forced her to pack up early and stumble to her truck, desperate for home, bed and sleep.

But tonight was book club. Vivian ran to the front door and yanked it open, and there was Maya, leaning on her porch railing, chatting with a woman Vivian didn't recognize.

"There you are!" Maya shook a finger in the air at her. "I was about to break your door down. I was worried about you."

Vivian pressed her palms to her heated face. "I'm so sorry! I'm supposed to be at your grandmother's house right now, aren't I?"

Maya smiled, and Vivian caught the traces of relief in her expression. "It's okay. Grandma's not upset or anything. She just got worried and sent Trisha and I to make sure you were okay."

Her expression tensed. "*Are* you okay? I really was getting ready to bust your door down."

Uneasy guilt settled on Vivian's shoulders. By law, she wasn't required to tell Maya of her illness, so she hadn't. She'd wanted this job so badly and was sure she would be great at it, despite her lupus. But here the disease was, doing what it did so well. Slowing her down, tiring her out so it seemed that her limbs were moving through molasses.

"I took a nap. I guess I haven't been sleeping so well the past few days."

"Do you still want to come to book club?"

"Of course." Vivian glanced down at her clothing. "Give me just a minute to get changed?"

"Ahem," the other woman said with an exaggerated cough.

Maya jumped as if she'd been poked in the ribs. "I'm sorry. Sometimes I have the worst manners. Especially when I've been working out in the middle of nowhere for a few days. Vivian, this is my friend and your soon-to-be colleague, Trisha. Once we get the animal rehabilitation facility built, she'll be in charge of any injured animals that come our way."

"I'm glad to meet you," Vivian said. "It's

so exciting to be a part of such a new project. I can't wait for the buildings to be finished."

"You mean you're already tired of working out of a trailer on a construction site?" Maya's grin was contagious. Vivian was certain the less-than-ideal working conditions didn't bother her boss one bit. Maya was famous among field biologists for the years she'd spent in the most remote corners of the Rockies, studying mountain lions and other top predators. Rumor had it, Maya had only come out of the mountains long enough to email her research articles. But then she'd surprised everyone by returning to her hometown of Shelter Creek to help start a wildlife center here.

"I'm fine with the trailer for now," Vivian assured her. "I'm spending most of my time on Jace's ranch, anyway."

"Where you found California tiger salamanders," Maya said. "I got into town a few hours ago and finally checked my email." To Trisha, she said, "I leave her alone for her first week on the job and she locates previously unknown populations of an endangered species. I told you I'm good at spotting talent."

Trisha grinned. "I wonder if Jace sees it that way."

"Trust me," Vivian assured her. "He doesn't see it that way. I'm pretty sure he thinks I put those salamanders there deliberately, to thwart him."

"Uh-oh." Maya bit her lower lip. "Is he giving you a hard time? I'll talk to him. I swear, these cowboys around here all have such giant chips on their shoulders, it's amazing they don't look lopsided."

Trisha cracked up and Maya flashed Vivian a conspiratorial smile. "Caleb was pretty upset when I first offered him advice on how to prevent mountain lion attacks on his ranch."

Clearly there was a lot more to that story, but despite the missing pieces, Vivian felt the strain of the past couple of days lift from her shoulders. She needed Maya's humor desperately. She was working every waking hour to come up with a solution for Jace and the cattle he wanted to graze in Long Valley.

She'd always fallen for the underdog. Colin had been that for her. A skinny, cerebral guy who got sick a lot, who seemed to need Vivian's care in order to be okay in the world.

And Vivian had loved him and wanted to make life okay for him, so she'd stepped up and given him all the comfort she could.

She'd worked so hard to create a home for him. They'd worked together on projects of his choosing. She'd helped him type his notes and write his papers. Then she'd stood back while he took all the credit for their success.

And then she'd gotten sick. She couldn't know for sure, but sometimes she wondered if she'd caused it with all that self-sacrifice. By taking on all the stress so Colin wouldn't have to feel any.

She had worked so hard to gain Colin's affection, to keep him by her side. Afraid to ask for anything she wanted or to pursue the projects that interested her, because if she did, it might upset him. Or his love might disappear.

And, sure enough, when the tables were turned and she was the one who needed nurturing, when she wanted him to step up and care for her, he couldn't. As he explained in his wedding-day note, caring for someone sick just "wasn't in his nature."

In other words, she'd been a total fool. And this week she'd fallen right back into that same old pattern with Jace. He looked down at her with those gorgeous blue eyes, and she immediately went into rescue mode. And, once again, she'd done it at the expense of her health.

A psychologist could have a field day with her. Would probably say something about her father walking away when she was born and her mother having to work constantly from then on to make ends meet.

But today had been her wake-up call. No more long hours for Jace. She'd try to be quick and efficient, but she wasn't going to make his problems her own.

The image of little Alex, so excited about the salamander, ached in her heart. She understood that the root of Jace's frustration and urgency was that he wanted to do right by his nieces and nephew. But that was Jace's job. Not hers.

"I'm going to go get dressed," she told Maya and Trisha. "Would you like to come in and wait inside?"

"Nah, we're fine out here." Maya plunked down on the porch steps with a happy sigh.

"Maya's always happier out of doors," Trisha

added. "And I've been working at the veterinary clinic all day so I appreciate the fresh air."

"Okay, I'll be right back."

It only took Vivian a moment to pull on some jeans and a sweater, splash her face with water and comb her hair. She rarely wore makeup, so there was no need to worry about that. Still, she wished her first visit to the book club wasn't one where she was showing up late and half asleep. The fatigue still clung to her like moss on a tree. Parasitic. Draining.

When she went outside again, the cool evening air helped revive her a little, and jogging to Maya's truck with Trisha and a big dog Maya introduced as Einstein had Vivian smiling. Einstein sniffed her with one ear flopped forward. It wasn't until Maya picked him up and set him down in the small back seat of the truck cab that Vivian realized the dog only had three legs. Trisha climbed in next to him saying, "Scoot over, Einstein," leaving Vivian to sit in the front.

"This is quite a welcoming committee," she told Maya. "I've never been chauffeured to a book club before."

"Well, that's what you get for napping." Maya glanced her way as she started up the engine. "Are you sure you're not overdoing it? I looked at the notes you sent me, and you've accomplished a whole lot of work for the first week on the job. Maybe you should take tomorrow off."

"I can't," Vivian told her. "I've got a biologist, Orin Redmond, coming from Sacramento to take a look at Jace's ponds. He's an expert on the tiger salamander. I think he's going to bring a team of grad students from UC Berkeley up here to do a survey of Shelter Creek and a few other local ponds."

"Wow, you are on it." Maya flashed her an admiring smile. "Thank you. But I can meet with him if you'd like."

Vivian gazed out the window as Maya navigated them through the adorable streets of Shelter Creek, the clapboard houses nestled in the shade of big oaks, kids playing in their front yards before their parents called them in to dinner. It was tempting to take a day off. To give herself time to sleep and to wander this town so she could get to know it better.

But no. Just two more days until the weekend. Then she could rest. Then she could wander. She'd come out to California determined to work hard and live well despite her illness. She couldn't let one day of fatigue send her running for cover. "You are welcome to join the meeting. In fact, it would be great because you know a lot more about possible habitats around here than I do. But I'd really like to be there, as well, to see this thing through."

"I figured you'd say that." Maya shot her another smile as she pulled up in front of a lovely old two-story Victorian-era house. "But this weekend you have to take it easy. Boss's orders. Except on Sunday, when I'm hoping you'll come to a barbecue at Caleb's ranch. We're celebrating our engagement."

"Congratulations!" Vivian's first instinct was to say no. Maya was her boss, and of course she was just inviting her to such a personal event out of obligation.

But then Trisha leaned forward from the back seat and put a hand on Vivian's shoulder. "Please say you'll come. Now that Maya and Caleb are engaged, I don't have any single gals to hang out with. I need you there!"

There was no denying Trisha's plea and Vivian didn't really want to. A barbecue on a ranch. It was so…so Western. She'd take some photos to send to her mom and her friend Charlotte back in New Hampshire. Proof that she was hanging out on real ranches with real cowboys and cowgirls. It was still all so unreal. "Okay, I'll go."

"Oh, good." Trisha gave her shoulder a light squeeze. "You'll have fun. Caleb's ranch is really nice."

Maya turned the engine off and leaned back in her seat, as if she were gathering strength. "Well, girls. Are you ready for an evening with The Booze Biddies?"

Trisha burst out laughing. Vivian looked from one to the other in confusion. "I thought we were going to a book club."

"Oh, yes, they talk about books sometimes." Trisha reached into her tote bag, pulled out a copy of a novel Vivian recognized from the bestseller lists and waved it vaguely in the air. "But mostly they gossip and drink cocktails."

"Well, I guess that's good for me, since I haven't read it."

"Trust me, no one cares. I'm sure they'll be more interested in getting to know you than anything else. They're kind of…" Maya paused, as if trying to find the right words "...involved?"

"Meddling," Trisha added.

"Enthusiastic," Maya said.

"Okay!" Vivian couldn't remember the last time she'd smiled so much. "I get the picture. And even if they are a bit...um..."

"Nosey?" Maya supplied.

Vivian giggled. "Okay, yes, even if they're nosey, I'm still grateful that they, and you, have included me. It's strange being new in town. It's nice to have a plan."

"Trust me, they will fill your days if you let them," Trisha said. "They've taken up the cause of mountain lion conservation, they've been trying to set me up on dates and they organized the entire community to rebuild Caleb's ranch this summer. And now they're working together to raise funds for the wild-life center. Eva, the founder, is one of The Biddies. She used her savings as the seed money for the project."

"They sound like amazing women."

Maya put a hand to Vivian's shoulder. "I hope you still feel that way after this evening. Are you ready? You might never be the same."

It was meant as a joke. Just a humorous threat. But Vivian kind of hoped it was a promise. She didn't want to be the same. Didn't want to be the stressed, mousy, people pleaser she'd been back in New Hampshire. She wanted to be strong, independent, a problem solver, someone who accomplished things. She wanted to have fun and have friends. And if The Book Biddies could help with that, she was on board.

TRISHA AND MAYA had tried to warn her, but nothing could have prepared Vivian for the mile-a-minute action of a Book Biddies meeting. She'd just followed Maya and Trisha into the grand old living room and found a seat when a beautiful older woman in a colorful tunic, leggings and motorcycle boots flitted into the room with a tray of full glasses.

"Champagne!" she said, passing out the flutes.

"What are we celebrating?" Trisha asked. She'd taken a seat next to Vivian. "By the way, that's Eva," she whispered.

Oh. *The* Eva. The driving force behind the wildlife center and Vivian's job. Vivian had spoken to her on the phone just the once, when she'd first called to inquire about the posting, but she hadn't actually met her yet.

"Full funding for the Shelter Creek Wildlife Center! A friend of a friend of a friend connected me with a very wealthy nature-loving venture capitalist in San Francisco who grew up in this area. He has provided the last fifty thousand dollars. We can complete the building!"

A cheer went up around the room.

"That's amazing, Eva!" Maya's grandmother, Lillian, clasped her hands together in delight. "What wonderful news!"

"You started building the wildlife center before you had all the money?" Vivian asked of no one in particular.

"We had faith," said the woman with curly hair and a sensible brown cardigan sitting in the armchair next to Vivian. "I'm Priscilla, by the way. Priscilla Axel. I was Maya and Trisha's teacher when they were young."

"The best teacher ever," Trisha added, leaning across Vivian to give Mrs. Axel's hand a squeeze.

"Nice to meet you," Vivian told her.

Eva stopped in front of Vivian and handed

her a glass. "Vivian. It's so nice to finally meet you. Welcome to Shelter Creek."

"Thank you for having me." Vivian flushed as she realized her words made no sense. Ugh. Sometimes it seemed like she'd never get any better at social situations. "I mean, thank you for hiring me."

Eva's smile was a warm welcome. "From what I hear, you're off to a fantastic start. I look forward to getting to know you. But for now, I have champagne to distribute." And she was off across the room, moving with the smooth grace of someone far younger than she seemed.

"Look at this gorgeous hair!" A perfectly made-up older woman with bleached-blond hair had crossed the living room and was reaching for Vivian's ponytail. "Do you always keep it tied back? Have you ever considered adding just a few extra highlights? It's such a beautiful brown, and if you broke it up with larger streaks of blond it would really show the depth of the color."

"This is Monique," Mrs. Axel told Vivian. "She gets a little excited and forgets her manners."

"I'm sorry!" Monique pulled her hands

away and clasped them in front of her ample bosom. "It's nice to meet you, Vivian. Come by the salon soon and let me play with your hair. Monique's Miracles. Right downtown next to Chaparral Books."

"I will," Vivian promised before she realized that she was people pleasing again. She didn't really want to change her hair. "I mean, I'll think about it."

"Monique, don't pressure the poor thing. Her hair is just fine as it is." It was Annie, whom Maya had met at the town hall meeting. She had a folding chair under her arm that she plunked down on the other side of Mrs. Axel's armchair.

"Of course it is. But it would be nice with highlights, too." Monique's smile was totally unapologetic and she gave Vivian a pat on the head. "Welcome to Shelter Creek. We're all so glad you're here." She gave a little wave, walked over to the big couch under the window and sat down next to Maya and Lillian.

"Monique can come across a little strong, but she's the nicest person and she really is a genius with hair." Annie put a hand to her gray, streaked bob. "She put something she calls lowlights into mine. I was skeptical, but now I love it. Anyway, I'm so glad you could join us tonight. We were worried you'd gotten shy on us or something."

Vivian shook her head, flushing because she *was* shy and she'd been shy at that first town meeting when she'd tried to speak into the microphone. It was amazing how she'd found her voice a little bit already since coming to Shelter Creek. Maybe it was a good thing she had to work with Jace. He was so frustrated with her and her discoveries that it forced her to push back at him.

Annoyance rose at just the thought of him. He might be a good man for taking in those kids, but it wasn't her fault his pond was home to endangered salamanders. There was no need to be rude or to try to make her feel guilty simply because she'd been the one to spot the little creatures.

Maybe she'd tell him that straight up if he was rude again. She remembered him lecturing the elk by the pond the other day and smiled. He might be annoying but he was also kind of funny.

Which was not something she should think about. She couldn't get sucked into his problems when she had plenty of her own.

Her thoughts had taken her completely off track and she pulled herself back to her conversation with Annie. "I can be shy sometimes but I'm very glad to be here." She pretended to take a sip of her champagne, then set her glass down on an end table. Lupus was notorious for damaging people's kidneys. The last time Vivian had been tested everything seemed fine, but she wasn't going to add alcohol into the equation. She couldn't afford to.

"Vivian, we are so glad to have you working at the wildlife center." Eva, perched on the couch now, raised her glass in Vivian's direction. "Our second full-time employee. It's so exciting."

"And Vivian has already uncovered our first big wildlife dilemmas." Maya explained to the group about the elk and the salamanders—and Jace's quandary.

"Poor Jace." A woman Vivian hadn't met yet bustled in from the kitchen with a tray of crackers and cheese. "He's already given up so much. It seems like that man just can't get a break." She set the tray on the coffee table. "I'm Kathy Wallace, by the way. I'm Lillian's neighbor."

Kathy's smile was so kind that Vivian immediately felt at ease with her. "Nice to meet you," Vivian told her. "Are you talking about Jace's rodeo career?"

"It took Jace years to work his way up to the top of pro rodeo," Annie explained to Vivian. "He finally made it, started winning, made a little money, got a few sponsors and it seemed like his hard-won dreams were coming true. Then his sister got into all that trouble and there was no one else to take the kids."

"And Jace always looked out for Brenda," Kathy added. "So of course he stepped in to take her kids. He wouldn't know how to do it any other way."

"Well, good thing he did," Lillian said. "He may be struggling now, but it's the best decision." Lillian glanced at Maya and the love in her expression was a sight to behold.

"Aw, now you're going to make us all cry." Maya's tone was silly but she put her hand over her grandmother's. "My grandmother raised me after Social Services took me away from my own parents."

"Well, it's really a shame about Jace's rodeo career, but aren't those kids cute?" Mrs. Axel sighed. "I met them at the market the other day. That little Alex and Amy are really bright. They almost made me want to go back into teaching."

Vivian thought of Alex, so animated at the pond the other day. All those words tumbling out of his mouth because he'd been excited about the salamanders. She'd promised herself she'd keep her distance from Jace and his family. That she wouldn't get too involved. But if she could get Alex talking about salamanders, maybe eventually he'd start talking to other people about other things.

No, that was not her problem. Not her responsibility. If Jace brought Alex down to the pond, of course she'd welcome his help. But she wasn't going to take on worry that wasn't hers. Stress made lupus worse. And she really didn't want to get worse.

"And of course there's Carly, his teenaged niece." Maya sighed. "I've been trying to get to know her. Jace brings the kids by to visit the horses and hang out on the ranch, but Carly either doesn't come with them or won't talk to anyone if she does."

"Well, those are challenging years." Lillian gave her granddaughter an affectionate smile. "You weren't exactly smiles and rainbows back then, either."

Maya grinned at her grandmother. "I'm sure I was very charming, in my sullen, teen-aged way."

"Maybe Carly would like a job," Eva said. "Once we get the building finished we could use someone to help out a few hours a week at the front desk. She could file, answer the phone, help us with our social media, things like that."

"It's a great idea." Maya brightened. "I'll mention it to Jace."

"I love that we're already calling it *the wildlife center*, when it's really still just a trailer parked on a construction site," Kathy teased.

"Dream big and big things happen." Eva folded her arms across her chest defiantly. "We should all be proud of ourselves. We only came up with the idea this summer. But we've already found the land, started construction, hired two employees and become fully funded. Ladies, I propose a toast to our alter egos, the wildlife-saving Cougars for Cougars."

Everyone in the room raised their glasses and Vivian did, too. But while they all drank, she set her glass down with a sigh. It was hard to feel festive when the wildlife center's work was causing Jace so much trouble. And when he blamed her for a lot of it. He thought of her as some kind of Snow White, living in a fantasy world with her animal friends. A woman who'd never known hardship. Who'd never had her plans end in disappointment. Ha.

Still, it shouldn't matter what he thought of her. He was just a frustrated rodeo star, overwhelmed by his new life as a dad and taking that stress out on her. So why was her mind on him so often? Why had she looked for him the last couple days when she'd been working in his valley?

She'd come to Shelter Creek to be like these women around her. Strong. Independent. Not needing a man in their lives to feel fulfilled. She'd given up so much of her life to Colin. She would not do the same for Jace.

She leaned over to where Maya sat, two seats over, and put a hand on her arm. "Maya. I think I'm going to take you up on your kind offer of taking tomorrow off."

Maya raised her glass with a smile. "Good decision. Relax and get some rest. I'll set everything up with the visiting scientists."

Vivian leaned back in her chair with a sigh of relief. She needed this break. Needed a fresh perspective. Needed to remember that Jace Hendricks was just a handsome, troubled cowboy with bad luck when it came to choosing a ranch and nothing more than that.

CHAPTER EIGHT

"UNCLE JACE, can we ride Newt today?"

Jace looked down at Amy's hopeful up-turned face and gave her hand a squeeze. "Not today. Caleb and Maya are having a lot of people over. Not just us. They're celebrating their engagement."

"But we haven't ridden Newt in ages," Amy protested.

"Amy, you can't just expect to ride other people's horses." Carly's lecturing tone showed just how often she'd had to take the role of parent over the past several years. "That was a special treat. Caleb was being nice to us until we got our own horses."

Jace shot Carly a grateful look. Today was a good day in teenage land. Carly had been helpful all morning and hadn't protested about going to the barbecue.

"Carly is right. We have our own horses

now. You and Alex took turns riding Ike and Coral just yesterday afternoon."

Jace led the kids down the lane toward Caleb's recently rebuilt barn. That's where his buddy and Maya were having their engagement barbecue. It was typical for them to celebrate in the most casual way possible.

Amy's little hand tugged at his own. "But Uncle Jace, I want to ride every day."

Jace suppressed a smile. Amy had fallen in love with riding, and she was pretty good at it, so he must be doing at least one thing right with the kids. Even Alex seemed to like horses, though he was much shyer than Amy around them. Carly seemed interested, too, but stood back and let the little kids enjoy Ike and Coral.

Jace had been watching the local want ads, hoping that a sweet, younger quarter horse at an affordable price would miraculously appear. He figured when spring came around, if a lot of Carly's friends were on the high school rodeo team, she'd feel pretty left out if she couldn't participate.

Of course, there was the small task of teaching her to ride between now and then, but Carly was a tough cookie. She'd excel at anything she set her mind to.

The problem was, when Jace asked if Carly was interested in her own horse, she gave him a shrug so noncommittal he was sure she'd practiced it in the mirror. So he had no idea what she really wanted.

He glanced down at Alex, clinging to his other hand. "How about you, champ? You want to ride every day, too?"

Alex glanced up and nodded once. For the past few days they'd had a little more communication going. Nothing like the day with Vivian and the salamander, but at least it was an improvement.

Somehow Jace had to work a little more riding time into their schedule. His days were packed already, as he tried to cram all the ranch work into the hours the kids were at school. And then, this week, the elementary school had closed for a teacher work day, making *his* day a whole lot more complicated. It turned out that stringing a barbed wire fence wasn't very entertaining for a six-year-old and an eight-year-old.

He'd tried to make it like a picnic, packing snacks and a ball and telling them each to bring a few toys. He'd hoped they could hang out and entertain themselves while he worked on the fence.

But after a couple of hours, the novelty had worn off and they'd started to get sunburned because he'd forgotten to put hats or sunscreen on them. So he'd taken them back to the house and spent the rest of the day playing board games and trying not to think about the work undone and the clock ticking down.

"Is Maya going to be a bride?" Amy asked.

"Yeah, that's what an engagement is." Carly's unspoken *duh* was loud and clear to Jace, but Amy wasn't fazed.

"I want to be a bride someday." She looked at her older sister, suddenly uncertain. "Was Mommy ever a bride?"

Jace felt his stomach turn over, as it did every time the kids mentioned Brenda. He didn't have the vocabulary to explain to them why she'd made the choices she had. Yet he felt like he owed them something. Some way to make her actions make sense. Except how could choosing drugs over your own kids ever make any sense?

Carly glanced at Jace and swallowed visibly, like she wasn't sure how to answer, either. He'd have to try his best.

"People are brides when they decide to get married. Marriage is when you say to someone you love that you are going to spend the rest of your life with them. And you usually have a big party to celebrate. I don't think your mom ever got around to throwing that party."

"And then she went to jail," Amy said. "And now we can't see her anymore."

"You'll get to see her." Carly took Amy's free hand. "When Mom is ready for a visit she's going to let us know."

That was something Jace didn't even want to think about. How was he going to bring himself to take these sweet kids into a prison? He knew at some point they'd have to go, but he was almost grateful that Brenda had said she didn't want the kids to come right now. It seemed like the one unselfish thing she'd ever done.

Carly picked Amy up and twirled her around in a circle. "Come on, Amy-bug. Don't be sad. We're at Caleb's ranch and we can at least visit Newt and all of the other animals.

And Maya's dog, Einstein, will be there, and you like him so much."

Jace let out a breath he hadn't realized he was holding, thankful that Carly was big-hearted enough to shed her grumpy attitude when her sister and brother needed her.

At the same time, he wished that things were different. That Carly could have normal teenage worries instead of trying to console her sister over the loss of their mom.

He needed to find that horse for his niece. Carly deserved a friend like that. Maybe he could ask around at the barbecue today.

Jace glanced down at Alex. "You want a piggyback?"

Alex looked alarmed and shook his head.

Jace stopped and knelt beside him, trying to make eye contact, the way he'd seen Vivian do down by the pond. "Are you okay? When we talk about your parents? Does it make you sad?"

Alex nodded.

Jace wanted that enthusiastic kid he'd seen in Long Valley to come back. "You know you can talk to me about stuff if you want. We can even talk about salamanders."

He thought he saw a faint twitch at the corner of Alex's mouth, but the stoic boy just nodded. Jace wished he could figure out what was going on in Alex's head. He'd signed him and Amy up for counseling at school, as Amy's teacher had suggested. Maybe that would help him talk more.

Or maybe Alex just needed salamanders. And Vivian.

Vivian. Her dark hair and pale skin, her stubborn mouth and pink lips, had been on his mind way too much the past couple of days. She shouldn't be, but Jace couldn't help admiring her determination. She was so bright that she made him realize how much he didn't know. He'd barely made it through high school and never taken a class since then, while she could spout facts about all kinds of things and make plans with ease. While he bumbled around, blaming and uncertain.

Yet her intelligence, her hard work, all the stuff that drew him to her, were also the rocks under the water, threatening to take his whole ship down. Thanks to the loan he'd managed to wrangle from the bank the other day, her salamander wouldn't totally ruin him. But he still had to fence off new pasture and the delay in getting cattle would set him back.

And he doubted Mrs. Sherman would accept delays.

He could explain to the social worker that he'd run into an endangered species and his business might not be up and running according to her timeline. But he had a feeling she'd just use the salamander as an example of how unpredictable ranching was. And what a poor career choice he was making. And did he really expect to make enough money to support three kids?

Yeah, maybe he wouldn't mention the salamander just yet.

"Uncle Jace?" Carly broke into his thoughts. "Earth to Uncle Jace."

They'd reached the barn and Carly was setting Amy down in the dust. She backed away a few paces. "I see a few friends from school over there. Is it okay if I go talk to them?"

Jace followed the motion of her hand and spotted several teenagers hanging out beneath one of the old oaks that shaded the area in front of Caleb's barn. He squinted, trying to recognize any of them, but he'd been away from Shelter Creek too long. He wasn't familiar with this new generation of kids. But he did see that two of the kids in the group were boys and he didn't like that.

"I don't even know who your friends are," he blurted out.

"They're good kids. I met them at school."

He should just be grateful she had friends. But his protective instinct kicked in. "Why don't I come meet them?"

There it was, the inevitable eye roll. "Uncle Jace, I'm fine. These kids are tame compared to the ones I went to school with in LA. Seriously. Can I just go hang out with them for a while?" Her pink, glossed lips pressed together in a frustrated line, and she shifted her weight to one hip, practically tapping her foot with impatience.

"Okay. Check in with me in about an hour. And make sure you eat something."

Only a small eye roll this time, and an actual, somewhat grateful smile that he'd spared her the mortification of introducing her uncle to her friends. "Thanks, Uncle Jace."

"Hey!" Caleb strode up just as Carly ran off. "Glad you could make it, buddy."

Jace had always thought of himself as a pretty big guy, but when Caleb pulled him in for a brief hug and a thump on the back it put him in his place. He slapped his friend once on the shoulder blade, still getting used to this happy version of Caleb. He was jovial now, eager to talk, excited about all the work he was doing on his ranch. A few months ago, Caleb had been a lot like Jace was now. Lost and a little broken. Trying to resurrect a family ranch after years of total neglect.

Then Maya had helped Caleb get a grant to show other ranchers how to deter predators like mountain lions and coyotes. And with those funds and Maya's love, and by starting therapy with the VA hospital in Santa Rosa, Caleb was transforming right in front of Jace's eyes from a morose and angry guy into one of the most enthusiastic people Jace had ever met. It was a little disconcerting how fast his friend was changing, but it was a relief. And Jace figured he deserved a little credit. He'd been the one to yell at Caleb and tell him to go get some therapy. He was just glad his lecture had worked.

If only it was as easy to fix his own life.

"Caleb, can we go say hi to Newt?" Amy pressed her palms together in a plea and batted her long rusty eyelashes at Caleb.

"How do you resist these kids?" Caleb

asked Jace. And it was true. With her orange curls and wide smile, it was hard to say no to Amy. Plus she didn't take no easily. The kid was probably going to be queen of the rodeo someday, but Jace hoped she'd also be a lawyer. She'd be great at it.

"You can go as long as it's okay with Caleb," Jace told her. "But keep your brother with you and do not go inside any of the stalls or animal pens."

"It's okay with me," Caleb said. "As long as you just go to the barn. Don't wander any farther. It will be dark pretty soon."

Jace watched the kids run toward the barn, hand in hand, wondering for the millionth time what real parents would say. Would they let their kids out of sight like this?

But if Amy and Alex were going to grow up on a ranch, he'd have to learn to trust their common sense. He turned to Caleb. "Thanks. How's it going? Congratulations again on your engagement. Glad you finally grew a pair, my friend."

Caleb burst out laughing, his white teeth a contrast to the dark stubble of his day-old beard. "I'm glad, too. And glad she said yes. There was this moment, after I pulled the ring out, that I wondered what the heck I'd do if she said no."

"She wouldn't say no. You two were always meant to be. You both just needed some time to figure everything out. I'm happy you finally did."

He glanced around for Maya and saw her talking to Vivian over by the barbecue. Vivian looked relaxed in faded jeans tucked into leather boots, a quilted jacket over her plaid shirt. Her hair was loose, blowing in the light breeze, and Jace swallowed hard. He'd never really met a woman like her. Smart enough to know more than him, strong enough to stand up to him and gorgeous enough to make it hard to look away.

But he had to. There was no room in his life for a relationship, and even if there was, he and Vivian were way too different. Jace turned to Caleb. "I realize you're not drinking these days, but I sure could use a beer."

Caleb was studying him with a knowing smile. "I'm sure you could. Come on, I'll show you where the cooler is."

"While you do, tell me about those kids over there. The ones Carly is talking to. Who are they? Who do they belong to?"

Half an hour later Jace had the scoop on Carly's friends and was working his way toward the bottom of his beer. He was talking with Annie Brooks, a good friend of Maya's grandmother, who had a ten-year-old gelding who might be just perfect for Carly. Better yet, Annie said she barely rode him anymore, due to arthritis in her hip, and she'd be happy to lend him to Jace until he could afford to pay her. It was too good to be true, and the beer and Annie's kindness infused the evening with a warmth and a sense of relaxed well-being that he hadn't felt in a long, long time.

Until he remembered Alex and Amy. Scanning the crowd of about forty people, he realized he couldn't see them. He excused himself from Annie to go find them. On the way to the barn he checked the food tables, the trees, the picnic area and the stage where a country band was warming up. They must still be in the barn talking to Newt.

But when he got to the barn it was empty. They were gone. Jace hurried from stall to stall, calling their names and checking behind each door. He'd lost the kids. Mrs. Sherman was right. He wasn't fit to be their parent.

"VIVIAN! WAIT FOR US!" Vivian glanced up from her salamander search along the tiny creek to see Amy and Alex pelting down the bank, feet pounding, arms flailing. She winced as Amy's leg came within millimeters of a poison oak bush.

"Slow down, you two!" she called, laughing breathlessly as they crashed into her and threw their arms around her.

"Are you looking for salamanders?" Amy asked. "Alex told me you found some in our ponds. I wanted to go look for them, too, but Uncle Jace says he doesn't have time right now." She stuck out her lower lip in a perfect pout. "He says that a lot."

"Your uncle is a busy guy," Vivian reminded her. "He's trying to fix up that big ranch and get it running so it will make money for you all."

"We're going to have cows!" Amy bounced up and down. "A lot of cows."

"It will be fun to have a lot of cows." Vivian tried to ignore the twinge of guilt. Because of her discovery, these kids wouldn't have cows as soon as Jace had hoped.

Alex knelt down and started studying the

sluggish trickle of water left in the creek bed at this time of year. "Are there salamanders?"

"I haven't found any, but I saw the creek and figured I might as well check while I'm here. It's a little early in the fall for them to be out and about, though. Especially here, because this is more of a seasonal creek."

When she saw the question on the kids' faces she answered it. "That means it gets a lot of water from the rain in winter and spring, but mostly dries up in the summer and fall."

"Like the LA River."

Vivian had seen pictures in her ecology books of the cement channel as a what-not-to-do example. "Yeah, like that."

She glanced around for Jace or Carly or someone who was watching over the kids. "Where is your uncle?"

"Uncle Jace said it was okay for us to go look at the horses in Caleb's barn," Amy explained, kneeling down to trail her hands in the water.

"How did you get down here, then?"

"When we got to the end of the barn, the doors were open and we saw you." Amy, sensing trouble, threw her little brother under the bus. "Alex wanted to come."

Alex, busy peeking under bushes for salamanders, didn't seem to notice.

"That was nice of you, Alex, but I need to get you two back to your uncle."

"Pleeeaase!" Amy begged. "I haven't found any salamanders yet."

Vivian decided it wouldn't hurt to teach them one thing before taking them back to Jace, since it was in their best interests. "I really don't think we'll find any salamanders today. But take a look at this." Vivian pointed to the bushes growing a few yards away. "That plant is called poison oak. If you touch it, it will give you a really itchy rash. You have to be careful not to even let your clothes brush on it."

She led Amy a little closer for a better look. "See how the leaves come in groups of three? And they're kind of rounded at the edges. Sometimes they can be green and sometimes they're red, so they can be kind of tricky to identify."

Amy regarded the plant solemnly, then went and pulled her brother over by the arm. "Alex, you can't touch this plant." She explained everything that Vivian had said, almost word for word.

"Okay." Alex turned away to go back to his salamander hunt and Amy wandered over to join him. The kids were so cute, crouching by the creek like miniature explorers, and Vivian didn't have the heart to take them back to the party just yet. She went to join them. "What do you see in the water?"

"A water bug!" Amy pointed to the water strider. "And over on the other side there's something green."

Vivian squinted. "Oh, wow, it's a banana slug!"

"I want to see!" Alex walked right into the water, which, thank goodness, was only ankle-deep, but still, his shoes were soaked in an instant.

"Alex, you're all wet!" Amy admonished.

Oh, no. What was Jace going to think of this? Alex was oblivious, standing in the water, examining the big yellowish-green slug.

"It's huge," he said. "Amy, come look!"

"No—" Vivian started, but it was too late. Amy sloshed across to join her brother. "Ew! Vivian, it's weird."

Then they heard Jace's voice up the hill above the creek, "Amy! Alex!"

Vivian could hear the edge of fear sharpening his words. "Down here," she called and then turned to the kids. "Come on. Your uncle sounds worried."

They splashed back across the creek, their clothing soaked and muddy. "Oh, no, you two are a mess." She took them by the hands and led them across the gravel to where the trail sloped up toward the barn. At the base of the trail they froze, shoulder to shoulder, as if closing ranks against the world. "What's wrong, guys? We need to go find your uncle."

Alex glanced at Amy. Amy looked at Alex. Vivian took in their suddenly pale faces and realization rolled over her in a sickening wave. They were frightened. They were worried they'd done something wrong and they were terrified of the consequences. Which begged the question of what consequences they'd faced in their past.

"It's okay." She knelt down in front of them and put a hand on each of their forearms. "Your uncle is just worried. Grown-ups get scared when they can't find little kids."

Jace must have followed the sound of her

voice because he ran down the hill toward them, denim-clad legs leaping bushes, until he landed with a thud in the gravel of the creek bed. Chest heaving, sweat beading on his forehead, all of his worry came tumbling out in a roar. "I told you two not to leave the barn!"

The kids jumped as if struck. Vivian faced Jace and put her hand up. "Slow down. They're fine."

He glared at her, but he did take a step back. "Do you have any idea how worried I was?"

The kids moved a little closer to Vivian. "I'm sorry you were worried," Vivian told Jace. "But try to calm down. Your angry tone is scaring them."

Jace's gaze locked onto hers and she saw the guilt there. The fear. He'd been terrified, and she could understand why. Losing track of your kids was a big deal. She'd keep talking and give the guy a minute to compose himself. "The kids saw me down here and came to join me. We were looking at a banana slug."

"They're all wet. You let them go in the creek?" At least his voice was lower now, though she sensed the agitation radiating off him like a force field.

"Well, *let* isn't exactly the word."

"And you didn't think to tell me that the kids were with you? I was worried sick."

Now she was the guilty one. "I got caught up in their enthusiasm."

"You should have brought them straight back to the party."

Maybe he was right, but she was so tired of him blaming her. For the elk, the salamanders and now this. "Or maybe you should have kept a closer eye on them in the first place."

Jace winced as if she'd slapped him. "You're right. I shouldn't have let them go to the barn on their own. But I need you..." He paused, as if trying to find the right words for maximum damage. "I need you to stop meddling in my life."

"Meddling?" Anger heated her skin from the inside out. She turned to Alex and Amy. "Do you two want to go throw rocks into the creek?"

They both nodded and ran off to the water's edge, their feet squishing wetly over the gravel. Vivian angled her body to keep an eye on them and let her anger roll out in a quiet murmur, so only Jace could hear. "Meddling? I'm doing *my job* at your ranch, Jace. The job assigned to me by my boss. So if you have a problem, I suggest you take it up with her, since you're here at her party today. And I was at the creek by myself. The kids ran down here *on their own*. Would you have preferred that I left them here? Alone?"

He was silent for a moment. Good. He certainly liked to dish out blame. Maybe it was time he learned to take a little.

"I'd have preferred that you brought them to find me. But I'm sorry. You're right. I'm blaming you for all kinds of stuff that's not your fault." He pulled off his straw hat and ran a hand over his forehead. The lines around his mouth, between his brows, were etched deeper than usual.

"Do you want to tell me what's really got you worried?"

He sighed. "I've been under a lot of pressure. It's no excuse. But the social worker in charge of the kids thinks I'm just some messed-up ex-rodeo cowboy who won't be able to make my ranch a success. She gave me six weeks to show her I can do it. And it seems like everything's been going wrong since. I'm running out of money and time. But I have no right to take it out on you."

Vivian brought her palms to her cheeks. "Oh, no. What will she do?"

"I've got to come up with some solutions fast, or I might lose the kids."

"Have you talked to Caleb? He's your good friend. He might have some extra pasture you can lease for cheap. Buy your cattle and get them grazing on his land, while you fix up your own."

Jace gave her a grim look. "I've thought about it. But I hate to ask him for a favor when he just got back on his feet himself."

Pride. She understood that. The fear of being a burden. It had propelled her three thousand miles across the continent.

"You've got a lot at stake. I guess you need to ask yourself what's more important. Pride or the kids."

He huffed out a bitter laugh. "When you put it that way, I'll talk to Caleb."

It was almost easier when he was being rude. This humbler Jace tugged at heart-strings that had no business responding. Whatever his problems, they weren't hers. They couldn't be hers. Still, she had one more thing to resolve before she could leave. She walked over to where Alex and Amy were dropping pebbles into the water.

"You guys, your uncle understands that you just got really excited about the creek. But next time you cannot just run off, even if you spot someone you know, like me, okay? You have to follow his directions."

They nodded solemnly.

"He cares about you a lot. He wasn't truly mad, he was scared he'd lost you."

They both nodded again.

"I'll see you soon, okay?"

Amy crossed the space between them and threw her arms around Vivian's waist. "Bye, Vivian," she said, peering up with her big green eyes.

This wasn't making it easier for Vivian to keep her distance. "Bye, Amy." Vivian stepped out of Amy's embrace and waved to Alex, who gave her a little wave back. When she turned, Jace was watching her with a slightly stunned expression. She waved at him as she walked past but didn't stop to talk again. His combination of surly cowboy and overwhelmed dad were two layers that didn't quite fit together. It was like looking at a photo that was slightly out of focus. It made her eyes tired. It made *her* tired.

She started up the trail, smiling a little when she heard Amy start to teach Jace about poison oak. But this whole incident was just another reminder for her. She had to stop getting tangled up in things that weren't her business. She'd come to Shelter Creek to focus on work and her health. To get away from the stressful emotions of her old life and the work she'd once shared with Colin.

The last thing she needed was to get emotionally involved with Jace and his kids and his problems. Or to let him keep blaming her for things that weren't her fault. That kind of stress would defeat the whole purpose of her cross-country move to start a new, independent life. Stress would make her sick. Lupus guaranteed that.

She'd actually come down to the creek today to escape from stress. Because though the party was lovely, it was also to celebrate… well…an engagement. And the last party she'd been to like this had been her own.

She'd been so full of hope that night. She'd been so ready to take that next step with Colin. Being at this party had uncovered the

CHAPTER NINE

A FEW DAYS LATER, Jace led Amy, Alex, Carly and two of Carly's friends down into Long Valley, feeling ancient as he listened to the older girls talk about bands and actors he'd never heard of. Well, he had wanted to get to know Carly's friends, and this was a good way to do it, he guessed. Though if he heard "Ooh, he's hot" one more time he might have to cover Amy's ears because she was listening with rapt attention.

Jasmine and Jessica, Carly's buddies from school, were obsessed with some band on YouTube called Boys Will, and they'd been comparing the physical merits of several of the band members for the past fifteen minutes. Maybe it was time to change the subject.

"How did you three settle on studying the elk for your science project?" he asked.

"I was talking to Maya at her engagement party," Carly said. "And she introduced me to

Vivian, that scientist who's been studying the wildlife in the valley. Gosh, Uncle Jace, you didn't tell me *anything* that's been going on."

He sure hadn't. The last thing he wanted to do was worry her. "I figured you wouldn't be interested."

"I wouldn't care that our valley has tule elk all over it? They're kind of rare, you know." She addressed her friends. "This scientist, Vivian, is so cool. She said she'd be here today and could give us some advice on our project. She also said there are these really rare endangered salamanders in our valley, but they're super hard to see."

Jace figured he should be grateful to Vivian for making science cool for the kids, but instead he was uneasy. He hadn't thought she'd be on his ranch today. She and Maya had been supervising college interns who were surveying other ponds around Shelter Creek for the endangered salamanders, so he hadn't seen her since their disastrous argument at Maya's party.

He was an idiot and a weakling, blaming her for—what had he called it? Meddling. And after she'd put him in his well-deserved place for that, she'd calmly suggested a solution to his current dilemma. Ask Caleb.

So Jace had swallowed his pride and asked him. Caleb had offered him the pastures on the west side of his ranch. He'd even seemed happy to help Jace and refused to take any rent money. He said so many people had pitched in to get his ranch started, he was just paying it forward.

Jace had his first cattle coming tomorrow. Once he had calves to sell, he could use that money to fix the water system on his ranch and get his own pastures fenced. Because even though Long Valley spread out below them like a green oasis, it was really more of a mirage, something he needed but couldn't actually use.

The screeching noise of an elk bugling rose from the valley floor, making all the kids jump.

"What was that?" Carly, out front, stopped in her tracks, halting all of them.

"It's the noise the male elk make when they're…" Jace paused, not sure how to explain without saying too much. "Trying to get the females' attention."

"*That* gets the girls to like them?" Jessica asked.

"Well, that, banging their antlers together and running around trying to separate females from the rest of the herd."

"Kind of like creepy guys at a party," Jasmine said, and the three teens cracked up.

Jace was just about to ask what Carly and her friends knew about parties and creepy guys when Amy called out, "I see Vivian!"

"Come on, let's go see her!" Carly started running and the other kids pelted after her, skidding and sliding down the steep trail.

"Slow down," Jace called. "Don't scare the elk!" But he was too late. The kids didn't hear him. They were laughing and squealing, and when they hit the floor of the valley they kept on running.

But so did the elk, spooked by the kids, trotting with heads held high in alarm, bunching together to move across the valley and then picking up speed as a group. Running toward Vivian.

What was she doing over there, anyway? She wasn't near the pond, she was out in the open, looking at something down in the grass.

"Vivian!" Jace shouted, throwing himself

down the trail. But she was too far away to hear him. As he watched in horror, her head came up at the sound of pounding hooves. She raised her hands, waving them in the air to try to stop the approaching herd.

"Get to the rocks!" He was yelling advice that had no hope of reaching her, but she started to do just that, sprinting for a group of boulders that jutted at odd angles from the valley floor.

The kids had stopped several yards from the base of the trail and when Jace reached them, Carly looked at him in horror. "What do we do?"

"Stay here. I think she'll be okay."

Vivian was closing in on the boulders, racing for her life as the elk charged toward her in a rumbling wave.

"Take the kids back up the hill past that old fence," Jace told Carly. "Stay close together." He took off running again, with no clear plan as to what he was going to do. One lone man running after a few dozen stampeding elk.

Vivian made it to the rocks, leapt onto the lowest boulder and used it to scramble onto a taller one. Moments later the elk parted to avoid the rocks and flowed past her in a chaotic current. Jace stumbled to a walk, weakened by the intensity of his relief.

The elk must have realized there was no real threat because they were slowing. Eventually, some began to trot, then walk, then break off from the group and return to grazing, until Vivian was perched on a rocky island surrounded by a sea of peaceful brown rumps.

Which was better than a stampede, but not perfect. She was stranded. She couldn't possibly walk safely through the herd.

Jace wished he had Tioga, but he was on his own. Stopping by a shrubby willow that grew near the middle pond, he dropped his backpack on the ground and broke off a couple of branches. Then he carefully skirted the herd until he was in a position to drive them up the valley again and away from Vivian's rock.

Glancing back at the hill, he made certain that Carly had taken the kids high enough to be out of harm's way. He had a flash of pride when he saw that not only had they climbed the hill, they'd found a boulder to sit on, as well. Smart kids.

Vivian turned toward him and waved. He waved his branches back at her, then slowly, carefully, walked toward the elk, fanning the willows in front of him. The trick here was to scare the elk enough to move them, but not so much that they charged.

"Get on!" he called, as if they were cattle. "Get going! Get on." He waved his branches over his head.

It was working. The elk moved away, heads bobbing as they broke into a trot. One male stayed back, as if he might defend his herd, so Jace stopped, jumped up and down and yelled some more. The male studied him haughtily, as if embarrassed by Jace's ridiculous behavior, and finally turned and trotted off.

With a whoop, Vivian climbed off her boulder and ran toward him. "Thank you!" Jace dropped the willow branches and she threw her arms around his neck and hugged him so hard he staggered back. She didn't let go so he wrapped his arms around her, taking in her warmth, her strong body, her breath on his neck. She was alive and unharmed. He'd been so scared that she wouldn't be.

He let her go, relief making his laugh shaky. "You're okay? That was a pretty good sprint you did there. You might have broken a few records."

"For elk escape? Maybe so." She turned to look at the herd. "I thought I wasn't going to make it. What spooked them in the first place?"

"The kids started running down the trail when they saw you. I hadn't talked to them about how they should behave around elk. They scared the herd."

The reality of what had happened, of what could have happened, ran like ice water down his spine. "I'm sorry, Vivian. You might have been hurt. And it would have been my fault."

Her cheeks were bright pink. She should get out of the sun. Jace led her toward the pond and the shade of the willow where he'd dropped his backpack.

"Here." He pulled a water bottle out of the side pocket. "Drink this."

"Thank you." She took a few sips, closing her eyes as if relishing the cold water, and then drank some more. She wiped the neck of the bottle off with her T-shirt, giving Jace a glimpse of her pale, toned stomach that he wished he could unsee. Because holding her in his arms after almost losing her, so warm and alive and soft and strong, had left him wanting to hold her again.

But she must hate him. The last time he'd seen her, he'd blamed her for his own poor parenting choices. And today his carelessness had almost killed her.

The kids came toward them, walking quietly and carefully.

"Are you okay?" Carly reached for Vivian's hand. "I'm so sorry, Vivian. It was my fault. I got everyone to run down the hill."

"It's okay," Vivian assured her. "I survived. But if you are going to study elk, you have to know how to act around them. No running. Stay far away and watch them through binoculars. Talk quietly or whisper." She surveyed the group, hands on her hips. "Agreed?"

All the kids nodded and Jace felt like a fool for not having this conversation with them before they started on their hike.

"Good. Well, girls, you have something exciting to put into your project already. Not too many people have witnessed an elk stampede. Now, how about we go back to those boulders and sit up there? I'll help you take some notes on your elk observations."

All the kids wanted to go with her, so Jace followed along and within minutes they were all seated on the rocks watching the elk. Even

Alex and Amy wanted to be involved, so Carly shared her paper and pencils with them.

Jace looked over Alex's head at Vivian. "Thank you for doing this. Especially after the stampede. And after my behavior at Maya and Caleb's party."

"Don't get any ideas that I'm doing this for you, Jace Hendricks. You're nothing but trouble. But these kids are future scientists. So I'm happy to help them."

He liked that she could tease him when she had every right to yell at him. "You're a good person, Vivian."

She grinned at him. "You *finally* figured that out?"

It was hard to look away from her deep brown eyes. A strand of her hair had flown up and was draped across the brim of her hat and Jace reached across to tug it back into place alongside her pretty face. "It took me a while. I'm slow like that. But I'm catching on."

VIVIAN GLANCED DOWN, breaking the bright blue intensity of Jace's gaze, but she could still feel it on her skin. Why was he being so sweet? And *why* had she hugged him? It had been pure impulse, gratitude that he'd chased those elk away. But once she'd been in his arms it had been something else entirely. Sheer comfort. The peace of being surrounded by so much strength and warmth. And Jace. His face buried in her hair, his muscles taut across his chest. He'd smelled like fresh air and salt. She hadn't wanted to let go, which had made her let go immediately. He was difficult. He was always upset with her. He was all kinds of complication that she'd sworn to avoid.

It was easier to deal with Jace the jerk than this nice guy. Maybe he'd just been rattled by the stampede. She was trying to play it cool, but truth be told, she was rattled, too. If she hadn't looked up when she did, if these boulders hadn't been there, she might have been severely injured or worse.

Sitting on top of those rocks, with elk swirling all around her, she'd had a strange disembodied moment of irony. Here she was, trying so hard to stay healthy, watching everything she ate and drank, tracking all of her various aches and pains and rashes and other lupus symptoms in a journal. It would be too pathetic if she did all that and then was killed by a herd of upset elk.

She glanced at Jessica's paper. The girl was

sketching one of the bull elk and it was really beautiful. "Jessica, you're an artist."

The girl smiled shyly. "I enjoy drawing."

Amy peeked over Jessica's shoulder, her eyes wide with awe. "I want to draw like that."

"I'll show you sometime," Jessica offered. "When we don't have to do all this stuff for school."

That was sweet of her. Vivian was glad she'd met Carly, and excited that she and her friends wanted to study the elk. When they reported back to their class, it would help educate the other teens on how to coexist with these amazing animals.

She glanced back at Jace and caught him watching her with an odd smile on his face. "What?"

"I'm just studying you. The kid whisperer. Trying to learn your secrets."

"What?" She shook her head. "I'm not a kid whisperer."

"Sure you are. You got Alex here to talk."

"That was a salamander, not me."

He grinned. "You're telling me I should be *grateful* to my endangered salamanders?"

"For some things, sure." She liked it when

they had this kind of banter. It was way better than arguing with him.

"You're not that bad with kids, Uncle Jace," Carly said. "You're just really uptight sometimes."

Jace gave his niece a pat on the shoulder. "Thanks, Carly. I think." Then he turned back to Vivian. "I've figured out some of your methods. You're enthusiastic, you listen, you ask a bunch of questions, you make stuff more fun that it normally is and you're a cool wildlife biologist who knows a lot about plants and animals. And while I can't replicate that last part, I am going to try my hand at some of your other tricks."

"I wouldn't say they're my *tricks*." Vivian felt her face prickle at his compliments. "I was just being a nice person."

Carly snorted. "Ooh. Burn."

Vivian grinned and held up her hand to Carly for a high five. Jasmine and Jessica giggled.

"Well, maybe I need to work on that, too. Rodeo doesn't do much for one's manners."

"Do you miss it?" This from Jasmine, whose sketch of an elk looked more like a cow. Not that Jace could do any better.

"Sure. Of course. But I don't miss worrying about getting injured. I don't miss living out of my truck half the time. And I like my new life. Even if it makes me uptight sometimes."

Carly grinned and glanced at Jace, who smiled back, and Vivian forgot pretty much everything else because he looked happy. She'd never really seen him that way before. His eyes under the rim of his hat reflected the blue sky, his smile lines crinkled and deep grooves dimpled his cheeks.

He was the most beautiful man she'd ever met. He belonged in an ad for saddles or jeans or something, and yet here he was, sitting next to her, smiling at her, telling her she was great with kids. It was disorienting.

She motioned to him to follow and climbed down the rock. When they were several yards away from the kids she stopped by a clump of coastal sagebrush and broke a sprig off, twisting it in her nervous fingers.

"Am I in trouble again?" Jace asked. He pointed to the sage in her hands. "Please tell me that's not endangered."

"This?" Vivian laughed. "No! It's just sage. It smells great." She handed him the crushed plant and watched as he inhaled its scent. "Nice, right?"

"Yeah. The smell of home. Now, what's up?"

Now she felt dumb, dragging him over here. But she'd never been good at reading people. Maybe that's why she'd always loved math and science so much. "Why are you being so nice all of a sudden?"

"That's why you called me over here? You're upset that I'm nice?"

"No! Yes. I'm not sure. You're just different."

"Maybe I'm tired of being a jerk. I'm not proud of how I've behaved around you."

He gazed out at the elk, twisting the sage between his fingers. "I've been carrying around all this resentment ever since I left the rodeo. I mean... I wanted to care for the kids. But it felt like who I was had been ripped away without my consent. But standing in the creek after you left the other day, I realized I've been taking that hurt out on everyone around me. Especially you. I'm sorry, Vivian."

"Oh." Lamest response ever but his explanation was a lot more than she'd expected.

"I'm gonna try to own it now. I chose this

life. I chose this ranch. And if there are obstacles, I need to deal with them like a grown-up. Not like a kid whose toy has been taken away."

"That's a good plan." Vivian smiled weakly. She'd thought he was a shallow, angry cowboy. And yet he constantly surprised her with his depths.

"And then there's the small manner of almost getting you flattened by a herd of elk. Almost losing someone makes you realize what they mean to you."

Vivian's heart thumped against her ribs. She took a step away. "I'm fine. I wasn't hurt." She glanced over at the rocks. "We should get back to the kids."

"All I'm saying is I'm wondering if we can start again. And have a more cordial relationship than we've had."

"Oh. Of course." Her face was so hot it must be beet red. He just wanted to be more polite. And she'd thought for a moment that he might have feelings for her. Not that she'd want him to.

Jace stuck his hand out as if to shake hers. "Jace Hendricks. Former rodeo rider, wannabe rancher and bumbling foster dad. Nice to meet you."

Vivian smiled despite her confusion and shook his hand. "Vivian Reed. Wildlife biologist. Nice to meet you, too." His hand was rough with thick calluses and warm as it wrapped almost all the way around hers. They shook, and it was hard to pull her gaze away from his, so bright and full of self-deprecating laughter.

This wasn't good. This kind of intimacy was unprofessional. And more than that, it was a vacuum, pulling her in, tangling her up in him and his moods and his family, and she couldn't do that now. Not when weariness was seeping into her bones and a headache was climbing up her skull. Maybe that run from the elk had sapped more of her strength than she'd realized.

This nice version of Jace, the sweetness he was showing her, was unsettling. She'd thought she loved Colin, but she sensed that if she allowed herself to feel anything for Jace, it would be so much more than anything she'd felt before. He was just overwhelming that way. And she couldn't do that to her heart—or her health—again.

"I should head home," she told him. "The kids are fine. If they have any questions about elk that you can't answer, they can look them up online. There are a bunch of really good websites available."

"Is everything okay?" Jace eyed her sharply.

"Absolutely. Everything is fine. I had an early start today, that's all." She walked back to the boulders and said goodbye to the kids.

"We don't want you to go!" Carly said. "Can you come by Friday after we get out of school and carve some pumpkins with us?"

"That's right. Halloween is this weekend." Vivian had forgotten. October was flying by. "What are you going to be, Carly?"

Her question was met with silence and Carly glanced at Jace.

"I guess we have to talk about that, don't we?" He looked a little alarmed.

"Can I be a witch, Uncle Jace?" Amy bounced up and down on the rock.

"I'm sure we can figure it out."

Vivian almost smiled, he looked so worried. Poor guy. Every single tradition must be new to him.

"So you'll come?" Carly asked. "To help us with the pumpkins?"

Vivian almost said yes and then remembered her resolution to keep her distance. To keep her life simple and focused on maintaining her health. "That is very kind of you, but I really don't want to intrude on your family activity."

"You wouldn't be intruding," Jace said. "The social worker is stopping by that day, too. So it's not like it's some private affair."

"Please, Vivian?" Amy looked like a little cupid with her hands pressed together at her chest.

It would be so fun to carve pumpkins with them. But then she'd be even more involved. It was a slippery slope.

"Please, Vivian?" Alex had set his notebook down and was staring at her through his dusty glasses. His plea was the last straw. She couldn't say no to them. Not for this special holiday. Not when Alex was talking.

"I'll stop by. I may not be able to stay long, though, okay?"

There. That was a good compromise. She'd be there long enough to make them happy, but not long enough to get too involved.

"That would be great," Jace said. "We'll see you Friday. We're starting around four."

Vivian waved goodbye and headed toward

the first pond, where she'd left her backpack. As she walked the dirt track to her truck, she glanced over her shoulder and spotted them all huddled together on the rock. Jace was pointing to something on the other side of the valley. For an instant Vivian stopped, wanting to be there, to see what it was he was looking at. To hear the kids' responses.

But that wasn't her role. It was Jace's family, not hers.

Vivian headed for Rusty, grateful that Jace was learning to connect with the kids. Glad that maybe she'd played a small part in that. But now she had to tread carefully. Because this is what she did. She got overinvolved in other people's lives. Made their lives her own, even. It's what she'd done with Colin and look where it got her. She wouldn't make the same mistake here in Shelter Creek.

CHAPTER TEN

JACE WATCHED THE last few cattle trot down the chute and closed the gate behind them. He shook hands with the truck driver, handed him a check and watched him pull away down the road toward town.

He wondered, again, how Vivian was doing after the stampede yesterday. She'd seemed to get over it pretty quickly, but she must have been scared. Nothing less than sheer terror would send her flying into his arms.

Not that he'd minded. Holding her like that had been an unexpected revelation. She'd fit against him like she belonged there. Like they should stay that way, holding each other, for a lot longer than they had.

Jace shook his head, trying to rid himself of the memory. It had too big of a hold on him, left him with hopes that were unrealistic. Someone like Vivian wouldn't be interested in a guy like him. She'd just been frightened.

That was all. Though there was that moment when they shook hands and agreed to start again…

How he got to all this wishful thinking he'd never know. He'd always been practical, definitely not some romantic daydreamer. He needed to get his focus back on his work.

Caleb was waiting for him, leaning on the fence watching the two dozen Angus. They were keeping close together, wary of their new surroundings but eyeing the good alfalfa Jace had set out for them. A few of the bold finally left the group and wandered toward the hay and the others soon followed, filling the afternoon with the comfortable sound of chewing.

"That's a good-looking herd you have there," Caleb said as Jace approached. "You're off to a nice start."

"I hope so." Jace leaned his forearms on the top rail. "They're all grass fed, and I intend to keep it that way."

"It's the best market around here. If you're interested, down the road, maybe we can help each other market our beef. I've been thinking about growing my herd, as well."

Jace elbowed his buddy. "I thought you

were working with Annie Brooks on breeding some prize-winning sheep."

"Well, I am. But I've got a big ranch. There's room for both. Once I kick you off, that is." Caleb shot him a grin. "Nah. Just kidding. Take your time. Your cattle are welcome here as long as you need a hand."

"I appreciate your help," Jace told his friend for probably the tenth time that day. The cattle represented hope to Jace. Evidence that his business was finally getting started. His future. The kids' security.

"Happy to do it. You put up with so much from me this past year. It's the least I could do. But there is one thing I want to talk about."

Jace glanced at Caleb, instantly wary. Caleb wasn't much of a talker. "What's up?"

"I think you need more help." He held up a hand when Jace opened his mouth to protest. "Look, I may not be great at math, but I'm sure you didn't make a fortune during your rodeo career. Then you bought that ranch, but you haven't fixed it up. And, meanwhile, you've got to feed and clothe three kids. So why don't you tell me what I can do to help get you on your feet?"

"You're already doing something." Jace nodded toward the cattle. "Right here."

Caleb clapped a big hand to Jace's shoulder. "What's going on, buddy?" Though both men were tall, Caleb was huge, with broad shoulders and big hands that sent Jace staggering a bit with one friendly tap.

"Fine. What's up is that most of the money I had went into mending the fences around Long Valley. And now I can't use it because it's full of elk and endangered salamanders."

Caleb nodded. "Maya's been filling me in on that."

"I got a loan to cover these cattle, the fencing for the rest of the ranch, and also to get the old well going, fix the pipes, prop up the barn, all that stuff."

"And who's doing the labor?" Caleb glared at him as if he already had the answer. "Let me guess. You're trying to do it all by yourself."

"Well, yeah. Labor's expensive."

"Not when you ask your friends to help."

Jace shook his head. "You've got your own ranch to run. This is my problem to deal with."

"You mean it's your pride."

Jace wasn't in the mood for a lecture. "I've got to go get the kids from school."

"Liar. You don't have to be there for another hour." Caleb's voice softened. "Don't you remember what you said to me just a couple months ago? That I had to be willing to reach out for help? That I shouldn't be so stubborn about trying to handle everything on my own?"

"Well, yeah. You were drinking and fighting, and you were about to lose Maya for good."

"Yes, I was. And even if, at the time, I was a little upset, I appreciated that you were honest with me. So now I've got to be honest with you. Stop trying to handle everything on your own. Because you're not alone. This whole town will come out and help you fix up your ranch. They did it for me, and they'll do it for you."

Jace shook his head. Caleb was delusional. "You're a war hero. You fought for our country. Your parents were respected in this community and your sister passed away in a terrible tragedy. People wanted to help you. But I'm not you. I'm no hero."

"What do you mean you're not a hero? You

gave up your life's dream to help these three kids. You walked away from a successful career for them. If that's not heroic, I don't know what is. And then you got a bad deal with the valley. Maya told me that between the salamanders and the elk, you might never be able to graze it. That could have happened to anyone. People are going to want to help you get on your feet."

"No." The word came out louder than he'd meant it to, and from a place inside Jace that he'd shut the door on long ago."I'm the son of the town drunk. I'm the kid who didn't even finish high school, I was so eager to get away from here. For most of my career, I barely had a dime to my name. My sister is a criminal. I can't ask people to come out here and fix my ranch up for me. I've got to do it myself."

"Why? What are you trying to prove?"

The question gave Jace pause. What was he trying to prove? That he was worth something? That he could create something despite the hand he'd been dealt? He didn't have a clear answer.

"I'll tell you what I think is going on, and you can tell me if I'm wrong," Caleb said. "You're still clinging to the idea that you're this big rodeo star. You only got to wear that mantle for a few short months and you don't want to let it go. If you ask for help, that dream is well and truly over."

The words sliced like a blade. "That's not true."

"It's not?" Caleb gave an exaggerated shrug. "Huh. Guess I got it wrong, then. And I guess you won't mind too much if I ask Maya's grandmother and her book club friends to organize a barn raising for you?"

Jace was caught. Say no and he'd admit his friend was right. Which he was. Jace *did* have a chip on his shoulder. Because he had nothing left of his old life except the admiring way people looked at him when he walked through town. If he had a barn raising, everyone in Shelter Creek would know he was desperate.

Heat rose behind Jace's eyes, and at first he had no idea what it was. It had been so long since he cried and so many weeks since he'd felt much of anything. A big part of him had gone numb the day he'd heard about the kids, and he'd stayed that way, a fish out of water gasping for air, trying to survive until someone threw him back into his native waters.

Except there was no going back. This ranch, these kids, this town, this was it for him now. And Caleb was here to remind him that he'd better adapt quick or he wasn't going to make it.

Jace had a sudden memory of walking toward the arena down in Abilene last summer, his gear bag slung over his shoulder, the hot Texas sun beating down hard. He'd had his hat cocked to match his attitude, a sponsorship check in his pocket, and a photo of his backside up on a billboard selling jeans. In that moment it had seemed as if everything had come together—all the hard work and brutal falls and lean years—to this perfect point.

That memory wavered and dimmed, as if it belonged to someone else, the old Jace, who'd lived a completely different life.

"Okay." The word came out heavy with bleak acceptance. "Okay let's do it. Let's see if anyone is fool enough to give up their Saturday to help me fix my ranch."

"You'll be surprised. In a good way. I promise." Caleb held out his hand as a peace offering.

Jace shook it, pressing his lips together to

keep any more emotion inside where it belonged. "Thanks, Caleb. I think."

Caleb laughed as they walked to their trucks. "Now you can go get those kids from school knowing that pretty soon they'll have a really nice ranch to come home to."

Home. The kids deserved it, even if he had to rely on charity to get it. And that was the challenge. To let go of the image he'd cultivated his whole life, that he was okay, that he had it handled, that he was a tough cowboy who took care of himself. Maybe that was the lesson here. To learn to rely on others a little more. To admit that he needed a hand. Then maybe he could move forward with a little more ease. And a little more hope.

"I CAN'T BELIEVE the progress they've made." Vivian tipped her head up to examine the roof of the new Shelter Creek Wildlife Center. "It's framed! I mean, it's starting to look like a building."

"Isn't it incredible?" Maya's eyes were wide. "Only a few months ago, this was just one of Eva's crazy ideas. And I was heading back to Colorado to keep going with my research, and you were up in New Hampshire studying beetles."

"Hey, don't underestimate beetles. They're pretty cool," Vivian joked. "But being here is better." And she meant it.

She was amazed each morning when she opened her eyes and the California sunlight flooded her cottage. She'd loved her cozy, safe life with Colin in New Hampshire. But maybe that was because she'd never tried anything else.

"Isn't this divine?" Eva strode up, wrapped in a poncho woven of brightly colored yarn. She owned a gallery in town and her love of art and design extended to her unique wardrobe.

"We were just saying it's a dream come true," Maya said.

"I just met with the contractor this morning, and he told me he thinks they'll finish by next summer, as long as the winter isn't too wet."

"Since when has a winter in Shelter Creek been too wet?" Maya glanced around at the brown hills rising behind the center. The wildlife center was being constructed on the western edge of town, on a plot of land Vivian was shocked to learn had been donated by Bunny Chadwick, of all people. Bunny had been so abrasive in the town council meeting, that Vivian had been surprised she really did walk her talk. Years ago, Bunny had donated most of her family's historic ranch to the state as a wildlife preserve, and now she'd given this land for the center.

"And once it's built," Eva continued, "you two can move your office out of that trailer and into a real building."

"Am I late?" Trisha's voice was breathless as she held tightly to a leash attached to Maya's dog, Einstein. Even though he only had three legs, the big dog was pulling Trisha along. Einstein's huge ears were up. Well, one was up and the other always flopped over. "Here's your boy, Maya. He missed you."

"Einstein had a sleepover at Trisha's last night because Caleb and I went out to try to trap a lion near Juan Alvaro's ranch. We didn't catch the lion, though."

Einstein celebrated their reunion with an awkward happy dance. "Einstein, settle down," Maya commanded, and the dog instantly slowed. "Trisha, it's okay to be a little firm with him. Now that he's realized he's not going to be dumped by the side of the road again, he's getting kind of bossy."

"You're right." Trisha handed Maya the purple leash and ruffled Einstein's big, soft head. "But it's hard to be firm when he's such a cutie-pie. Plus he was pretty good until he saw you."

"Maya, did you happen to see Annie around the ranch?" Eva asked. "She's been awfully closemouthed about her relationship with Juan. But I saw them the other morning, early, at Shelter Creek Café. *Very* early," she emphasized with a wink.

"They're definitely dating," Maya said. "But I don't know what will happen. They both love their own ranches and they're set in their ways."

"It's romantic. Love can find us at any age." Trisha gave Eva a mischievous grin. "You might be next, you know."

"Or you, young lady." Eva clapped her hands together. "So, are we going to take the tour?"

Today they'd been given the go-ahead to enter the structure and make sure they were happy with the way the architect's plans were coming together in real life. Eva led them through the framed building, pointing out where the offices would be, the bookstore, the classrooms and the small museum to teach visitors about local wildlife. Around the back would be a veterinary clinic as well as cages and enclosures for injured animals.

Eva pointed to the large swath of vacant land between the back of the center and the hillside beyond. "Eventually, we'd like to fence in this area between the building and the hills so we can have a sanctuary for animals who can't be released back into the wild."

"Can you imagine?" Maya turned to Vivian and Trisha. "We could have an aviary for injured birds and habitats where disabled animals could live out their lives in peace. And people could walk through and learn about them."

Her enthusiasm was infectious, and Vivian could picture it, too. She was excited that she'd get to be a part of it. *As long as you stay healthy* warned the voice of doom that lurked in Vivian's mind. The voice sounded suspiciously like her mother's. Maybe because Mom had kept Vivian on the phone for what felt like hours the previous night. Her mother had been researching various obscure symptoms of lupus, and she was convinced that Vivian needed to come home and take a desk job in her mom's real estate office in order to fend off the disease.

To which Vivian had said no, nuh-uh, nope, not going to happen.

Maybe this job was strenuous and could cause a flare-up. But right now it also made her happy. It gave her a chance to make new friends and be a part of this amazing project. Not to mention sore elbows and shoulders from hauling herself up on boulders yesterday to escape stampeding elk.

She hadn't mentioned those particular aches and pains—or the elk—to her mother.

"Trisha, are you okay?"

The concern in Maya's voice pulled Vivian out of her thoughts. Trisha was leaning on a low boulder a few feet away.

"I'm fine." Trisha waved a hand in front of her suddenly red cheeks, as if to fan herself. It was hot today. Was Trisha suffering from heat exhaustion? Fall in California was so different than what Vivian was used to. She wasn't homesick, but she did miss the cool, crisp fall weather.

"I'll get some water from my truck." Vivian ran for Rusty and grabbed her water and cell phone. If she needed to call an ambulance, she'd be ready.

Sprinting back to the shelter, she was relieved to see that Maya and Eva had moved Trisha into the shade of the framed building. "Here. Drink this." Vivian pressed the bottle into Trisha's hand, noticing that Trisha's other hand was draped over her stomach. Nausea. That could mean heat exhaustion for sure.

Maya put a hand to Trisha's forehead. "It's cool. That makes me nervous. Trisha, did you drink any water today?"

"Yes. I'm fine. I just got a little dizzy for a moment, that's all."

"You weren't just dizzy, you were green," Eva said. "Do you think you might have a stomach bug?"

"Maybe…" Trisha stood, her hand still on her stomach. "Maybe I'll just go home and rest for a while."

"Trisha, are you…" Maya held up her hand, palm out, as if to stop herself. "No. Never mind."

"Pregnant?" Trisha finished for her and let out a long breath, like she'd been holding it in for a while. "Yes. I am." Tears welled up in her eyes. "So I understand if you need to find someone else to run the wildlife rehabilitation program."

"What? No! Trisha that job is always yours if you want it. Your having a baby makes no difference whatsoever. Why are you crying? This is *amazing*!" Maya put her hands on her friend's shoulders. "You're going to be the best mom!" Tears were streaming down her cheeks when she turned to Vivian and Eva. "We're having a baby!"

Trisha pulled Maya in for a hug and when they parted Trisha's expression was pure relief. "I was planning to tell you soon. I was just waiting for the first trimester to be over. It's over tomorrow and I wasn't sure what you'd think."

"What we'd *think*?" Eva clasped her hands together. "This is great! We are very happy for you! And for us. It's been so long since I had a baby to spoil! My own kids don't seem to want any children and they both moved to Chicago, which I try not to take personally."

Vivian was trying to process the news. A baby! A little tiny person to cuddle and spoil. Her heart went out to Trisha, who had been carrying this secret alone. Vivian knew so well what that was like. Except Trisha's secret came with a happy ending, while hers...well, hopefully her lupus wouldn't ruin everything, though it was always a possibility. But she wouldn't let that thought spoil this moment. "I am so happy for you," she told Trisha. "Truly. Congratulations!" Trisha held out her arms and Vivian gave her new friend a hug. "But you should still get out of this sun."

"Oh, gosh, we are not thinking straight." Eva took charge. "Trisha, are you okay to drive? Go home and rest. Or maybe you should see your doctor? Who is your doctor? Someone in town? Can I drive you there?"

"I think I'm okay," Trisha said. "Maybe I'll go home and put my feet up for a bit, though."

"That's a good idea," Maya agreed, taking Trisha's arm and leading her toward the cars. "We can have this meeting another day when it's not so hot."

They all watched as Trisha slid into her compact car and started down the road toward town. The sound of her car faded away, leaving only the buzzing of insects and the faint rattle of dry grass in the breeze.

Then Eva turned toward Maya and Vivian. "She didn't mention who the father was."

Maya nodded slowly, still watching the road, though Trisha was now out of sight. "And she hasn't dated anyone, that I know of, since we've been friends. But we've only been friends since July."

"And it's October now," Eva said thoughtfully.

"Three months." Vivian did the math. "One trimester."

"So the question is," Eva mused, "what was Trisha up to three months ago? And with who?"

"No sleuthing," Maya admonished. "If she wants to tell us who the dad is, she will. If she wants to have this baby on her own, then that's her choice, right?"

"Right." Vivian said the word so emphatically that the other two women looked at her, startled. She tried to explain. "It's her body and her health. And it's a modern world. Women can have children all kinds of ways. They don't need a man around if they don't want one."

"Yes, indeed," Eva said.

Phew, dodged that one. But it was true.

Someone's health issues weren't anyone else's business. Which was why Vivian was here, pretending her joints didn't hurt the way they did right now, pretending she wasn't falling into bed exhausted at eight o'clock each night. Her health was her private business, and Trisha's baby and its father were private, too.

But, like Trisha, Vivian wasn't sure she could hide her symptoms too much longer. The pain, the fatigue, everything seemed to be getting more frequent. She just hoped that if she had to tell Maya she was sick, her boss would be as understanding with her as she'd been with Trisha.

CHAPTER ELEVEN

JACE SET LEMONADE and cookies on the picnic table in his front yard. He'd built it himself from some of the discarded wood around the property, and it had turned out pretty well. He looked around with pride, hoping that his attempts to clean up the ranch would meet with Mrs. Sherman's approval. He'd been up since dawn getting ready. Cleaning the house, top to bottom. Sweeping the porch. It still wasn't fixed but at least it was clean.

The yard had to impress her. He'd borrowed Caleb's tractor to haul all of the old equipment and debris behind the barn. He'd weed whacked and then scraped this area down to the dirt, added edging, weed cloth and gravel so they had a real picnic area.

He hadn't been able to afford a play structure like Mrs. Sherman had suggested, but he had set out logs and stumps in a pattern where the kids could jump from one to another. And he'd padded the ground underneath with woodchips, of course. Safety was the name of the game when you were under the eagle eye of Mrs. Sherman and Social Services.

Jace glanced at his phone. The social worker was due to arrive in twenty minutes. He'd set out the tarps and pumpkins on the ground near the table. He'd even bought those kid-friendly carving sets so no one would get hurt. Maybe he was finally getting some kind of grasp on this parenting thing.

He walked back into the house, where Alex was reading in the shabby armchair Jace had found at the flea market last week. Amy was doing a puzzle, also a flea market find, by the empty fireplace. And Carly was nowhere to be seen. Probably upstairs in her room.

Jace paused in the doorway, trying to take in the scene through the social worker's eyes. The house was clean. The old plank floor was spotless. The tall windows looking out over the coastal hills were crystal clear. He loved this house, had loved it from the moment he saw it. Despite the fact that it was saggy, weathered and needed years of repair, it had elegant bones. Those Victorians knew how to do things right. The high ceilings still sported chandelier medallions, even though the chandeliers had been replaced with cheap brass fixtures sometime in the eighties. The trim around the ceiling was decorated with plaster flowers, and the baseboards and door-frames were wide and solid and carved in lines and scrolls.

But despite all the vintage detail, his fresh paint and scrubbed floors, the room felt bar-ren. And he realized then what was missing. Decoration. Those small touches that made a place into a home. Art on the walls. Some-thing on the mantel. Candles, maybe?

Well, that was the next step. Maybe Carly would want to help him with that. It could be a fun project for them to do together.

Hey, check it out, he was thinking kind of like a dad. A good dad, even.

Alex and Amy looked so peaceful, he al-most hated to disturb them. But they had a schedule to keep if they were going to be all together having fun when Mrs. Sherman ar-rived. "Hey, Alex? Amy? Almost time for pumpkins."

"Where's Vivian?" Amy's head popped up

so fast her curls bobbed all around her head. "Is she here?"

"No, she said she'd probably just stop by for a little bit, remember? Can you get your shoes on and come outside to the picnic table?"

Miracle of miracles, they both scrambled up and ran to the front hall to get their shoes.

He started up the stairs, pausing at the landing. Carly's door was directly across from the top step. "Carly?" he called. After a long moment, her door cracked open and there she was, her blond-streaked hair, so like Brenda's, pulled into a ponytail, her phone in her hand and an irritated expression on her face.

"I'm doing homework." The earbuds in her ears and the fact that he could see the name Stephanie on the screen of the phone belied her statement.

"Let's go get our pumpkins carved. Plus the social worker is coming." As her expression closed like a door he added, "There are cookies. And it will only take about an hour."

"Okay." Jace heard her say, "Steph, I have to go." And then she flung the door open again and followed him downstairs.

"Is she going to try to take us away?"

Carly's question stopped him on the bottom step. When he turned, Carly sat down on the landing, as if voicing the question had knocked the strength right out of her legs.

Jace floundered around for something to say that wouldn't scare her. But he wouldn't lie to her, either.

"She doesn't think I'm an ideal parent for you guys. She doesn't like the ranch much, she wishes I had a steadier job. But I'm trying really hard to show her that I can do this. That I can be the right person for you and your brother and sister." He paused, realizing he'd never even asked her about it. "Do you want to stay with me?"

Her eyes went wide, like she was shocked to be asked. He realized she'd probably never been asked about much of anything. She'd just been swept along in the flood of her mom's chaos and addiction, trying all on her own to keep her and her siblings' heads above water. Her answer was especially savvy, considering.

"What are my other choices?"

"Some other foster family. They might be more experienced at this parenting thing than I am. They might live in a town or a city, somewhere a little more interesting than a ranch way up above Shelter Creek."

She shook her head so quickly, so vehemently, that he knew that this place—and maybe even her uncle—had gotten under her skin. Maybe even into her heart. "No. I mean, it's all been hard. I miss my mom, but I also don't miss her. You know? And then I feel bad about that."

Guilt. He was very familiar with that. Lived with it every day. If only he'd been the kind of guy who settled down into one job, in one place. Maybe he could have gotten Brenda to come live with him. Maybe he could have helped her get settled and clean. Maybe he could have kept all of this loss from happening to these kids. But he hadn't been that kind of guy. Not then. Though, ironically, through necessity, he was forced to become that guy now.

"I don't think emotions are things we should apologize for. They just are what they are, you know? You've got reasons for feeling the way you do."

Carly nodded slowly, as if really listening to his words. The afternoon light streamed in from the small window on the landing, casting gold all over Carly. Jace had the strangest feeling it was some kind of sign that things were shifting for them.

Or maybe it was just wishful thinking. Because if he'd learned one thing in his months with Carly, it was that teenage girls were even more of a mystery than they'd been when he was a teenager. They slept, ate, dressed, functioned in an entirely separate realm, a parallel universe of friends and phones and music and thoughts. His best hope was to try to get a glimpse of Carly's reality every once in a while and to try to talk her into spending some time in his.

"Carly, you're a good kid. You worked hard to help your brother and sister. I hope now that you're here, you can relax a little more, have fun with your friends and get involved in stuff at school. I hope you can talk to me about what's going on in your life. Who knows? Maybe I can help a little. Believe it or not, I was your age at one point. And I didn't have the easiest relationship with my own parents, either."

"What happened to them?" Carly asked. "I think I met them when I was little, but my mom never talked about them."

It was hard to talk about a relationship so complicated and damaged. "Your mom and I grew up in a pretty uneasy home. Maybe a bit like how it was for you, having your mom be so unpredictable. Our dad was gone a lot. He drove trucks all around the country. But when he was home he'd get angry about the smallest stuff. And he'd drink at night. My mom worked, cleaning houses, doing alterations, she had a bunch of businesses going to make ends meet. And she was real quiet. She was scared of my dad, I think. Your mom and I, we just tried to keep out of the way, you know?

"Anyway, my dad's drinking finally went on the road with him. He crashed his truck, went off a cliff...and he died. Ten years ago now. And my mom moved away, to Florida. She had cancer by then, but never told us. Not until the very end. I got down there to say goodbye. Your mom, well, she didn't show. I'm not sure what happened."

Carly nodded, her face almost blank, like all this sadness was commonplace information. And maybe, for her, it was. Hopefully, before she went off to college, Jace could give her some of the happy childhood she'd missed.

"Hey, I was talking to Annie Brooks at the barbecue last Saturday. She has a really great horse she doesn't ride anymore and she's looking for someone to take care of him. Would you like a horse of your own? Maybe we could get you confident enough in your riding for you to join the high school drill team this spring."

Carly's eyes went wide, then pooled with tears.

Oh, God, he'd blown it. Said the wrong thing. Made her feel like a charity case. Or maybe she really hated horses and had just been going along with…

She launched herself down the stairs and threw her arms around him, almost knocking him off the steps. Once they found their footing she pulled away and he saw that Carly wasn't just crying, she was smiling so wide it was like she still carried that sunbeam from the window with her.

"I'd love a horse. All the kids at school have been talking about drill team and their horses." She stepped back and wiped her eyes with the heels of her hands. "I'll take really good care of it if you show me how, I prom-ise."

"I'll show you," Jace husked out through a throat that seemed to have closed up. Christ, these kids had a way of grabbing his heart and twisting it around in ways he'd never imagined. All these feelings he didn't even have names for. Pride in this girl he barely knew for holding her head up and persisting, even when she must feel so lonely and lost sometimes. Sadness that she hadn't told him how she felt. "How come you never answered, when I asked if you wanted a horse?"

Her smile faded. "I don't know. I guess I just didn't really think it could happen. I didn't want to get my hopes up."

"You can ask for stuff, okay? I may not be able to give you everything you want, but I'll try."

She met his eyes, her expression shy. "Thanks, Uncle Jace." She hugged herself like she couldn't believe her luck, then some-thing cooled the joy in her eyes. "We have to make a good impression for the social worker. She can't take us away from you."

"Don't worry. I think we're on track. Just act natural. And if she asks about how you're doing, be honest." He drew a breath. "Even if there are things about me that you don't like. I want you to be truthful, more than anything."

She nodded. "Where are the littles?"

"Outside, at the picnic table." Jace picked up his box of utensils for pumpkin carving and handed Carly a stack of bowls to carry. "They've probably eaten all the cookies by now."

"Oh, great, Uncle Jace. Even I know better than to give them a sugar rush before Mrs. Sherman shows up."

Jace was laughing as he followed her outside.

CHAPTER TWELVE

THEY FOUND AMY chasing Alex around the picnic table. At first Jace worried that they'd gotten into one of their disagreements, but miraculously, or maybe it was the sugar, they were both laughing.

"We left you each a cookie," Amy called proudly.

Considering there'd been a dozen on that plate, Jace wasn't sure that was much of an exercise in self-restraint. He caught Carly's I-told-you-so look and laughed out loud. "Well, live and learn, I guess. Okay, sugar monsters, come settle down. We have to get started on the First Annual Hendricks Family Pumpkin Carving Celebration."

Alex and Amy ran to the tarps and sat down by their pumpkins. Carly grabbed the last two cookies and sat down, too. Jace took a knife out of the box and knelt next to the kids. "Let me cut the tops off for you, okay? Then you can scoop."

"But I want to carve a face," Amy said.

"You will," Jace assured her. "After we scoop out all the stuff inside."

He sliced around the stem and pulled the top off, smiling as Amy peered in.

"Whoa!" She looked up at Jace with her big green eyes. "There's a lot of stuff in there!"

"Haven't you carved a pumpkin before?" Jace glanced at Carly, shocked when she shook her head.

"Never?"

Alex and Amy shook their heads, too.

He tried to disguise his disbelief, but emotion made his voice a little raspy. "Well, it's a good thing we're doing it today." They'd do it right. Save the seeds and roast them. In fact, they'd do every holiday right. He'd try to make up for all the traditions and fun they'd missed out on over the years.

Jace quickly sliced the tops off of Alex's and Carly's pumpkins, too. Then he grabbed the plastic bowls he'd brought out, and the big spoons. "So the next step is to scoop out all the orange stuff inside. And put the seeds in this separate bowl here."

"Well, look at you all. Have I interrupted a family project?" Mrs. Sherman was crossing the rough grass from the driveway. Jace had been so engrossed in the pumpkins that he hadn't even noticed her driving up.

"Mrs. Sherman!" Carly jumped up like she'd been struck by lightning. "How are you? Would you like to sit down? Here, let me pour you some lemonade."

Carly was no good at acting natural.

"Why, thank you, Carly." Mrs. Sherman's brows were rising, never a good sign. But she sat down and took the offered lemonade. "What a nice picnic area." She gave Jace what felt like her first genuine smile. "You've made so many improvements to this yard."

Relief loosened some of the tension in Jace's shoulders. "It's a work in progress."

"Well, it's good to see progress. I also noticed new fencing on the way in. But I thought you were focused on fencing off that valley down the road for your cattle. Did you change your plans?"

"Yes. We ran into a few problems in that valley," Jace told her.

"We have endangered salamanders!" Amy announced.

"And rutting elk!" Alex chimed in.

Mrs. Sherman's brows nearly disappeared into her hair this time. "Rutting? What an interesting word choice." She glanced at Jace, her smile devolving into a tense line.

"Vivian taught it to me," Alex said, sensing her disapproval and meeting it with a touch of defiance. But, hey, the kid was talking. Hopefully Mrs. Sherman would focus on the quantity of his words more than the quality.

"And who is Vivian?" Mrs. Sherman asked.

"There she is!" Amy yelled the words with the same enthusiasm she might have if a circus parade had made its way up their road. Instead, she was pointing at Vivian's old red truck, huffing and puffing its way up their driveway. Maybe Jace would offer to take a look under the hood. Years of living out of his truck had taught him a thing or two about engines, and Vivian's needed help.

Vivian parked by the house and climbed out. She glanced around, spotted the kids' frantic waving and started toward them. All three kids scrambled up from the table and ran toward her, Alex and Amy leaping and tumbling like puppies in their enthusiasm.

Mrs. Sherman turned toward Jace and repeated her question.

"Vivian is the wildlife biologist who is studying the endangered salamanders and the elk Alex and Amy mentioned. Remember those protesters in my driveway? It turns out they were right. That valley I was fencing off for grazing is where the local elk get their water. The town is funding a study to find out exactly what kinds of animals are living there and what to do about it."

"And how does this affect your plans for the ranch?" Mrs. Sherman's eyes were kind, at least, but Jace knew he had to pick his way carefully through his answer.

"I took out a loan to fix some of the other fences and repair the water system on the rest of the property."

"Oh." She pressed her lips together in an expression Jace was beginning to dread. "That's not ideal. You need financial stability."

"I'm working on that, too. I've got twenty-four head of cattle. I'm grazing them on my friend Caleb's land."

"Caleb, who you got arrested with."

Why did she have to turn every good thing

into a negative? "He's also organizing a barn raising for me. A bunch of folks from the community are going to come out and help me fix my fences and barns. So next time you come, you'll see even more big changes."

His gaze found Vivian and the kids. She was walking toward the picnic table, listening to something Carly said and giving her a high five. Then Alex and Amy, apparently deciding she was walking too slowly, took her hands and began to pull her forward.

"Amy, Alex, let go of Vivian." Jace started forward, exasperation rising. "That's not polite, kids."

Alex let go right away, but Amy clung to Vivian's hand. Vivian stopped, knelt down, and said something quietly to Amy that Jace couldn't hear. When she rose, Amy walked more calmly by her side. Another example of Vivian's kid whispering. Jace made a note to try it himself the next time he couldn't rein Amy in. Though if he got down to eye level she'd probably take it as an invitation for a piggyback.

"Mrs. Sherman," Amy called proudly. "This is our friend, Vivian."

At the word *friend*, the social worker

glanced at Jace with an assessing look. "I see."

Jace hated the way he strained to read Mrs. Sherman's face. The same way he used to try to read Ma's when he was a kid. Looking for the emotional forecast for the family. Concern in Ma's eyes had usually meant Dad was pissed off or drunk or both, and trouble was coming.

"And we've been helping her do science," Amy said proudly.

"Nice to meet you." Vivian extricated her arm from Amy and reached out to shake hands with the social worker.

"And Carly is studying the elk for school," Amy went on, oblivious to the adult introductions in progress.

"Really?" Mrs. Sherman's face brightened at the girl's enthusiasm and the coil in Jace's stomach unwound a little. "Carly, you're doing a science project?"

"Yes, ma'am," Carly answered, and Jace glanced at her in alarm. She never spoke that politely. Maybe it had been a bad idea to tell her how much Mrs. Sherman's visits mattered. He wouldn't want the social worker to think he was coaching the kids to act a certain way.

But Mrs. Sherman just smiled. "I'm so glad. Are you enjoying school?"

Carly shrugged. The polite facade could only take her so far. "It's okay. I'm making some friends, so that's cool."

"And Jace, have you met Carly's friends? Have you had them over here at the house?"

"Jessica and Jasmine have been over." He noted the surprise in Mrs. Sherman's expression and gave himself a mental pat on the back. "They've been working on the elk project together."

"And Jace, you're supervising the project? To make sure the girls are safe? Elk can be dangerous."

"Well—" Jace started.

"There was a stampede," Amy interrupted proudly. "Vivian had to run away and climb on rocks to be safe."

"Amy, why don't you show me your pumpkin?" Vivian asked. She smiled gently at Mrs. Sherman. "It wasn't really a stampede. And the children were far away up the hill when it happened. They were completely safe."

Mrs. Sherman gave a curt nod. "Good to know."

Vivian rolled up the sleeves of her pretty pink flannel shirt and strode toward the tarp. "Okay, kiddos, who needs help digging out some goop?"

All three kids followed Vivian to the tarps. The change in mood when she was around was palpable. Maybe Jace should be jealous that the kids seemed to like her a lot better than they did him, but right now he was just glad she was here. Glad to see everyone smiling as Vivian shoved her hand into Amy's pumpkin and brought out the slimy, orange insides. Glad to see Alex laughing as she chased him around making monster hands.

Mrs. Sherman watched the chaos with a slight smile on her face. "Things appear to be going well, Jace. You all seem a lot more settled."

"I'm happy you think so." He kept his voice casual but relief washed through his system. He'd been dreading this visit. Afraid she'd see only what he hadn't done. What he didn't have yet.

"But be careful. They all seem pretty attached to Vivian. Is she someone you're serious about?"

Jace gaped, trying to figure out her meaning. "Serious?"

"Well, it's not a great time to start a relationship. The kids are still getting used to you, and you're establishing your bond with them."

"Hang on." Jace didn't know whether to laugh or worry that she was prying into the nooks and crannies of his personal life. Though she'd have to look long and hard to find anything interesting these days. "I'm not dating Vivian, if that's what you're implying."

"Well, whatever you're calling your relationship with her, the kids seem to be very attached. And even though she's sweet and enjoys them, what's going to happen when her work in your valley is over? How are the kids going to feel when she disappears from their lives?"

"Well, she lives here in town. She's not disappearing."

"Just be careful, Jace. You don't want the kids to think that everyone they care about is going to walk away. They have enough abandonment issues as it is."

Maybe Jace had issues, too, because the idea of not seeing Vivian made the future seem a little bleak, as if Mrs. Sherman had just put some kind of filter in front of his eyes that dimmed the colors of the landscape.

He and Vivian weren't involved with each other, but he thought about her way too often. Wished he could hear her opinion on whatever was going on in his day. Wondered what it would be like to trace the tattoo on her wrist. Imagined running his fingers through her hair, to see if it was as soft as it looked.

But Vivian wasn't the slightest bit interested in him. For one thing, she was brilliant, while he was barely educated. And she saw him as a grumpy, obstructive cowboy. He hadn't given her much reason to view him otherwise.

"I hear you," he told Mrs. Sherman, and his answer seemed to satisfy her. She nodded once, so vigorously her curtain of stick-straight hair swayed at her jaw.

There were a few beats of awkward silence while they both watched the kids. "Do you want to carve a pumpkin?" Jace finally asked.

Mrs. Sherman glanced down at where Vivian and the kids had returned to scooping out pulp and sorting seeds. "Well, maybe

CHAPTER THIRTEEN

"I HAD NO idea our booth was going to be so busy." Maya's grin told Vivian that she was delighted with the chaos around them. It was the first Saturday in November and the Shelter Creek Fall Festival was underway. The wildlife center's booth was a huge success. If you could count being totally overwhelmed by kids as success.

Every family in town must be here and the elementary school campus was packed. There were the usual school-sponsored booths, like face painting and pin the tail on the turkey. But unlike the school carnivals that Vivian remembered from her childhood, community agencies and businesses also had activities. Shelter Creek Tack and Feed had provided a petting zoo, the Blackberry Bakery was running cakewalks, and the Creek Café was making a killing selling coffee to all the tired parents. Farm Girl Fashions was getting kids dressed up to participate in a fashion show, Eva's gallery had easels set up so kids could paint and a local ranch had provided a hay ride. The big old cart horses had been very patient as they circled the block around the school with load after load of kids and their families.

All the proceeds from the paid activities would support the school's art and music programs.

The fledgling Shelter Creek Wildlife Center was here with a free activity, and a few other community groups had set up free events, too. The fire department was giving truck tours, the sheriff was letting kids sit in his squad car and the high school clubs were running field games out in the grass. The library's bookmobile was parked nearby and the librarians were out front organizing a Harry Potter trivia contest. The free events ensured any kids who couldn't pay for the fundraising activities still had a good time.

"Are you ready to take over for the next round of origami?" Maya asked. "I promised Trisha I'd give her a break and supervise all of our stuffed friends."

They'd borrowed some taxidermied specimens of native animals from a natural history museum in Marin County, farther south, and sworn they'd return them in perfect condition. That meant they had to be on constant patrol to keep the stuffed coyote, bobcat, raccoon, opossum and red-tailed hawk safe from curious sticky fingers.

But the animals were a great opportunity to teach. Vivian had spent a lot of the morning watching over them and talking with kids about the animals' adaptations for survival in the wild. She loved the children's questions and was astounded by the connections they could make. One little boy had compared the hawk's talons to dinosaur claws, which led to an entire discussion of evolution. That little boy knew more about dinosaurs than Vivian did, that was for sure.

"I'm not sure I totally have the origami pattern down, but I'll give it a try," Vivian assured Maya.

"Well, you're way better than me when it comes to working with kids," Maya said. "I have no idea how you have so much patience. You always know just what to say to them."

"I like kids," Vivian mused. "It's their enthusiasm for everything, you know? The world is new to them and they've got such a wide-eyed sense of wonder and excitement."

"Maybe they're that way with you because you can guide their energy. To me they just seem really wiggly and unpredictable." Maya glanced over at Trisha and the stuffed creatures. "But here goes nothing."

"I can do that instead," Vivian offered. "If you'd rather do origami."

Maya looked at the squares of paper, held down by geode paperweights, another thing that caught the interest of a lot of the kids. "No, thank you. I can't face another fold. I may not be able to talk about the animals in kid language, but at least I know a lot about them."

Vivian laughed. "Okay, origami it is." She went to the folding table they had set up and pulled the chairs out to signal that the activity was now open. She, Maya and Trisha had met with Priscilla from The Book Biddies last night, learning from the former teacher how to make origami cranes. But that didn't mean Vivian was going to remember how to do it today. Especially because it was afternoon now, and they'd been here since morning. Her mind was getting that horrible, fuzzy fatigue that she was pretty sure was another special delivery from her lupus.

She reached for the directions Priscilla had written out and studied them one more time.

Hearing footsteps, she looked up to see Amy and Alex running full tilt for her table, along with a few kids Vivian didn't recognize.

"Vivian!" Amy ran around the table and hugged her. "We miss you. Why haven't you come to visit us?"

"Oh, guys, that's so nice of you, but I'm not working on your ranch much now. I'm doing lots of paperwork in the office instead." She was working on the official report and recommendations for Jace's valley, which would be submitted to the town council next week. She missed getting to spend her days in that beautiful landscape, but it was probably better that she had some time to rest.

"But being stuck inside isn't as fun as being with you," Alex complained. "We want to go to the valley and look for animals."

He reached out for a hug, so Vivian leaned down and gave him one. Then she turned both kids gently back to the table. "Why don't you introduce me to your friends and we'll make some paper cranes."

"But I don't know how to make a crane." Alex was anxious, as always, about anything new.

"Don't you worry about that. I'll show you," Vivian assured him.

She got them seated and was introduced to Madison, Hannah, Charlie and Gabe, their classmates from school. The next hour passed in a flash as they folded cranes and chatted. More kids joined in, sitting on the ground when the table filled up.

"You're like the pied piper of children."

Vivian looked up from where she was seated on the ground, helping a group of kids fold their paper. Jace was standing just outside the group. She hadn't seen him since they'd carved pumpkins last week. It had been such a fun afternoon. So easy to hang out and joke around with Jace and the kids, and even the social worker, who hadn't seemed nearly as formidable as she'd imagined. "How are you, Jace? Want to fold a crane?"

"Yeah, come on, Uncle Jace. Make a crane with us." Alex and Amy had come running up at the sight of him and were now trying to pull him down to sit on the pavement next to Vivian.

He hesitated, then plunked down next to her in a cross-legged position that seemed almost comical on such a big man. Especially one in cowboy boots and a cowboy hat.

Amy and Alex sat down on the far side of him and started shaping their cranes expertly, chatting with each other and comparing their creations. Vivian saw Amy take Alex's paper and redo one of his folds. She almost intervened. Sometimes Amy could be so bossy, Vivian worried it might stifle Alex. Then she caught herself. They were fine and not hers to worry over.

Jace was watching them, too, and Vivian wondered if he'd also noticed Amy's behavior. Maybe not. His expression was relaxed, like he was just enjoying being with them, which was really sweet and made her heartbeat speed up.

She attributed that to some kind of innate, biological response. She needed to do something, or say something, to distract herself while she got used to him again. His smile with his even, white teeth. The striking blue of his eyes. That dark stubble on his jaw that made her want to run her fingers—no. What was she thinking? No fingers. No stubble.

"How was your Halloween?" she blurted.

He turned to look at her. "It was good. We went into town and the kids had fun. I survived my first trick or treating as a parent and no one got hurt. I even survived the sugar rush afterward."

She laughed, trying to picture the chaos of the kids, especially busy little Amy, with too much candy in their systems. "What were their costumes?"

"Amy was a witch, Alex was Harry Potter and Carly went to Jasmine's house to pass out candy, because apparently she's way too old for costumes."

"Did you get any photos?"

"Thought you'd never ask." Jace pulled out his phone and showed her several snaps of the kids posing on the sagging porch and running toward houses to ask for candy.

The photos were adorable and for a moment Vivian almost wished she could have been there to see them herself. *Don't get involved.* It was her mantra these days along with *make self-care a priority.* "They look great. You're now officially a parent because you have all these kid photos on your phone."

He grinned at her and put the phone away. Then he picked up a piece of paper. "Okay, teacher, teach me what to do here." He turned his paper around at funny angles, deliberately comical.

"Here, put it on the ground. I'll show you." Vivian leaned forward and moved his paper so it was in the correct position in front of him. Her shoulder brushed his and stayed there, leaning into his arm when she demonstrated the first fold. He was so warm and solid, and it was nearly impossible to think when they were touching like this. Of course, she'd always been aware that Jace was handsome.

But now his warmth and strength were right here, reminding her of the way she'd run into his arms after the elk stampede. Something she'd thought about way too much already. She could feel his breath on her ear and she scooted back as soon as she got the first fold done. "Now do three more just like that," she said all in a rush because she was actually a little dizzy.

Which was ridiculous. Hopefully it was because she was tired and not because of Jace being all sweet, showing off his nice neat folds to Alex and Amy.

She was relieved by the small tap on her shoulder. It was little Hannah asking her how to make the beak just right on her crane. And then Hannah's mother was there, thanking her and taking Hannah by the hand, and Vivian realized that other booths were packing up. It was almost three o'clock—festival cleanup time. Next there'd be a barbecue at the park, just a block away, and then a dance at the old Shelter Creek Livery Stable. The big barn had recently been turned into an event space.

Vivian rose and started collecting unused paper and abandoned cranes.

"Uncle Jace says we're going to get barbecue now." Alex appeared at her side and slipped his hand into hers. "You're going to come with us, right?"

She still felt a thrill every time Alex spoke like this. He'd come so far. "That's very nice of you to ask, Alex. But I have to clean up our booth and drive all this stuff back to our office." Vivian was grateful for the built-in excuse. Otherwise she'd want to get barbecue with them. She'd missed them. But she wasn't a part of their family. She had no reason to be on their ranch anymore. And she was already more attached to them than she should be.

Plus, she was tired, so tired, and she knew she had to listen to her body to maintain her health. There wasn't room in her life for these kids and this cowboy.

She noticed Jace watching her from a few yards away. She led Alex to him. "Alex is ready for his barbecue now. And I've got to clean up all this stuff."

"Thanks for doing these activities." Jace motioned to the booth. "You helped give the kids a really good day."

"We helped, too." Amy drew herself up importantly. "We delivered a bunch of straw bales this morning, to decorate the school booths."

"Well, wasn't that nice of you?" Vivian glanced at Jace and they shared a small smile at the girl's pride. "You all did your good deed for the day. Did the bales look nice?"

Amy nodded, positively glowing. Vivian remembered the first time she'd met the kids, how they'd been tentative and a little sad, like they still carried the shadows of their past experiences inside. But those shadows were gone, at least for now. Chased away by this beautiful, bright November day, this fun event and Jace's steady care.

"It's an honor to be part of something like this," she told Jace. "I had a lot of fun." Then she noticed the small piece of paper in his hands. "Oh, let me see your crane."

He handed it to her with a chagrined smile and their fingers brushed as she took it. The feel of his calloused skin against hers froze her hand. She glanced up to find him watching her with a new intensity in his blue eyes.

Vivian quickly examined the crane and tried to figure out what had gone wrong, because it didn't look very crane-like at the moment. "Hang on." She turned around and set the mangled thing on the table, unfolded a few parts, refolded them and then straightened the neck and beak. She handed it back to Jace. "Here you are."

He took it more carefully this time, so their fingers didn't touch. He examined her handiwork, an expression of delight on his face. "You're amazing," he said. "You take all my messes and turn them into something a lot better."

Vivian's heart gave a lurch as the meaning of his words sank in.

"It just needed a few tweaks," she told him weakly. "You had it mostly right."

He laughed, a low cynical sound. "Story of my life."

And she remembered that he'd almost been a champion, had been so close before he had to walk away. "It's not a bad story. Most people's stories are probably more like that, really."

And here she was, trying to make things better for him again. Just like she had for Colin. Old patterns, ingrained so deep. "Enjoy the barbecue." She glanced over at Trisha, who had backed her car up close to their booth. Maya was trying to fit the stuffed coyote into the trunk. "I'd better go help."

"Right." Jace hesitated, as if he had something else to say. But then he tipped his hat her way, a gesture she never quite got used to, it seemed so old-fashioned. "Thanks for the bird."

"It's a crane," she told him. "In Japan it's a symbol of peace."

He smiled and lifted the crane to look at it a little more closely. "Peace is good. I'm glad you and I are more peaceful now, too. No more arguing. Just carving pumpkins and making cranes."

That peace might not last once he saw the report with her recommendations for Long Valley. Which he'd hate. And then he'd be angry at her once again. "A truce." It was the only honest response she could give.

"Uncle Jace, the other kids already went to the park. Can we go?" Amy bounced up and down in front of Jace like an adorable pogo stick.

"Yeah. We'll go." Jace looked at Vivian. "You're sure you don't need our help to clean up?"

"We're fine, thanks."

He nodded and took the kids by the hands. "Come on, you two. We need to find Carly."

Vivian watched them walk away. They really looked like a family now, and for a fervent moment Vivian wished that things were different. That she wasn't sick. That she had more time and energy and ability to devote to them. That she could be part of their family, too.

HIS ATTEMPT AT being a fun, easygoing parent was not going well. Jace had promised himself that today he'd try to be less rigid and more in the moment with the kids. But after the barbecue, the kids had gotten this idea that they wanted to go to the barn dance. Some of their friends from school were going, and even Carly, who'd joined them for some food, wanted to go.

Jace suspected that the boy who'd walked her back from the sack races and introduced himself as Travis in an embarrassed, foot-shuffling way might be the reason Carly wanted to stop by the dance.

So Jace had agreed, but now he was standing by the big barn doors, as far away from the dancing as possible, trying to keep an eye on the kids but also be invisible. He wasn't opposed to dancing as a rule, but one of the moms from Amy's class had cornered him soon after they arrived and introduced her friend Leslie, who had apparently just gone through a divorce and needed a "cowboy like Jace" to show her a good time.

Where Jace came from, that phrase implied a lot more than dancing. Leslie, who'd immediately dragged him onto the dance floor to sway to some slow song, seemed to be aware of that implication, too. And not averse to it.

Six months ago, maybe Jace wouldn't have been averse, either. But now Jace was a dad, not a bull rider, and more than that, Leslie wasn't Vivian. And somehow Vivian had become the standard by which Jace judged all women. He wanted anyone he got involved with to be smart, kind, funny, brave, strong and beautiful. In other words, he wanted them to be Vivian.

He'd made an excuse, something about checking on the kids, and escaped Leslie to hide out here like a coward.

He peeked around the corner again. The kids were fine. Alex and Amy were eating cookies and busting out some ridiculous dance moves with their little buddies from school. Carly was chatting nearby with Travis, Jasmine and a couple of other teens Jace didn't know. They were holding their paper cups of punch just like grown-ups might hold a cocktail at a party. It was kind of cute and kind of bittersweet. He didn't want Carly to grow up so fast.

Jace stepped all the way outside and leaned on the barn door. The barn was set just two blocks off Main Street, next to a big gravel public parking lot and a pizza shop. As he inhaled the good pizza smells, Vivian's old truck pulled into the lot. Vivian parked, hopped out, shut the creaky cab door and started toward the pizza place.

"Hey, Vivian," Jace called before he'd even really decided to do it.

She glanced over, saw him and waved. She hesitated but finally came toward him. She was still dressed in her jeans and wildlife center T-shirt, and there were shadows below her eyes, dark smudges that Jace wished he could wipe away. No wonder she was tired. She'd been at the Fall Festival when he dropped off the straw bales this morning, and she'd been there packing up when he and the kids went for food at the end of it. That was a long day.

"Are you getting some fresh air?" She climbed the steps to the deck. "Or did too much dancing wear you out?"

"Nah. Just..." he glanced over his shoulder "...hiding."

She was so serious a lot of the time, her smile always startled him. "What?" She peeked around the barn door like she was a detective and whispered, "Who are we hiding from?" Then she laughed, realizing the answer on her own. "Let me guess. Some of Shelter Creek's single moms?"

"How did you know?"

"I hear stuff. You're a hot topic around town, Jace Hendricks."

He was happy to see her like this, teasing and carefree. "Well, maybe I need to give them something to actually gossip about. How come you're not in the barn?"

"At the dance?" She shook her head. "I barely know anyone in town yet. And I don't feel like being a wallflower. Plus..." she pointed across the parking lot "...I'm starving. And there's pizza over there calling my name."

"Is that place good?"

"You haven't had it yet? It's amazing. It makes up way too much of my diet."

"Well it must suit you, then."

She froze. "Are you giving me a compliment?"

Something about hiding here, outside the barn with her, made him reckless. "Yeah. I am."

"I don't even know what to say to that."

"You could say thank you."

"Thank you." She pointed toward the pizza place again. "Well, I'd better go. That way we can end this little chat on a high note, before we start squabbling."

He didn't want her to leave. He'd been doing nothing but staring at her, wishing for more time with her, all day. This feeling in him had been building since they'd met, since she'd changed things for him and the kids. But he hadn't realized exactly what he wanted until the social worker said he shouldn't have it. "We can't squabble. You gave me a crane, remember? Our truce?"

"Jace Hendricks, if I'd known a paper crane was all I'd need, I would have brought you one the first day on the job."

He laughed. "You should keep a supply on hand for the next rancher whose plans you're going to turn on end." He didn't want to go any longer without her close to him. "Dance with me?"

She folded her arms across her chest and eyed him suspiciously. "I thought you were hiding."

"I won't need to hide if you're there to protect me." He shouldn't do this, should keep his distance, but it wasn't even really a choice anymore. Instead it felt like he was meant to hold her.

"I don't know. I'm not much of a dancer."

Vivian peeked through the door again. "What are they doing?"

Jace peered in over her shoulder. "A two-step. C'mon, I'll show you."

"That's real dancing. I never learned how to do that. I'll probably step on your toe, break your foot, cripple you, and then how will you run a ranch and chase after three kids?"

He glanced down at her cute white sneakers. "This may be the first time I've seen you without hiking boots. I think my feet will be fine."

"My dignity won't." She glanced inside again. "I'm sure there are plenty of women in there who would love to dance with you, if you just come out of hiding."

"I don't want to dance with them. I want to dance with you." She was caving. He could tell. Some of the exhaustion he'd seen on her features earlier had faded. "Come on. Don't you ever just want to have fun?"

She looked stricken. "I have fun."

"How, exactly?"

"Well, there's the book club." She motioned toward the pizza place. "And food."

"*That's* your fun?"

"I love my work. So that's fun, too."

"Well, I don't have much fun these days, if we're being honest. So come dance with this boring old parent. Give me just a few minutes of adventure."

"Adventure is the right word, if you dance with me."

Jace grinned. She was funny, sweet and humble. So quick with her replies. The idea of having her in his arms was heady, like he was about to go downhill on a roller coaster. "I was a bull rider. I'm up for the challenge." He held out his hand, and with an embarrassed smile, she put her hand in his.

Her fingers were small and cool and he wanted to hang on for a lot longer than a dance. How could someone's hand be soothing? Calming? But somehow hers was. He glanced back at her, wondering if she felt anything like the emotions rushing through him now. Probably not. She was probably wondering how in the world a smart girl like her got talked into dancing with a washed-up rodeo cowboy like him. But she smiled shyly and there was something there, a warmth in the depths of her brown eyes, that had him wondering if maybe she felt this thing between them, too.

The band was playing a cover of an old Tim McGraw hit and Jace pulled Vivian close. "Put your hand in mine, the other at my shoulder." She did and Jace congratulated himself on asking her to dance, because she fit perfectly in his arms. She was just tall enough that he didn't have to slouch too much. Her slim, strong shoulder felt incredible under his hand and he pulled her a little closer.

"Okay, so it's a six-count dance. Start on your right foot. We're going to take two quick steps, and then two more that are twice as long." He counted her off, murmuring "Quick, quick, slow…slow," in her ear as they danced in place to practice. After a minute or two she seemed a little more relaxed. "Ready to move?"

She laughed softly. "You mean we have to take this on the road? I don't know about that."

"Let's just go a few steps sideways." They tried that and she did okay. She was way better at this than she'd let on. "Okay, how about you go backward?"

"Can I have one of those back-up signals, like a truck has?"

"Beep...beep," he offered, and her smile lit up her entire face and if he could, he would have stopped and tried to memorize the delight on her features because it was so pretty. But the two of them were moving and he had to make sure they didn't crash into any of the other dancers.

So he focused on steering them safely around the dance floor, and after a few minutes he even gave her a little spin and brought her back in again, and when she looked up at him, breathless and proud, he realized he'd completely missed out all those years, partying in bars with whatever woman happened to be available. Because he'd never danced with someone he was falling in love with before. And it took dancing to a whole new level.

The music faded away and Jace twirled Vivian one more time, then stepped in and caught her, dipping her slightly. When he set her back on her feet she was laughing breathlessly, her mouth open slightly, revealing her cute white teeth. His own breath caught as every part of him said *this*. *This* was what he wanted. Vivian in his arms, smiling up at him. Vivian having fun, with him.

Her gaze met his and her smile faltered. She wanted to kiss him, he could tell, and no way could he resist because he wanted it, too. So he let himself focus on the deep brown of her eyes and brushed his lips over hers. Her arms were on his shoulders from the dance, which was pretty nice, but nothing compared to the feeling of her sliding them around his neck, going up on her tiptoes and kissing him back.

The barn fell away, the crowd, the kids, too. All the reasons they shouldn't be doing this right here in the middle of the Shelter Creek Fall Festival just evaporated because all he wanted was that kiss, and another, and to find a way to keep kissing her for as long as possible.

But Vivian seemed to realize that they were putting on a show. She gasped against his lips and pulled away. "Oh, no!"

Jace glanced around. A new song was starting up, people were moving and he had no idea who'd seen them kiss. He didn't care. He just wanted to do it again. "That's not really the reaction a guy hopes for when he kisses a girl."

"The kids. Jace, we can't get involved."

"I think we might be involved already." He reached for her hand, but she pulled away.

"My work. Your ranch. This is a bad idea."

"The way you just kissed me didn't feel like a bad idea."

She flushed, put her hands to her cheeks, turned away and walked toward the door. He followed. Out in the open air of the deck, she stopped. "I'm going to get my pizza now. Thank you for the dance."

He didn't want her to go. "What just happened between us, that chemistry, those feelings, wasn't just a simple dance."

"It's all it can be. I really don't want to get involved with anyone. Not right now. I'm new in town. I'm…" Her voice trailed off. She shrugged. "I just can't."

He cast around in his mind for what to say, what to do, to keep her here with him a little longer. "You're smart, Vivian. And funny. And so sweet. I'm not saying I deserve to go out with you. But I'd sure like it to happen."

She touched her lips with her fingers as if

she was remembering their kiss. "I'm sorry. It's not a good idea. I'll see you later."

He'd tried. There wasn't much more he could do, but the disappointment weighed him down. He leaned against the barn wall, hoping it would absorb some of the heartache. "Enjoy your pizza."

"Yes. Yes, I will." She turned and Jace watched her go lightly down the steps and across the street. He hoped she'd turn around and come back, agree to go out with him. But she didn't, even though he watched her until she was through the door of the pizza restaurant.

He'd just have to give her some space and hope she'd decide, as he had, that this was special. This was worth chasing. But it had to be her decision, so he set aside the overwhelming need to follow her and went inside to check on the kids.

CHAPTER FOURTEEN

"VIVIAN, HAVEN'T YOU spent enough time out on this ranch?" Annie Brooks grinned as she slid on a pair of thick leather gloves. "Now Jace has you stringing wire, too?"

Vivian smiled at the Book Biddy, who was so much more at home out here in the dry brush than she had been in Lillian's living room. "I wanted to do my part." Though the truth was, Jace hadn't asked her to string wire. Jace didn't even know she was here. Vivian had deliberately shown up to the barn raising late and texted Maya to find out which section of the ranch they'd been assigned to. Then she'd walked straight out to the pasture to join Maya and Trisha.

"Team Maya," Trisha said as she walked by with a huge pair of wire cutters. "We all have to represent."

"Exactly," Maya said, carefully picking up a big reel of barbed wire. "If the wildlife center is going to work well with ranchers, we have to help them out, too."

Vivian wanted to help Jace. She wanted his ranch to be a success. But she wanted to hide from him, too. Ever since the barn dance yesterday evening, she couldn't think about him without remembering that kiss, so sweet and powerful.

Of course she couldn't date him. That was why she'd run out of there like a big chicken. She'd promised herself she'd keep life simple. Focus on her health. Not get involved with anyone.

She had a pattern in relationships. She got involved with men who needed so much from her, and then she gave too much. And then she shattered when they moved on.

And he would move on. Because she was sick. And there was a good chance she'd get sicker. And nobody wanted to be with someone like that.

She'd been trying to reframe their kiss in her mind so it didn't mean anything more than it was. Hadn't she moved to California for an adventure? To feel alive again? A dance and a kiss in a barn with a gorgeous cowboy was just part of that adventure.

Vivian glanced at Annie and saw she was hauling a big metal post driver all by herself. "Hang on!" Vivian couldn't help but tease the tough rancher. "You may be a woman of steel, but you can still ask for help."

"When we're working with tools from my youth, I guess I have to. I've got a gas powered one of these and I should have thought to bring it. Or we should be doing this in winter when the ground is wet," she grumbled.

"I think Jace is in a hurry to get some cattle out here." Maya grunted, hunching down to attach a strand of barbed wire to the post they'd already set. "He's using Caleb's land now, and while we don't mind, Caleb says it stings Jace's pride. I'm glad he let everyone know he was in trouble so we can help him get on his feet."

Vivian was glad, too. Glad not to be the sole witness to Jace's financial dilemmas. Glad he'd finally found the courage to reach out to the town and ask for help. She carefully unrolled the coil toward the corner post that someone had driven in already, making sure to keep the line straight.

"Here, I'll measure." Trisha came up next

to her. "No one is letting me do anything exciting."

"You're pregnant. You have to take it easy." Vivian marveled at Trisha's calm and happy nature. If she were all on her own and pregnant, she'd be a lot more nervous and stressed. Trisha seemed to be taking it in stride.

"I'm pregnant. Not broken. Sheesh. If I hadn't spilled the beans and just worn some baggier clothes instead, you wouldn't even know I was knocked up."

"I'm glad you told us," Vivian said. "And you can't blame us for being excited for you. And wanting to take care of you a little." She set the wire down to help Trisha drive a stake into the ground where the next fence post should go. "Have you said anything to your family yet?"

Trisha shook her head. "My mom and dad live in Italy now. They moved there for my dad's work and loved it so much that they rarely come back. I guess I'll have to give them the news over the phone at some point."

"Do you still live in the house where you grew up?"

"Yes. I'm lucky that way. My parents paid off the mortgage on it a long time ago. As long as I pay the taxes and keep up with repairs, I'm all set."

The information was a relief for Vivian. She liked Trisha a lot and she'd wondered how her new friend was going to support a child on her veterinary technician's salary. Fortunately, when the wildlife center building was complete, Trisha would be helping rehabilitate any animals brought there, which would supplement her income.

"How do you stay so calm?" Vivian finally asked the question that kept rising in her mind. "If I was going to have a baby, I'd be freaking out."

Trisha laughed. "Well, of course I was really worried at first. I mean, I definitely didn't expect to be pregnant at this point in my life or to be dealing with it all by myself as a single person. But I like kids. It's exciting to think that I'll be a mom. And I know I'll do whatever it takes to give my baby a really good life."

"And there's no way the father will…"

"No." Trisha cut her off. "There is no way."

"Sorry, I shouldn't have pried."

Trisha grinned. "Trust me, when the word

gets out in this town, you will not be the only one asking. I may as well get used to it."

"Okay, ladies, coming through." Maya dropped a couple of metal fence stakes on the ground. "Isn't this cool? It's like a work bonding thing. Big companies pay a lot of money to have their employees practice this kind of teamwork. And we're doing it for free. *And* we're helping Jace."

"And I'm grateful for it. I really am." Jace came striding up with another metal post driver on his shoulder and Vivian tried not to notice the way his muscles moved under his T-shirt as he carefully set it on the ground. Or the way the low-slung tool belt accentuated his hips. With his cowboy hat tilted down to block the sun, the man was beautiful. "You all are getting more done than the high school rodeo boys."

"You got the rodeo team working out here?" Annie glanced his way in admiration. "How'd you manage that?"

"They're here doing their community service hours. *And* I promised I'd take the assistant coaching job, come spring," Jace admitted.

"Brilliant." Annie clapped her gloves together. "They'll be so lucky to have you and all of your experience."

"Yeah, well, I'm not known for my amazing abilities with kids." Jace glanced at Vivian. "But I'll try."

Vivian's heart ached for him. She'd looked him up on the internet when she got home last night. He'd been kind of a big deal in the rodeo world. It must have been so hard for him to walk away. Now to revisit it, but behind the scenes at a local level, must feel like he'd fallen hard. "You're fine with kids," she assured him. "They'll love having you as their coach."

He responded with a wry smile. "We'll see."

"Ahem." Maya cleared her throat and Vivian flushed bright red. She'd forgotten they had an audience who knew nothing about the time they'd spent together or the conversations they'd had.

"Are we ready to drive the next stake in?" Vivian asked brightly. "Trisha just marked the spot." She tried to ignore the questioning looks of all the other women.

"I've got it," Jace offered. "I actually came out to tell you that Maya's grandmother has set up coffee, donuts and all kinds of other good food over by the barn, if you'd like to take a break."

"That sounds excellent." Trisha handed Jace the tape measure. "I'm ready for a break."

"I wouldn't mind some coffee," Annie said.

"I'll join you." Maya fell in alongside Annie, then over her shoulder, she said, "Hey, Viv? Catch up to us when you're ready." She gave Vivian a quick wink and Annie elbowed her. They left giggling like girls.

Had they heard rumors about the kiss at the dance last night? Or maybe whatever was going on between her and Jace was more than a little obvious.

Vivian turned to see Jace looking at her with an almost shy smile, though she'd never use that word to describe the cocky cowboy.

"You seem to have something to say."

He nodded. "I have a lot to say. First thing is that I wouldn't ever have said yes to the coaching if it weren't for you. Thanks for showing me how to be around kids. And how to just be."

"What do you mean?"

"I didn't really know how to behave around people. My whole world had been so transient for so long. Chasing the next rodeo, the next good ride, the next buckle. I never really learned how to exist without that chase. How to be peaceful. Watching you around the ranch and with the kids, well, you taught me how to slow down."

She had no idea how to respond to such a big thank you. "I'm glad I could help."

"And I wondered if you'd reconsider going on a date with me."

It was hard to remember why she shouldn't when he looked at her like that.

"Why do you even want to? Most of the time we're like oil and water."

"That just makes it more interesting."

Vivian had a brief flashback to the old Jace. The one who barely spoke, and when he did, his words came out angry. And now here he was, smiling that confident smile, his hat tilted down at a rakish angle, leaning on a fence post and saying words that flowed over her like warm water, tempting her to relax into them. To believe them.

She knew better. She'd believed sweet words before and been so very wrong. And Jace hadn't even guessed the truth about her. If he knew she was sick, he wouldn't be standing here asking her on a date.

She should tell him. The words rose inside, almost spilled out, and then she bit them back. No. Revealing her secret meant she'd have to trust him not to reveal it to anyone else. It wasn't fair to ask him to do that. To burden him with a confidence. She wasn't ready to tell Maya and Eva yet. Or any of her new friends. It was so lovely to get to know them without that sick-person label, without that pity. And maybe her lupus wouldn't ever flare up and they'd never have to know.

"Look, Vivian, maybe you're scared, or someone hurt you, or I'm just not your usual type. But we have something together. You and me, we have a spark, a connection, and I care about you a lot. So I hope you'll change your mind. I hope you'll go out with me. Just give me one evening, one date, and if I'm wrong, I will back right off."

It was only one date. And hadn't she said she'd come here for adventure? But dating someone was a big step.

"Why do I feel as if I just stepped off a cliff and I'm hanging in midair, like one of those old Bugs Bunny cartoons?" Jace was grinning, but his eyes held a degree of vulnerability that Vivian had never seen "You know the ones?

Where the character runs off a cliff and there's a minute when they realize what they've done and *then* they fall?"

"I didn't take you for a cartoon guy."

"But you must know I'm old-school. When Alex and Amy wanted some cartoons the other day, I pulled those up on my laptop."

Vivian was distracted for a moment by the idea of Jace on a laptop. She'd mainly seen him out around the ranch. Doing rancher stuff. And dancing. Though even that had been in a barn. The idea of him on a computer was intriguing. Another dimension of him that she hadn't discovered yet.

"I'm still hanging here, Viv."

Viv. He put a lot into that one syllable. A gentle note. Almost tender. And something warmer, too. "Okay. One date. So you can satisfy your curiosity or whatever this is."

"Sure, I'm curious. And a whole lot more than that." His smile could chase the fog away. "How about tonight? A late dinner."

Tonight she'd be a mess. Way too tired after this kind of ranch work. Ugh. Maybe she should just tell him she was sick. It would end things right here. But no one disclosed their medical history to avoid dinner with another person. And here she was, being so serious, when she'd come out here to California to get away from that type of limited thinking. "Would tomorrow be okay?"

"Tomorrow will be fine."

"Just one date, Jace. We should keep this casual. We're both busy people. And we don't want to have a negative impact on the kids or anything."

"One casual date, then. I'll pick you up at eight?"

"Eight's fine. Do you know where I live? It's on Buckeye Court. The last house by the old fence. Number ninety-six."

"I'll find it. Now go catch up with your crew. You all have done some great work out here. You deserve a donut or three."

Her blood was racing so fast, she didn't need a sugar rush. But she nodded and left. As she walked away across the field toward the barn she swore she could feel his eyes on her back. She peeked over her shoulder, and sure enough, there he was, watching her leave. He was too far away for her to read his expression but he tipped his hat, letting her know he'd seen her looking.

JACE STOOD ON an old crate and tried to absorb the number of folks gathered around him. There had to be at least fifty people, all drinking lemonade or beer, tired and dusty in the golden light of the setting sun. The town of Shelter Creek had turned out for him today, and they'd changed everything.

"Excuse me," he called out. "I'd like to say something before you all head home."

The crowd shifted, moved closer, until Jace felt like a soapbox preacher on a Sunday. He cleared his throat and tried to ignore the way his heart was thumping harder in his chest. He'd never done much public speaking.

"I just wanted to say thank you for coming out here today. You've transformed my ranch and I will never stop being grateful for that. The barn looks incredible, the fences are up, the pipes are fixed and the water troughs are full."

Everyone started clapping and smiling, and Jace was grinning ear to ear by the time they finished.

"My buddy Caleb and I are going to bring my cattle over tomorrow and I can't wait to see them grazing right here on my own land."

A few people clapped again. This was so

weird, he felt like a politician or something. But he pushed forward because his heart was way too full not to try to express his gratitude.

"I came here with no job and three kids who needed a home. We were all pretty lost at first. But the people of this town welcomed us and gave us fresh hope for the future. Lillian, Annie and all the ladies in that book club of yours, thanks for organizing this barn raising today."

"It was our pleasure," Lillian called out through the applause.

"Caleb." Jace searched the crowd for his friend and saw him standing hand in hand with Maya a couple of rows back. "Thanks for talking some sense into me."

"Likewise, brother," Caleb said.

"I hope every one of you will always feel welcome here at North Sky Ranch. Stop by and check out how your handiwork today is making a difference for us. Watch us grow into something special. And know we couldn't have made it happen without the incredible work you all did here today."

The crowd burst into applause and cheers. That's when Jace spotted Vivian, standing off to the side with Trisha, her eyes shining so bright with something that looked a lot like pride. Maybe he wasn't the greatest public speaker, but if he'd touched something in Vivian's guarded heart, that was an additional reason to celebrate.

Jace raised a fist, let out a whoop and made his way through the crowd, shaking hands and saying thanks to each and every person. He'd grown up feeling like an outsider in his hometown, and come home feeling like a stranger. But there was no doubt in his heart that he belonged here now.

CHAPTER FIFTEEN

JACE WIPED HIS damp palms on his jeans and turned up the radio for some courage. He'd pulled over a block from Vivian's house, trying to keep his cool. Because the truth was, Jace Hendricks, legendary ladies' man on the rodeo circuit, was nervous. He hadn't actually been on that many dates. Sure, he'd met women in bars and enjoyed partying. And he'd even had a few relationships over the years. Though, in truth, those mainly involved him taking the woman out for drinks and a good time whenever he happened to be passing through town.

He'd never been worried like this. Never wanted so badly for a date to go well. Because the truth was, the outcome of a date had never really mattered too much before. Maybe, in the past, he'd had hopes that the night might go somewhere. But he'd never wanted to impress a woman and show her that he was worthy of her, even while knowing full well that he wasn't.

He had to try, though. Because Vivian mattered. She was special, the whole package—beauty, intellect, learning, strength, humor and that quiet way she made the people around her feel like everything was going to be okay.

And then there was that kiss. That one kiss that had burned its way inside him and become an ember that wouldn't die, that just kept glowing whenever he thought of her.

He wanted her in his life. But he had no idea if he could make her see that he was worth taking a chance on. He had no idea, really, what was in her heart.

All he could do was try to show her that he wasn't just passing through her life, like some cowboy out on the circuit. He'd thrown his rodeo heart into this ride, not just for a few seconds but for a lifetime, right here in Shelter Creek.

"WHAT A NICE PLACE." Vivian glanced around the bar of Black Oak Bistro, which had to be the fanciest restaurant in Shelter Creek. Jace had gone all out for their date, and maybe that was the problem. She wasn't prepared for this Jace. Wasn't prepared for the way he'd shown up on her doorstep in black jeans and a fancy Western shirt and a leather coat.

She'd instantly felt like an idiot. She'd spent her life around other scientists, had never been one for dresses, if she could help it. She'd prepared for their date by finding a clean black T-shirt and some jeans without holes or grass stains, and figured she'd been doing pretty good. Until Jace showed up at her door looking like a country-and-western star.

She'd mumbled something about being behind and left him in her tiny living room while she frantically raided her closet. To her relief she'd found a ruffled red sweater her mom had given her for Christmas last year and her one pair of black slacks. Finished with a pair of heeled boots that she'd bought on a whim after Colin had dumped her and her winter wool coat, she was somewhat presentable.

But now it wasn't just the clothing that felt too fancy, it was this entire date. Vivian picked up her water glass, then set it down again. The hostess had asked them if they'd like to start with a drink in the adjacent wine bar, and Vivian had instantly said yes. Sitting next to this fancy version of Jace at a bar had seemed a lot less intimidating than sitting across from him at one of those white-cloth-draped tables.

But she'd forgotten that she didn't drink wine anymore. It had been a little awkward, just ordering water at the wine bar. And she suspected Jace would have preferred a beer, though he gamely chose a glass of the local cabernet.

Her sweater was hot and itchy and the boots smashed her toes into a point. She wished she'd offered to plan their date. She would have chosen a hike or a trip to the beach, something where they could both be comfortable. She peered at Jace again. He was a former champion bull rider. Maybe he was used to fancy places like this.

Though maybe the problem wasn't this restaurant. It was her. She'd been with one man since college. She had no idea how to date. Her brain was frozen, like a computer processing too much data at once. She couldn't come up with one interesting thing to say. It had almost been easier to talk with Jace when he was glaring at her all the time. At least then she hadn't been expected to make small talk.

Jace swirled the cabernet in his glass. "I'm not a big fan of wine but it is kind of neat to drink something that was made right down the road. Though if Caleb was here, he'd launch into a lecture about how the wineries are replacing all the ranches, and this has always been a ranching community."

"And what do you think?"

He shrugged. "I guess I never held this town in my mind the same way he did. I never thought much about coming home and making some kind of life here. So when I got back and saw the town had changed, it didn't bother me as much." He took a sip of his wine and a satisfied look lit his face. "And some changes are good. Are you sure you don't want a taste?"

"Just one." Grateful that he hadn't asked why she'd refused her own drink, Vivian took the offered glass and sipped. The wine was rich and fruity and just a little sour. "I'm no judge of wine, but that's yummy." She handed the glass back.

"Yummy." He grinned. "That should surely be a category when people are judging it."

"I guess it's a little subjective, though."

He laughed outright. "That's the scientist in you. Sometimes subjective is just fine. If we worry too much about being objective, nothing fun would ever happen."

"What?" She opened her hands in mock outrage. "Science is fun."

"I guess I was talking about this. You and me. We don't make a lot of sense, objectively. I've got three kids to wrangle and a ranch that is only avoiding bankruptcy because the town stepped up to rescue me." Jace set his glass down and reached for her hands. "But I really want this thing between us, anyway."

It was hard to think with his hands around hers. His skin was rough from hard work, his hands strong and broad. And then there was the whole question of what she wanted versus what she *should* do.

What she should do is tell Jace she was sick. That she wasn't going to date anyone seriously. That she couldn't afford to get involved, to get stressed, to put her focus anywhere but on her own self-care.

What she should explain to him is that

when she'd stood at the door of that church and learned that Colin wasn't coming, it had broken something inside of her. Her ability to trust, or maybe the kind of faith that had made her believe in happily ever after.

But he was gazing at her with such purpose and emotion, and whatever self-discipline she had inside melted away under his intense scrutiny. How could she not want this? This tough cowboy whose heart was so big he'd sacrificed everything he had and all that he was for kids he barely knew? A man who could warm her with a look, a small joke, a simple dance lesson.

"This is the part where you say you want this thing between us, too," Jace reminded her softly. "Or you can tell me to get lost. And I will. I promise."

"I want it," she assured him, ignoring the alarms going off inside. He should know that she was ill. He should know what he was getting into. But this moment was so perfect, so romantic, and she wanted so much to just enjoy it.

His grin, all white teeth and that dimple that ran down his cheek and made her want to trace it with her finger, was the reassurance she needed. She could be with him, even if it was for just a little while. She could experience what it felt like to be wanted by this charismatic man, whose rodeo story and self-less choice made him larger than life. A quiet scientist like her might not hold his interest very long, anyway. So she'd just keep things casual and enjoy this time she had with him, while it was here. Maybe it would heal the parts of her that Colin had broken, and that was something good.

"Hey, do you like this restaurant?" He glanced around with subdued humor. "I mean, we can stay if you want, but it's kind of…"

"Stuffy?" she supplied.

"Yeah. Not really my style, and I kind of sense it's not yours, either." He flashed her a sheepish smile. "I guess I was trying to impress you."

"I'm already impressed," she blurted out. Oh, no. She might as well be one of his rodeo groupies.

He looked genuinely surprised. "What with? My impressive parenting skills? My ability to purchase property I can't actually use? Property that's so run-down it takes a full day of my neighbors' charity to get even the most basic repairs finished?"

"It's just you I'm impressed with. You're a good man."

He looked down, studying their linked hands. "Tell me about this tattoo on your wrist. *Courage to fly?*"

"I got it before I left the East Coast. It reminds me to be brave."

He traced it with his fingertip, sending shivers along her spine. "I like it."

He released her hand so he could get his wallet and leave some money on the bar. Then he stood and she followed him out of the restaurant, grateful to be out in the open air. Once outside he turned to her. "I feel like I have so little to offer you."

His confession was abrupt in its honesty. But she felt the same. "Maybe it's about offering connection. Someone to spend time with."

"Is that what you want?"

She should have tried harder with the small talk. Because all of this cutting to the chase stuff was kind of terrifying. She needed to find a way to keep things lighter. Because light and casual was all she could really give him. "I want to get to know you."

"I want to kiss you." He pulled her slowly toward him, put a gentle hand to her jaw and paused. "Does that count as getting to know each other?"

Her heart was hammering almost as hard as it had that day she'd had to run from the elk. Though tonight it was racing not from fear, but from the choice he offered. She should step back, make some kind of joke, but her feet wouldn't move and a "yes" rose on her breath before she could stop it.

He kissed her. A long, lush kiss that left her clinging tightly to his shoulders in case the ground moved beneath her feet. When he pulled away he seemed shaken, too. "Let's walk."

They started along Main Street and Vivian calmed her racing emotions by appreciating the clapboard storefronts that always made her feel like she'd stepped into a fairy-tale world. Most were old cottages that had been converted into shops, and the tiny front yards were filled with flowers. "This is such a sweet town."

"It's so different from when we were young," Jace told her. "It was run-down then. The feed shop was always busy, and the grocery, but most other places were pretty neglected. I can't believe I'm saying this, but I think getting discovered by the tourists may have saved this town."

"What were you like when you were young?"

She could see the tension that immediately formed in the crease of his mouth and the set of his jaw. "I was determined to get out of here. As fast as possible."

"Why?" She was prying now, but she wanted to know. Wanted to understand who he was underneath his handsome and confident veneer.

"My dad was a bully. I spent my childhood trying to avoid him or trying to protect my mom and my sister from his temper. We were lucky when he got a job driving trucks. It kept him away for long periods of time." He glanced at her, a flush along his cheekbones. "Those were the best stretches."

"I'm sorry, Jace."

"You never mentioned your dad."

"I didn't know him. He was just some guy my mom met once. She never told me much about him."

"And your mom?" He paused and turned toward her on the sidewalk. "It's so strange how I feel like I know you so well, but I've learned almost nothing about you."

"There's not much to learn. My life is pretty straightforward." Vivian winced at the lie but she wasn't going to bring up her illness. Not tonight when it would change the way he was staring at her—as if she was the best thing he'd seen in years. She reached for his hand and started walking again, so she wouldn't have to look at his eyes when she gave her lie of omission.

"I grew up in Brooklyn. I went to college at Cornell, got my master's in biology there, too. Then I went to work in New Hampshire with my boyfriend. Who later became my fiancé. And then we broke up."

He glanced over at her, dark brows raised. "Recently?"

It was almost physically hard to confess it, she'd avoided talking about it for so long. "Last spring. He ditched me at the altar."

Jace winced. "Ouch. That's bad. I'm sorry."

"Yeah, it was no fun." She hated that it might change how Jace saw her—as someone else's reject. But it was better than his seeing her as some kind of invalid, so she'd share this secret and keep the other. "But honestly, it's better than marrying someone who didn't really love me. I'm glad he figured it out, even if he didn't realize it until right before the wedding."

"Maybe it's selfish, but I'm glad he did, too. Is that why you came out here?"

"In part." There, that wasn't a total lie. "I realized that I'd always been with him. We worked together and he had a habit of taking the spotlight so I always seemed like his assistant. I wanted to strike out on my own, have my own work, my own projects, my own life. So I wasn't just running away when I came here. I really wanted something different."

"And you don't plan to go back?"

"No. I don't." Vivian thought of her mother with a brief flash of guilt. They'd talked on the phone a few days ago and Mom had sounded lonely and a little lost. Vivian wondered if maybe worrying about her illness had given Mom a sense of purpose that she didn't have anymore. Her mother never dated. She mainly worked on her real estate business, which had certainly paid off. She'd gone from a broke single mother raising her child in a beat-up Brooklyn apartment to one of the top real estate agents in Manhattan. But with work as her only focus, Mom hadn't made time for friends, for hobbies, for much of anything else. Maybe Vivian could gently suggest something when they talked on the phone next.

"And what did you study in New Hampshire?"

"Invasive beetles. They're a real threat to the native forests there."

Jace grinned. "Aha. So that's why you've spent so much time causing trouble on my ranch. Tule elk and salamanders must be a whole lot more exciting than beetles."

Vivian laughed. "They're certainly a lot cuter."

He nodded and pulled them into the Best Eats Delicatessen. "This is a far cry from my original plan, but do you want to take sandwiches down to the creek? I like being outside with you. And it's a nice night."

He was right about that. The fog was staying away and the warm afternoon had turned into a nice evening for early November. And a picnic was much more her style than white tablecloths and fine wine. "That sounds ideal."

She chose the vegetarian sandwich while he ordered the roast beef, and they added a couple of sparkling ciders and a bag of chips.

Shelter Creek meandered along just a block off Main Street, and Redwood Park was the perfect place to access it. They unloaded their feast at the foot of the old tree that gave the park its name. Some of the redwood's roots were exposed and crept along the bank to the water, giving them a natural bench to sit on.

They munched their sandwiches shoulder to shoulder. The day had faded and without the streetlights at the edge of the small park, they might not have been able to see the shallow creek at all. But Vivian could hear it, rippling over the stones on its way to the Pacific, and the solid strength of Jace's shoulder against hers made the moment even more perfect.

"I never thought I'd have a date like this." Jace crumpled up his sandwich wrapper and put it in the bag.

"What do you mean?"

"I haven't dated a lot, to be honest. I'd pull into a new town for a rodeo and meet a friend at a bar. And we'd drink, play pool, hang out."

"And by friend you mean a woman?" She sounded weak and jealous asking, but it wasn't really jealousy that made her pose the question. Okay, maybe a little. But mainly she wanted to know what she might be getting herself into. He was so experienced. She was so…not.

"Sometimes a woman, sure. Mostly a guy I'd worked with, either on the circuit or on a ranch during the off-season. There were fights, too. It's another thing that's not endearing me to the social worker. I have a record, Vivian. Drunk and disorderly. A few times."

"Why?" She honestly couldn't imagine him fighting. Since she'd known him she'd seen him upset, but it was mostly tamped down. Contained.

He shrugged. "I guess I spent a lot of time on the road still rebelling against all the stuff that happened to me when I was a kid. Still fighting against authority, or what I perceived to be authority, when really I was probably just fighting with the ghost of my dad. Becoming a parent has changed me. It's made me finally grow up and realize that all that stuff with my dad happened a long time ago. And I'd be dumb to let it keep driving me now."

Vivian tried to imagine it all. A life on the road, bars and fights, motels and trucks, rodeo arenas. Chasing a dream to ride a bull that was going to throw you off its back and maybe try to kill you in the process. "Tell me about being a bull rider. What was it like?"

So while she finished her sandwich, he regaled her with incredible stories about rodeos and travels and life on the road. He had so much energy when he spoke about it, and Vivian could feel how much he loved the rodeo and how hard it must have been to leave that life behind.

As they walked back to his truck Jace grew silent, and Vivian assumed he was missing what he'd had. "You can do a lot here, right? For the Shelter Creek rodeo?"

"I'm going to try to be involved. I'll coach the high school kids this spring. And I eventually want to raise bulls on my ranch. I figure if I can't ride them, I can raise them."

Vivian laced her fingers more tightly through his. "That's a good plan."

Jace slowed, stopped, pulled her in close. "But right now I have other plans." He bent to press his lips to hers, to melt her bones with the heat and the longing she felt there. "They involve you. And more nights like this one. What do you say? Are you up for another date with me? Being with you gives me a bigger rush than the rodeo. And it's a lot more fun, too."

"And a lot less dangerous." She raised herself up on tiptoe to kiss him one more time.

"Oh, I wouldn't say that," he murmured against her mouth. "Those bulls might throw me off, but you're holding my heart in your hands, Viv. That's pretty scary, too."

Those words. He had a way with them, straight from his heart to hers. They scrambled all the plans in her mind and broke all the rules she'd set. This was supposed to be just one date. Just one evening that she could cherish and add to her list of Independent Vivian's California adventures. She didn't have the time or energy for more than one date. She couldn't get involved and risk losing herself and her health.

But she forgot all that when Jace ran his fingers into her hair, when he brought his lips to hers and when he kissed her as if he'd never let her go…

CHAPTER SIXTEEN

"VIVIAN, WHY DO we have to go back to the house?" Alex pushed his small grubby hand into hers. "I like doing science with you."

"Because it's getting late," Vivian told him. "And your Uncle Jace will be home soon and he promised to bring pizza. We're all going to have dinner together."

"Pizza! Yum!" Amy said breathlessly. The steep trail out of Long Valley was wiping all of them out.

Poor Jace was going to need some comfort food. He'd driven all the way to the prison near Fresno where his sister was incarcerated. He had some papers for Brenda to sign, officially surrendering her parental rights. It was heartbreaking to think about a mother giving up her kids, but Brenda was adamant that she wanted Jace to have them. She'd realized just how much she had to learn about herself and her addictions. And she knew that even if she got out of prison early on good behavior, her kids would be grown up by then.

Just the thought brought tears to Vivian's eyes. These kids had become so precious to her, so important, she couldn't imagine being in Brenda's situation.

Jace was also going to scope out what the facility was like. Hopefully it wouldn't be too grim. If his sister agreed, he'd be able to bring the kids for a visit. It would be hard for all of them, but better for the children to have some kind of relationship with their mother than for her to just disappear from their lives forever.

Meanwhile, Vivian had agreed to look after Amy and Alex for the day. It wasn't the wisest choice, because despite her feelings for Jace, she was still trying to avoid getting too involved with his family. But it was hard to say no when Jace really needed her help. Carly had to spend the day finishing her project with Jasmine and Jessica, and Maya and Caleb both had meetings and couldn't watch the kids.

"We're studying crayfish in school," Alex said, his quiet voice still a surprise and a delight every time he decided to use it. "We're going to get one in our classroom."

"That's so exciting." Vivian wiped sticky sweat off of her forehead. She was in pretty good shape, but this hill seemed extra long and steep today. She'd felt sick earlier in the week, some kind of virus, and there was a dull ache behind her eyes that had come and gone for the past few days. But this afternoon the headache had settled in and decided to stay. And the fatigue was back, adding lead to her limbs.

"Yeah. The teacher said we can even do experiments with it. Nice experiments like finding out what it wants to eat the most."

"That's great, Alex."

She wished, suddenly, that she didn't care about his crayfish. Or about Amy's growing passion for horses or Carly's project. The more time she spent with Jace and the kids, the harder it was to stay uninvolved. And she needed that distance. The headache and fatigue dragging her down right now were proof that she had to keep her focus squarely on maintaining her health.

But still, it had been fun to have an entire afternoon out in Long Valley with Amy and Alex. Vivian had been almost sorry to see the sun dropping lower on the horizon as they hiked up the hill toward Jace's house.

Maya had asked Vivian to compare the vegetation maps in her report with the real landscape one more time before they turned it in to the town council. Alex and Amy had loved helping her with it today, but it was bittersweet. The report included her and Maya's recommendations. And they were recommending that Jace refrain from grazing cattle in Long Valley indefinitely.

Vivian still hadn't told Jace. Maybe she was weak, but she'd been enjoying their time together too much to poison it with conflict. But she couldn't put it off much longer. She'd tell him tonight, and if he was angry and blamed her, well, there wasn't much she could do. This was her job.

Maya had offered to break the news to Jace herself but, tempting as it was, Vivian wouldn't hide behind her boss. She was already a coward when it came to her health. She still hadn't said anything to Jace about her lupus. She should. She meant to. But whenever there was a moment to tell him, she felt like she was on the brink of losing this magical stolen time when he didn't see her as sick, when there was no pity or worry in his eyes. She wasn't ready for that to end.

She was in a mess. In the week since their first date, she and Jace had tried to be together as much as they could. From stolen kisses around the ranch to a couple more meals in town, they'd been finding precious moments to get to know each other. And now Vivian was sure of one thing. She was falling in love with him. Head over heels in love. And Jace seemed to feel the same way. His face lit up when he saw her, he was always looking for excuses to get her alone and he talked about them as if they'd be together forever.

Vivian knew she had to step back. She had to put some distance between them. She was in too deep, spending time with Jace when she should be resting and taking care of herself. Already it felt like she was falling into the same pattern she'd had with Colin, giving too much, trying to make her relationship perfect.

And then there was the guilt. If she pulled away to take better care of herself, would he think she'd been leading him on? Giving him false hopes for a future together?

For the millionth time, Vivian wished she weren't ill. Wished she were just a normal woman who could easily keep up with Jace and his kids. And wished she'd told him about her illness from the very beginning.

Maybe her recommendation for his valley was just the thing to force her to walk away. Because Jace wasn't going to be happy about it. He'd be angry, he'd push her away and maybe that would be for the best. Maybe it would help her remember all the reasons she'd planned to keep this simple and casual.

"Come on, Vivian!"

She looked up, surprised to see that Alex and Amy were way ahead of her on the hill. Usually she was the one pulling them along.

She'd better hurry, though. It was going to get dark soon. The days were getting shorter as November took them closer to winter. Maybe it was the shorter days that had her so tired lately. She'd been climbing into bed earlier, sleeping later in the morning, and it seemed like no amount of caffeine could ease her exhaustion during the day. She might have to skip the pizza and head home before dinner.

Sweat coated Vivian's back and chest now. She was overheating, despite the cool fog that had crept in from the coast. She tried to focus on the cool touch of the mist, but it seemed to do nothing to chill her heated skin.

Vivian forced her legs to keep moving up the hill. They weren't far from the top now, just a few more yards and then they'd be on flat pasture, about a five-minute walk from the house. What was wrong with her? She glanced down and the dusty path seemed to tilt one way, then the other, as if the earth was one of Jace's rodeo bulls, trying to throw her off. She staggered. Her vision blurred, the landscape spun and darkness flooded in.

JACE PARKED HIS truck in front of the house and tipped his head back against the seat. Visiting Brenda had been rough. She'd done some terrible things, but seeing his sister behind bars still hadn't been easy. The hopeless look in her eyes stayed with him. One more problem in life that he had no idea how to solve.

So he'd try to do right by her kids. He'd picked up Carly in town and he turned to her now. "Your mom says hello and sends her love. She's thinking a lot about the mistakes she made."

Carly had been silent the whole ride home from Jasmine's. He'd been waiting for her to ask about Brenda but she hadn't.

"I'm glad. I don't want to see her yet, though."

"I understand. We'll just play it by ear." He reached over and put his hand over hers. "On a happier note, now that we've fixed those stall doors in the barn we can bring Annie's horse over here. What do you think? Are you ready to be a horse owner?"

Her whole face seemed to glow. "Yes! I can't believe it! And Milo is such a good horse." They'd gone to visit the chestnut gelding a few times on Annie's ranch and Carly loved him already. "Thank you, Uncle Jace."

"Well, it's Annie we should thank. I'll be excited to have Milo here, too. Now, we'd better get inside before this pizza gets cold."

He scrubbed his palms across his face and shoved open the door of his truck. He was desperate for a shower. It had been a long day on the road and the prison smell lingered on his clothes.

He was twisting to grab the food when he

heard it. A faint shout. He turned and shaded his eyes, trying to see through the fog flowing across the pastures from the Pacific. "Vivian?" he called out.

Carly looked at him, eyes wide. "That's Amy." She started running toward the sound and Jace followed. They raced across the field at the side of the house, the shorn grass uneven beneath their feet.

"Amy?" Jace called. Man, this fog was thick. A marine layer, heavy with water, coating his skin in cool damp.

"Uncle Jace!" Amy's voice was faint, and there was a note of fear in it that had him speeding up, stumbling, passing Carly as he hit the narrow path that crossed the pasture and dipped to the valley. He vaulted the newly rebuilt gate and kept going.

"I'm coming! Alex! Amy! Where are you?" Blind panic turned to relief when he saw their two little figures, emerging from the mist. But something was wrong. They were out of breath and staggering.

"Uncle Jace," Amy gasped when they'd closed the space between them. She flung her arms around his leg. "Uncle Jace, it's Vivian. Something's wrong with her."

Alex was already starting back the way he'd come. "Hurry, Uncle Jace. She fell down. She's just lying there." His little voice was shrill with fear.

Calm. He had to stay calm. Jace stopped, took Amy by the shoulders and knelt so that he was at her eye level, just like he'd learned from Vivian.

"Amy, can you be a really big girl right now?"

She nodded, tears running in silent streams down her face.

"You have to try to stay really calm, okay? So we can help Vivian." Vivian who'd collapsed. Who needed him.

Carly came skidding up. "What happened?" Jace asked, trying to keep his voice steady.

"Vivian collapsed farther down the trail. She seems to be unconscious," Carly related.

"Can you run back to the house and dial 911? Stay on the line and talk to whoever answers. They'll ask you questions. The most important one is our address."

"North Sky Ranch. One thousand fifty three Coast Route Seven," Carly gasped, still trying to catch her breath.

"Okay. Take Amy, so she can help you explain what happened. Please hurry."

Carly took Amy's hand and the two ran off toward the house at a sprint.

"Come on, Uncle Jace!"

He took Alex's hand and they pelted down the trail until Alex stopped and pointed. There was Vivian, lying on her stomach, one arm outstretched, the other under her.

"Vivian!" The horror in his own voice reminded him that he had to stay calm for Alex. For her. He knelt beside Vivian, put a hand to her neck, another to her side. Thank God, she was breathing.

There was a cut on her forehead, a scrape on her nose. If she'd fainted she wouldn't have done a thing to break her fall. Could she have a head injury? A neck injury? Should he move her?

Her neck seemed fine, not twisted at a weird angle. In fact, she looked strangely peaceful, like she'd decided to flop down for a nap or something.

"Is she going to be okay?" Alex was beside him, a small hand on Jace's knee, like he needed the contact.

Jace gave the kid a hug. "We're going to do everything we can to help her. But you have to be really brave right now. Can you do that?"

Alex nodded and Jace wondered how many times life had already required this little boy to be brave beyond his years.

"Okay, I'm going to check her arms and legs, and then we're going to wait for an ambulance to come. Okay? I need you to stay with me and try not to worry." Jace pulled off his coat and laid it carefully over Vivian. And fought back tears when little Alex got up and pulled off his jacket and placed it on her, as well.

Please let her be okay. Jace repeated the silent prayer as he carefully felt her legs and arms. "I don't think she broke anything. Can you tell me how this happened?"

"We were walking home and I was telling her about the crayfish at school and how we were going to feed it stuff. And then she walked slower and was way behind us. I turned around and she was acting kind of like she was dizzy, and then she fell like this."

Maybe she'd had a seizure or something? Jace took her wrist and felt her pulse—faint but steady. He thought he heard a distant siren and strained to hear more. *Please let them get here quickly. Please let her be okay.*

"You and Amy did great, running to the house for help. I'm proud of you." The sirens were louder now, and Jace hoped he'd be able to take a real breath soon, but worry made it hard right now. Had he done everything he was supposed to do for her? Was he missing something, some sign of distress?

He checked her breathing again. She looked small, so frail. Her skin was so pale, but it was usually pale. Was it always *this* pale? Was she in shock?

The sirens stopped and through the fog he heard the metallic thud of doors opening and closing. "They'll be here to help her in just a moment," he told Alex.

The little boy wrapped his arms around Jace in a hug. It was so sweet and so unexpected, and it ripped something inside Jace into pieces. Vivian had become part of what they were, part of their family, and what the hell was he going to do if he lost her now?

He wrapped his arms carefully around Alex and kept his eyes on Vivian. He loved her quiet way of fixing things. The way a little ripple formed between her brows as she tried to solve a problem. The way she brought out the best in the kids and in him. He'd slowly come to rely on her, to count on her, to need her and…to love her.

And now he might lose her forever. *Please God, no.* He closed his eyes and made a silent promise to Vivian that when she came back to them he'd tell her exactly how he felt, all the words he'd been afraid to say because he didn't want to scare her or push her away. He loved her. He wanted to spend his whole life with her.

Maybe real love, the lasting kind, crept up on you. It started with interest, was fueled by trust, fired by need. He might not have recognized it, but he could see how he'd been living it, how he'd been loving her, for some time now.

"Uncle Jace, they're here!" Carly and Amy came flying over the crest of the hill, followed by two paramedics. Jace recognized Ryan Loring, who he'd gone to high school with.

"Jace, long time no see. This is Jodie." Ryan set a large black bag down next to Vivian.

The woman he'd called Jodie shoved her blond ponytail behind her and knelt to open the medical bag, pulling on gloves and handing a pair to Ryan.

Jodie checked Vivian's neck and then carefully put a neck brace on her.

"What are they doing?" Alex whimpered.

Jace moved the kids a few yards away. "They're protecting her neck before they do anything else. That way, in case she hurt it when she fell, they won't make it any worse when they move her."

"Can you tell us what happened?" Ryan knelt to take Vivian's pulse.

"I wasn't with them. The kids said she just staggered and collapsed. Like she'd gotten dizzy or something."

"Does she have a history of seizures? Or any other medical issue that you know of?"

Jace felt stupid telling Ryan he'd never asked about her medical history. Or shared his own.

Ryan and Jodie checked Vivian's limbs, then started setting up the stretcher they'd brought with them.

"Is there someone we can call who might know? Family?"

Jace racked his mind for what Vivian had said about her family. "Her mom lives in New

York. Maya Burton is her boss, she might have more information."

"We'll call her on the way to the hospital."

They carefully straightened Vivian's limbs. Ryan counted off and they lifted her gently onto the stretcher.

"Mama had to go on one of those once when we couldn't wake her up," Amy said.

Jace's stomach lurched. "I'm sorry that happened to your mom," he said quietly. "Sometimes people get sick and they have to go on a stretcher to the hospital for help."

"Mom wasn't sick, though," Amy said. "She drank too much drugs."

Jace pulled both kids in for a hug and included Carly with his gaze. "You guys have been through a lot. You are all very strong. This is different, though. Vivian must be sick with something. She doesn't drink or take drugs. We'll get her help and she'll be okay."

"I don't want her to go away," Alex said, his voice muffled as he pressed his face to Jace's shirt. "I don't want her to be sick."

Tears burned behind Jace's eyes and his voice came out rough. "I don't want that, either. I really don't."

"We're taking her to Santa Rosa Medical

Center," Ryan said. "Do you want to follow the ambulance?"

"I need to get the kids settled. Then I'll be there." Jace would call someone, Annie Brooks maybe, or Maya's grandmother, Lillian, to watch the kids at their house. He needed to be with Vivian.

"We'll have to carry the stretcher. The ground is too rough for wheels. Take my bag?"

Jace swung Ryan's medical bag onto his shoulder.

Ryan and Jodie lifted the stretcher with practiced efficiency and started up the trail ahead of them.

"Come on." Jace and the kids followed them up the path. At the ambulance, Ryan had Jace sign a form, then clapped him on the shoulder. "Good to see you after all these years, by the way. Though I wish it were under different circumstances."

"You'll take care of her, right?"

Jace hated the quaver in his voice. His weakness, when Ryan was so stoic and strong. Of course, Ryan was used to this kind of thing. And he didn't know Vivian.

"We've got her. She'll be fine. All her vitals were stable, and apart from a few cuts and bruises she doesn't seem to have any serious injury from the fall."

Maybe Ryan's words were just meant to soothe, but Jace clung to them like gospel.

"You're sure she isn't sick with something?" Ryan continued. "Has she mentioned feeling dizzy or having flu-like symptoms or shortness of breath?"

Jace glanced down at the kids but they were eerily stoic, standing quietly, probably trying to process this latest scary thing that life had thrown their way. He'd have to call their counselor at school and let her know what had happened.

"She's never mentioned a specific illness, but she took a day off earlier this week. Said she had a migraine or something and needed to rest."

"Could be flu," Ryan said, "though it's early in the season still." He glanced at the kids. "Did you get them their flu shots?"

"Not yet," Jace admitted.

"Get them tomorrow. And then every year. Right when school starts. I've seen too many complications, Jace." He reached into his shirt pocket and pulled out a card. "My number.

Call me if you have any questions when you get to the hospital."

Jodie was already in the back of the ambulance with Vivian. Ryan closed the doors, climbed into the cab and they were gone down the driveway.

"Is Vivian gonna be okay?"

Amy's small voice tore at Jace's heart. "She's going to get the best care."

"It's going to be okay, Amy," Carly said. "The doctors will fix whatever is wrong." She looked over Amy's head at Jace, old enough to realize that wasn't always true.

"Carly's right. She'll get any help she needs." Now that the initial crisis had passed, the aftermath of the adrenaline left his body shaky. He couldn't imagine how the poor kids were feeling. "Look, I'm going to drop you guys and your pizza off somewhere warm and cozy. Maybe at Maya and Caleb's? Or at Vivian's grandmother Lillian's house? And then I'm going to go to the hospital and check on Vivian. You three have a job to do. You need to eat pizza and try to relax. You saved Vivian today. But even superheroes like you have to rest."

Alex glanced up at him with a tentative smile. "We're heroes?"

Jace crouched down and gave his nephew a big hug. "Yeah, buddy. You sure are. Many times over, but especially tonight."

CHAPTER SEVENTEEN

THE BEEPING WENT on and on. Vivian reached out, groping for her alarm clock. What time was it? Had she overslept for work?

"Shh…" A cool hand took hers. "Vivian. It's Trisha. Can you hear me?"

What was Trisha doing in her bedroom? Vivian cracked open an eyelid that felt strangely dry and heavy. A beige railing lined her bed, and beyond it was a box-like machine with… She tried to sit up. "Where am I?"

Trisha leaned over her, holding her shoulders gently so she wouldn't get up. "The hospital. You fainted out on Jace's ranch. Lie down. Please."

Vivian lay back, taking in the ceiling tiles, the smell of plastic and disinfectant, the IV in her arm, the beeping—faster now because her heart was pounding. "I fainted? Why?"

Trisha reached for the call button near the bed. "They don't know yet. They're waiting for some test results. I'm just going to tell the nurse that you're awake. Okay?"

"But why…how did I get here?" It was so hard to think straight. It was as if the fog that had covered the hills earlier today had seeped into her brain, stopping thoughts in their tracks or sending them wandering off aimlessly into the mist.

The fog…it had been so foggy as they walked up the hill from Long Valley. Alex and Amy… "Oh, no…" Vivian glanced up at Trisha, fear souring her stomach and rising in her throat. "The kids. I was with the kids."

"They're okay," Trisha assured her. "They're fine. They ran to the house just as Jace and Carly arrived. Jace explained it all to me on the phone. He's just getting the kids settled with Maya's grandmother and then he and Maya are coming here to see you." She smiled slightly. "He was pretty distraught. I think that man is sweet on you."

Jace. Maybe he had been sweet on her, but he wouldn't be now. She must have terrified those poor kids. He'd trusted her with them and she'd let them down in the worst possible way. She should never have agreed to watch them in the first place. She knew she wasn't able to take on that kind of responsibility. Still swallowing panic, Vivian glanced at the small window. It was dark outside.

Trisha must have noticed the direction of her gaze. "You've only been here about an hour. All of your vital signs were stable. You just seemed like you were having a nice long sleep."

"That's crazy. How could I faint? People don't just faint."

"You were sick earlier this week, remember? Right now they think you might have the flu. It can do all kinds of strange things."

Vivian nodded, and forced herself to speak, to change everything with three words. "I have lupus."

"You do?" Trisha stared in obvious shock. "Why didn't you tell us?" She pushed the call button again. "Where is the nurse? They need to know about this."

Vivian fought back the tears. She wouldn't cry. It was pathetic enough to be lying here in a hospital bed.

"I wish I'd known." Trisha put a soft hand over hers. "I would have kept a closer eye on you."

Trisha was being kind. That was her nature. But now that she knew, it felt like some kind of ending. The end of Vivian's anonymity when it came to her health. The end of just being Vivian instead of Vivian-who-has-lupus.

She'd wanted so badly to be free of this disease, as if by moving across the country she could somehow leave it behind. But of course that wasn't possible, and here it was, tainting everything again—how people saw her, her ability to work, and now those poor kids.

Jace would never trust her now. And how could she trust herself? She couldn't be alone with the kids if she was going to pass out like this. It was proof that she should not have let herself get so involved with Jace. Vivian put her hands up to cover her face as best as she could with an IV in her arm. "Ugh. Trisha, I've been pushing myself too hard."

"You're going to be okay," Trisha assured her. "You just need rest."

A nurse came through the door, tall and athletic under her pale blue scrubs. "Hey, Vivian, I'm Diana. Great to see you awake. And looking way better." She smiled. "You even have some color in your cheeks."

"Thanks for your help, Diana," Vivian said.

"Of course." Diana smiled at Trisha. "I have to ask you to scoot back while I check Vivian over. The doctor will be in shortly."

"I'm just going to step outside and make a few calls, Vivian." Trisha pulled her chair away from the bed to make room for the nurse. "I'm sure everyone will be really relieved that you're awake." She gave Vivian a little wave and stepped outside into the hallway.

Everyone. Vivian closed her eyes to stop the tears that rose again. It was silly. Everyone she knew in Shelter Creek was so kind. But now they'd all be on eggshells around her, wondering if she was okay. Wondering if she'd get sick again. Vivian had loved these past weeks when she'd been seen as strong and capable.

And Jace. Would he be angry at her for not telling him about her illness? Especially now that she'd scared his kids? While Diana slipped the blood pressure cuff on, Vivian closed her eyes and pictured his beautiful face, a little battered, a little creased, but with those blue eyes full of humor and humility and love. She remembered how he looked when he was angry or when he was protecting the kids. She couldn't bear to see that look on his face again.

When she opened her eyes, another woman was there, a black-haired woman in a white coat who was studying Vivian's chart while Diana tidied up the counter.

"Hi," Vivian said.

"I thought maybe you'd dozed off." The woman stepped forward and her smile reached all the way to her dark eyes. "I'm Doctor Irma Martinez. You've had quite an evening."

Vivian tried to give the expected smile in response but her mouth felt stiff. "I need to tell you, I have lupus."

The doctor was so professional, her surprise barely showed on her face. "That's good to know. And it explains a lot. We ran some tests and you have the flu. I expect that the lupus made it more difficult for your body to fight it off." She wagged a finger gently at Vivian. "Going hiking probably wasn't the best decision."

"I'm a biologist. That's my job."

"Well, you should probably take a week or so off from that job. I'd like to keep you in the hospital for the next day or two, just to make sure that all is well."

Vivian struggled to sit up. "No, I can't miss work. There's a lot going on there right now."

"Try to stay calm." Doctor Martinez placed a gentle hand on Vivian's arm. "Your employer will understand that you have to take time off. You need to heal from the virus and get your strength up again."

Vivian leaned into the pillows and drew a few shaky breaths. She'd never told Maya about her condition. She'd so wanted to avoid that and keep her health issues private.

"Are you a field biologist?" At Vivian's nod, the doctor frowned. "You do know that too much sunlight can be injurious to someone in your condition?"

"I wear sunscreen and a hat. And sun-protective clothing," Vivian explained.

"Vivian, you should consider working in a lab or in an office. Being out in the field so much could be detrimental to your health."

"I don't want to talk about this right now," Vivian said, closing her eyes. "I'm sorry. Truly, but I can't." The stale hospital air was pressing in, and the choices and decisions she'd been avoiding ever since her diagnosis were pressing in, too.

"I realize this is a lot to take in. But if you don't want to talk about it with me, how about with your regular doctor? Do you have a primary care physician who has been helping you manage your disease?"

Heat flared on Vivian's cheeks because of course she should have found one the moment she arrived in Shelter Creek. But it had felt so good to have some time without medical appointments. To have a few weeks off from her diagnosis. Though that vacation was over now. She shook her head.

Dr. Martinez pressed her lips together as if holding back a reprimand. "Well, we need to find you one as soon as possible. I'll have my assistant see if she can find a good doctor in or near Shelter Creek." She paused. "It's important, you know, to keep on top of your condition."

"Yes, I realize that. Thank you."

"It's going to be okay. You'll learn to manage this disease. But do be extra careful when you get colds or the flu."

Vivian nodded again and the doctor and nurse walked out together. Trisha came in as they left, with Maya following.

"I heard there was some excitement out at Jace's ranch," Maya teased as she pulled a chair close to the bed. "And that it didn't involve endangered amphibians this time."

It was hard to smile when she could hear the brittle quality behind Maya's cheerful demeanor. Vivian took a deep breath, which was hard because her ribs hurt from the fall. "I'm sorry I didn't tell you when I was hired. I have lupus, and then I got the flu and the combination knocked me out. Literally."

Maya's cheer vanished. "Oh, gosh, Vivian, I'm so sorry."

She'd been expecting Maya to be upset. But her boss just sat down heavily and clasped her hands together. "I had no idea you were living with a chronic condition. We should have been managing your workload and your schedule, to make sure you stay healthy."

"You're not mad that I didn't say anything?" Vivian studied Maya's face for signs of anger. Or disappointment. But all she found was kindness.

Trisha approached and stood next to Maya. "It's okay, Vivian. How could we be upset with you for being ill? We just wish we'd known earlier."

"Trisha and I know what it's like to live with pain that others can't see." Maya glanced up at Trisha, who put a hand on her shoulder. "We were in a car accident when we were young. I was driving Trisha and Caleb's little sister, Julie. I lost control of the car and we crashed. Julie had removed her seat belt and she died. Trisha's leg was very badly injured."

Vivian gazed from Maya to Trisha and back again. "I'm so sorry. That's awful."

Trisha gave a reassuring smile. "It turns out, Maya and I both blamed ourselves and never talked about it. We were both pretty unhappy for many years. And my leg still gives me trouble. I'm sure you've noticed that my walk is uneven. So we definitely understand what it's like to suffer in silence."

Maya reached for Vivian's hand and gave it a reassuring squeeze. "Have you been feeling sick this whole time you've been working for the wildlife center?"

Vivian shook her head. "I mostly get tired easily. And I've been getting headaches. The doctor just reminded me that sunlight isn't great for lupus. She told me that field biology is the wrong choice, that I should get an office job." She pressed her hands to her eyes in a futile attempt to stop the tears that rose hot behind them. "I don't want an office job."

"We can make it work," Maya said. "We'll get some interns for the field work. You can supervise."

"Maybe you can work outside on all the foggy days," Trisha offered. Then she paused. "Though I guess you still get a lot of the sun's rays through the fog, right?"

They were too kind. So good. How incredible that Vivian had ended up here, with these two amazing women and The Book Biddies and Jace and the kids. But what Maya was offering was basically charity. Vivian had taken the job knowing it would involve a lot of fieldwork. Maybe it had been part of her denial process with lupus, refusing to believe that she'd have to curtail her time out of doors.

Maybe she'd just been too hopeful. Or too busy running from Colin and a life that had become so stifling and sad.

Her head ached, low and dull, and the fatigue she'd been keeping at bay was creeping back in. She couldn't think about this now, couldn't make a decision about work or anything. Not when her eyelids had gained a few pounds and were closing of their own accord. "Thank you," she told Maya. "You are so kind."

And then she slept.

THE WAITING ROOM floor was fifty-three tiles wide. Jace knew because he'd counted those tiles a few times now while he waited for Vivian to wake up. He also knew that it took him forty-seven steps to walk from the elevator to the waiting room wall, because he'd spent a good part of the last two hours pacing.

Maybe he should leave and come back in the morning. It had been a hell of a day, as the ache in his shoulders and the sharp pain in the hip he'd messed up years ago when a bull ran him into a fence reminded him.

But Vivian was in there alone and the kids were tucked up with Lillian, watching a Disney movie and eating popcorn. He'd talked with them on the phone, and while they were worried about Vivian, they all seemed happy to have time with Lillian and excited about the comforts of her cozy home.

"Mr. Hendricks?" A tall nurse in blue scrubs walked toward him. "I'm Diana. I've been Vivian's nurse since she was brought in. She's awake now. Would you like to see her?"

"Yes." It came out louder than it should have. "Is she okay?"

"She's fine. Just tired. The doctor wants her to stay in the hospital for a few days, for observation. We'll be moving her over to the main building soon."

"Okay, well…" Suddenly nervous, Jace glanced around. "Should I wash my hands or something?"

"Handwashing is always good. There's a restroom next to the elevator. Vivian is in room 3B, just down this corridor here." She pointed to a beige hallway lined with gurneys and equipment, where another nurse was pushing an elderly gentleman in a wheelchair.

"Thanks."

"Of course." Diana paused, then added, "She's still pretty wiped out. Just be really calm, okay? She's been through a lot."

Cripes, did he look like some big scary guy? Glancing down, Jace realized he'd thrown on black jeans and a leather jacket this morning, somehow assuming he had to appear tough if he was going to visit a prison. And he probably looked pretty exhausted, too. "I'll be calm."

In the bathroom, he splashed cold water on his face and examined himself in the mirror for a long moment. He looked old. There were new lines between his eyes. Worry lines that hadn't been there before. That's what parenting did to you. That's what loving someone and finding her collapsed on a hillside did to you. When you loved, you risked your heart every day.

Some would say he'd been brave every time he got up on the back of a bull. But now he understood that real bravery was trying to stay calm when the woman you loved was a rag doll in your arms. Bravery was comforting kids and making sure they were okay when every cell in your body was desperate to be by her side. Bravery was what he'd need to walk into that hospital room and be reassuring and strong, when all he really wanted to do was go down on his knees and beg her not to faint or get sick or hurt, or whatever was going on, ever again.

Jace walked to Vivian's room and paused at the door. She was so tiny in that bed. She was never big, but she'd seemed strong and solid and now she was a scrap somewhere under the thin hospital blankets. She was gazing away from him, toward the dark window, probably looking for stars or bats or some other wonder of nature that he'd never thought to pay attention to until he met her.

He'd spent his adult life on the road in search of excitement and escape. She'd shown him the wonder of the world right where he was.

"Hey," he said, but the word caught in his throat.

Still, she turned her head at the sound. "Hey," she answered. "You came."

He covered the distance between them in a heartbeat. Leaned over and kissed her forehead, closing his eyes for a moment to absorb her reassuring warmth and her sweet vanilla scent. "You're okay," he whispered as he sank into the chair by the bed. "I'm so glad."

Her brown eyes were almost black in the dim light. "Me, too. I'm so sorry I scared you. And the kids." She closed her eyes, her thick eyelashes wet with tears. "I really messed up, Jace. I was supposed to take care of them for you. To keep them safe…"

"You did." He leaned close, wrapped her hand in his own, smoothed her hair back from her forehead. "They're fine. They're at

Lillian's house having a movie night and a sleepover. Last I heard they were eating popcorn and singing along with *Moana*. They're happy."

She opened her eyes to look at him in hopeful, watery relief. "Really?"

"Yes. They're tough kids."

"But I must have scared them horribly. And I just keep thinking, what if we'd been farther away? What if they'd had to hike the entire way home alone? It was the end of the day, there are mountain lions out there. And coyotes. They could have been killed. I could have killed them."

"Viv, please don't make yourself crazy with the what-ifs. You were pretty close to the house when it happened. The kids ran home and got me and Carly. It worked out okay."

She brought her hands up to her face, covering all that fragile beauty. When she pulled her hands away, her jaw was set in a resolute line. "Don't you see? Amy and Alex shouldn't have to do that, ever. They're tiny kids and they already had to witness so much they shouldn't have, with their mom. They are supposed to be safe from that stuff in Shelter Creek."

"Honey, you fainted. You've been sick. The doctors said you had the flu. It could happen to any of us."

"The flu?" She bit her lip. Tears were seeping out from under her lashes again and they were killing him because he didn't want to see her sad or down. He wanted her smile and her gentle teasing and her quiet competence back. But right now she just looked... broken.

"That's what's going on, right?" Oh, no, this couldn't be one of those horrible stories where someone went to the doctor for a cold and came out with a cancer diagnosis. His stomach soured and he gripped her hand tighter. Swallowed down the fear. He'd promised himself he'd be brave. But no. Not Vivian.

"I have lupus, Jace." Four quiet words, spoken with gravity.

All he could hear was *not cancer* and the relief almost made him giddy. "Okay. That's an autoimmune disease, right?" He knew it was serious, but it wasn't cancer or something that would take her away from him. "The doctors will help you," he assured her.

"You'll rest and we'll do whatever they tell us to do to get you back on track."

She pulled her hand away to push herself up in the bed so she was sitting a little straighter. Her cheeks were flushed even though the rest of her was so very pale and he wondered if she had a fever. He repressed the urge to put a hand to her forehead—she'd probably push it away. He recognized the stubborn look in her eyes. But he made note of where the call button was in case she really was getting worse.

"You don't understand. There is no 'back on track' with lupus. It's endless. It's fatigue and random pain and weird rashes. It can even make your hair fall out."

"So we'll get you some cute wigs." He knew the moment he said it that he'd shoved his foot in his mouth. But when he found her on the trail, he'd feared he might lose her forever. A few bald patches seemed pretty minor in comparison.

"My kidneys can fail. I may even need an organ transplant at some point." She was ticking things off on her fingers now, following some list she'd been keeping inside. "I'm not supposed to be out in the sunlight and I'm a field biologist. I get headaches, and my joints might freeze up if I stay in one position too long." She closed her list-making hand into a fist. "Don't you get it? I've been lying to you, to myself, to everyone, these past few weeks. I'm not who I seem. I'm not a healthy person."

"I've seen you down in Long Valley, crawling on the ground looking for those darn salamanders and spending hours watching those pesky elk. And now I know you were doing all that while you weren't feeling so hot. That makes you the strongest person I've ever met, Vivian."

There were tears running down her cheeks and she shook her head. "We can't do this."

Something inside him curled up. Just curled up and slunk off to a corner to collapse. "We have to do this. We love each other."

"You love someone who isn't real. You don't really know me. The real me is tired and has to sleep a lot and is always wondering if my health is going to fall apart. I should never have gotten involved with you. Not without you understanding what you were getting into."

"Well, of course I wish you'd told me earlier on. But I get it. I do. It's hard to bring up health stuff. I just don't understand what, exactly, you're so worried about. Are you talking about your hair? Or that maybe, someday, you might have a messed-up kidney? Because that's okay. If you need help, I'll take care of you."

It was crazy how silent tears could say so much. They ran thick and heavy down her cheeks and he knew he'd somehow said the wrong thing.

"That's exactly it, Jace. You'd have to take care of me. You already lost your career, your dream, everything you'd spent years working for, so you could take care of Carly, Alex and Amy. Now you're going to add me to your list of responsibilities, too?"

"It's not like that. Bull riding *was* my dream, and it was hard to let it go. But you showed me how to walk this new path with the kids. And I want us to walk it together. That's my dream now, and it means a hell of a lot more than rodeo ever did. Those were eight-second rides. This is the long haul."

Vivian shook her head, the tears making her eyes red, her lids puffy, but she was still so beautiful to him. So beautiful and so precious. He tried to take her hand, but she pulled away. She'd gone somewhere inside, so deep and so miserable that he couldn't find her.

"Raising those kids is a long haul. And I

won't be one more burden on your back. I can't be. I moved out to California to create a life where I could be independent. Where I could focus on my health, on managing my condition, and stand on my own two feet. And then I got involved with you and I lost track of all that. And look what happened. I got the flu, pushed myself too hard for work and ended up scaring your poor kids. Jace, I need to simplify my life again. I don't have room in it for anyone else."

"But we have room in our lives for you, Vivian. I love you. You know that, right?" He was starting to sound desperate but he didn't care. She was closing the door on everything he'd envisioned for them. "I love you. And the kids do, too. You're a part of our family and we can help make life better for you."

She shook her head. "That's not your job, to make my life better. It's definitely not the kids' job. Jace, you're becoming a great parent, and those kids are so lucky and they love you so much. You're building a family with them, and you're filling their lives with all this good stuff they've never had before. If we stay together, I'll just detract from that. I'll be the sick person who's too tired for the pillow fights or movie nights. They don't need me, Jace. They need *you*."

"Viv, I know you're upset. But can we talk this out with your doctor?" He wanted her to stop, just stop talking, because with each word she was pulling apart the dreams he'd built.

She reached over and pressed the call button for the nurse. "I'm really tired, Jace. I want to rest now."

Diana appeared at the door. "Is everything okay?"

"Jace was just leaving," Vivian said, a grim determination Jace had never seen before making her face into a stranger's. "And my head hurts a lot. Could I get some more medicine?"

Diana looked from one of them to the other, as if she could feel the despair polluting the room. "I'll get the doctor. Jace, why don't you let our patient get some rest."

"Goodbye." Vivian's voice was oddly stilted. Eerily polite. "Thank you for everything."

Thank you? That was *it*? Vivian loved him. He was sure she did. He'd seen it, warming her face and lighting her eyes when she looked at him. He'd felt it in her kisses, and in her touch. But this wasn't the time to remind her. She was exhausted and she'd made it clear that she needed him to leave. So he nodded once and left the room, stumbling in a daze toward the elevator.

He'd spent his whole life in pursuit of goals, of winning rides and buckles and trophies and glory. But he hadn't known how to live until Vivian taught him how. How to stop and see and appreciate the world around him. How to be alive in the moments he was given, not just the seconds he was in the arena. She was his light, his guide, and he could be that for her, too, if she let him.

Or was she right? Would her illness affect the kids? Of course it would. But wouldn't her love affect them, too? It had already helped to heal them all, to bring them out of their past and into their new lives.

Jace summoned the elevator and stepped inside, welcoming that silent, timeless space between floors. He stared hard at the double doors and forced his breath to calm. Because when those doors opened, it would just be him, stepping out into a life without Vivian. He wasn't sure how to live that way anymore. But he would, if that's what it took to make her better.

CHAPTER EIGHTEEN

"VIVIAN?"

The voice lured her out of sleep, out of peaceful oblivion. Vivian opened her eyes, took in her hospital room and shut them again quickly. She wanted that mindless place, to rest, to avoid reality. To avoid what was waiting for her. A life without Jace.

But who was calling her? That voice was so familiar. The gardenia smell, too. Vivian sat up in bed so abruptly she jerked her IV. "Ow. Mom?"

Tori Reed reached for Vivian's hand, the one not tethered to the IV. "Oh, honey, I came as soon as I heard." Her mom's thick, bleached hair was tousled. There were shadows under her eyes and worry in her gaze.

"You didn't have to come." Vivian looked around the hospital room, evaluating the bright light that flooded in from the window. "Is it morning?"

"Yes. You were brought to the hospital yesterday evening."

"You flew all night? How did you even know I was here?"

"Your boss called me. I'm your emergency contact, remember? Maya is very sweet. She helped me get a ticket, find a hotel, everything."

Oh, Maya. So well-meaning. But she'd gotten it so wrong. Though how could she know when Vivian had never mentioned anything to her about being sick or about her mom's fears and doomsday predictions?

"You didn't need to come, Mom. I'm fine."

Her mom's eyes filled with tears. "You're not fine. You're in the hospital. You collapsed out in the middle of nowhere. You're so lucky, honey, that those children had the presence of mind to rescue you. What if you'd been alone?"

Yikes. How much had Maya told her? Vivian tried to lighten the mood. "If I'd been alone, I'd have woken up when the first vulture tried to take a bite."

"What? Vivian Reed, how can you even joke about that? It isn't funny!"

"Sorry, Mom. Just a little biology humor."

"Well I don't find it amusing. I don't find it funny that my only daughter is ill and won't do the things she needs to do to stay healthy."

"I *am* healthy. I eat well. I rest. I wear my sun-protective clothing…" She left off the word *sometimes*. She had to do better about that. "I had the flu and it was affecting me more than I realized. Now the doctors are just being extra careful because of the lupus."

"You should come home with me. You need someone to watch over you. Why don't you look for a new job somewhere in New York? Then I'll be able to look after you and still keep my clients in the city. I certainly can't move my business out here. Santa Rosa? How can they call this a city? And that little town you're living in? I looked it up on the internet when you first moved there. It's no more than a speck on the map between here and the Pacific Ocean!"

"Which is one reason I like it, Mom."

"But who will take care of you there?"

Jace. His name came unbidden and entirely misplaced. He was gone from her life precisely because she didn't want him to feel like he had to take care of her.

Still, the memory of him holding her hand,

smoothing back her hair… No. Her brain was going off on impossible tangents. Places she couldn't go because no one needed a partner who couldn't even get an average, everyday virus without passing out and landing in the hospital. Colin had certainly made it clear that he saw her as a burden. What if Jace ended up seeing her that way, too?

Maybe her mom was right. Maybe she should go home. As much as she hated Mom's hovering, she was family. She was obligated to hover. If Vivian had a real health crisis, which was a definite possibility, she'd be grateful for her mom's care.

"I don't want to get another job," she blurted out as if she and her mom had been having the conversation she'd just conducted in her own head. "I love working here."

"I'm sure it's very pretty, and California weather is nice, of course. But I can't fly out here every time you have a problem."

"I never asked you to fly out here, Mom."

"You need help, Vivian. I've read the articles. Lupus can be progressive. Many things can go wrong. What if you faint again and no one finds you? And don't go mentioning vultures again, please."

Mom kept talking, exploring all the possible ways, no matter how rare, that lupus might take Vivian down. Might make her an invalid. Maybe even kill her. Vivian closed her eyes and the words mushed together into a thick blanket, smothering her and her hopes for independence, for meaningful work, for health.

She'd moved to Shelter Creek to handle her condition on her own, in her own way. But look where that had gotten her. She'd scared the kids she loved. She'd hurt Jace. She'd worried Maya and Trisha.

It wasn't fair to stay. Maya, Eva and Trisha were motivated to make the wildlife center into something really special. They needed someone who could handle the level of fieldwork the job required. If Vivian stayed, they'd try to accommodate her disabilities, they'd have to, by law, but all she'd be doing would be getting in the way.

She opened her eyes. Mom had stopped talking. Maybe she thought that Vivian had fallen asleep.

It was hard to push the words out, they felt so heavy. "Okay, you're right. Coming out here was a bad idea. I'll come home. I'll find a new job in New York, just as soon as I can get out of this hospital."

Then she closed her eyes and tried to breathe, tried to accept what had to be done and tried to get used to the idea of a life without all of the people and the places she'd come to love in Shelter Creek.

IT WAS DAY THREE without Vivian. Jace glanced out the window to see if it was foggy. The atmosphere in the house was so gloomy, sometimes he wasn't sure if it was the weather or their hearts. The kids had been down, too, ever since Vivian got sick. They missed her. They'd wanted to visit her in the hospital, and Jace had to make all kinds of excuses about how she needed to rest, how she was busy getting help from doctors, when the truth was, she'd asked for space.

"Alex, finish your toast," he said, his parenting on autopilot for now.

"I don't like it. This bread has weird seeds in it."

If Vivian were here she wouldn't feel the same flash of annoyance that hit Jace. She'd just be excited that Alex was talking. She'd ask him why the seeds were weird and then engage him in some kind of activity where they pulled the seeds out, dissected them and discussed their nutritional value.

But Jace didn't have the heart to imitate Vivian today. "Try to be flexible," he told the little guy. "We're all pretty tired and cranky right now." Okay, so it wasn't one of Vivian's brilliant kid-whispering moments, but he'd acknowledged Alex's feelings and tried to appeal to his better side. And at least he hadn't just said "eat your darn toast," even though he kind of wanted to.

He got up and went to the kitchen to start the dishes, glancing back through the doorway into the dining room as he scraped the plates. Alex and Amy were chewing dutifully, all the joy wiped from their faces, and he doubted it was just about seedy toast.

Guilt turned in Jace's stomach. Mrs. Sherman had tried to warn him, but he'd been so swept up in his budding relationship with Vivian, so convinced she loved him back, that he hadn't been careful. He'd let the kids get attached. And now they felt abandoned.

Carly came in and rinsed her plate in the sink. "I miss her, Uncle Jace," she said quietly. "Why can't we go visit?"

With Carly, he could be more honest. "Vivian has a chronic illness that makes her weak," he told the teen. "It's not fatal or anything, it just wears her down. That's why the flu made her faint."

"So why can't we go see her? We could cheer her up."

Here was the hard part. Carly's innocence had been crushed at such a young age and now Jace felt he was taking a sledgehammer to the final shards. "She has to take a bit of a break to focus on her health. She doesn't think she has the energy or ability to be a part of our family."

"That's so lame." Carly's hands folded across her chest in teenage defiance. "She's already part of our family. And we don't care if she gets sick sometimes. What does she think will happen if one of us gets sick?"

"I tried to convince her," Jace said. "I told her we don't care that she has this illness. That we love her." He stopped, wishing the words back. He'd never admitted his feelings to the kids before.

"Are you, like, *in love* with her?"

Jace hedged. "Would it be weird if I was?"

"Well, it's always weird when old people

kiss and stuff. But we want you to be happy, Uncle Jace. And we love Vivian. She's awesome."

He couldn't help but smile at her description of him and Vivian as old. "I think she's awesome, too."

Carly put her hands to her hips in a gesture so full of adult disapproval that it was almost funny. "So that's it? You're just going to say 'oh well, too bad' and let her go? You just said you're in love with her."

"I am. But that doesn't mean I get what I want. I have to respect her wishes."

"But what if her wishes are wrong? I mean, for real, what is her plan? Just to sit at home for the rest of her life with no friends or family because she has a chronic illness? She isn't thinking straight. You have to go talk to her. You have to try again. Aren't grown-ups supposed to be all good at compromising? I mean, you're always telling us kids to do it."

Jace couldn't suppress a chuckle and it felt good to finally have something to smile at. "You're right. Adults *are* always telling kids to do stuff that we're really bad at."

"So, practice makes perfect. You should talk to her. Find out if she loves you, too. And if she does, then maybe she can have time for herself to make sure she's better, but also a little time with you and us, too."

"You make it sound pretty simple, Carly."

"Because it is." She gave him a triumphant smile and went into the dining room. "Come on, littles. Move it! We have to get to school."

Jace stood in the kitchen watching her round up her sister and brother and shoo them upstairs to get changed. It was a mixed-up world when the kids were more grown-up than the grown-ups. Carly was right. He should talk with Vivian. He had to try to show her that there was a compromise.

He understood very well how overwhelming he and the kids could seem. But he didn't need to lean on Vivian and her kid-whispering abilities as much as he had. He'd learned from the expert and he was doing all right. He wouldn't ask for more than she could give. Maybe there was a way to show her that…

CHAPTER NINETEEN

It was strange how little luggage she had.
Vivian had rented her cottage fully furnished,
and she'd mainly brought hiking gear with
her when she'd moved in. So here she was,
all her things packed into two suitcases, taking with her only what she'd brought. She had
no souvenirs from Shelter Creek.

She'd miss it. The dry, dusty, windy fall had
grown on her. She liked the cool mornings and
the hot afternoons. She'd been looking forward
to winter and the way the rain would turn the
brown hills green for just a few months out of
the year. She'd wanted to see the spring wildflowers. California's beauty was subtle for a
lot of the year, but according to Maya, nature
pulled out all the stops for springtime.

Maybe someday, if her health held up and
her heart healed, she'd come back and visit.
For now, she would stay at Mom's apartment
in Manhattan while she searched for a job.

She'd look for a research position, maybe. Something with flexible hours that would keep her safely indoors.

It didn't sound very fun. Not nearly as exciting as trying to manage elk or hunt for salamanders on Jace's ranch. Not as heartwarming as watching Alex and Amy carve pumpkins or climb on Jace like he was their own personal play structure. Not as joyful as watching Carly get to know her new horse, Milo. And never as perfect as sitting on the back steps with Jace at the end of the day, watching the sunset spread spectacular color across the sky. But her life would be more predictable and her health more manageable. Mom was right. Moving back east was the responsible thing to do.

She took one last look around the tidy little cottage and bit her lip to stop the tears that stung her eyes. Going forward without Jace and the kids was like moving on without her heart.

Pushing through the door onto her front porch, she stopped in shock. There were Book Biddies on her porch. Annie, Lillian, Maya, Trisha, Kathy, Eva, Monique, Priscilla, they were all perched on the railings and stairs, sitting on the porch floor and on the porch swing. And at the bottom of the steps were Jace and the kids.

Vivian's heart rose in her throat because she'd missed them all so much. The little kids were watching her wide-eyed, and Carly gave her a small wave. Jace was smiling at her with eyes made even more blue by the denim of his shirt. He wore his straw cowboy hat and he tipped it in a greeting that melted some of the resolve she'd relied on since getting out of the hospital yesterday.

"What is going on?" Vivian pulled the front door shut behind her and leaned against it.

Maya stood up from the swing. "We're here to see you off. Unless we can talk you into staying."

Amy let go of Jace and came pounding up the stairs to wrap her arms around Vivian's waist. "We don't want you to go."

The tears Vivian had been holding back threatened to spill over. She knelt down and gave Amy a big hug to distract herself. A terrible idea because, hugging the girl tight, it occurred to Vivian that she'd never do this again. She'd never hold this little person in her arms, never get to see her grow up, never have to answer any of her millions of questions ever again. Vivian's tears spilled over. She needed some space or she'd just lose it. "Amy, thank you for the cuddle. Can you please go stand with Uncle Jace for now?"

Amy looked at Vivian solemnly and used her fingers to try to wipe the tears trailing down Vivian's cheeks. Then she ran back to Jace, pressing her face into her uncle's faded denim thigh.

Vivian swiped her sleeve across her eyes. Kathy reached into her purse and pulled out a packet of tissues. Each one had little frogs printed on it.

"Thanks." Vivian accepted a tissue and looked at the circle of people around her. "You all have been wonderful. I can't thank you enough for making me feel so welcome in Shelter Creek."

"You're *still* welcome." Lillian was sitting cross-legged on the porch, her back supported by the railing. "You're a part of our community. If you're leaving because you miss the East Coast and you really want to live there, we understand. But if you're leaving because you think you're alone here, or you're worried about not having family, please stay. Because everyone here feels like you are family."

"I felt it that first night when I met you in the town hall," Annie said from her perch on the railing. "I could see how much you wanted to do a good job, get to know the community and make a difference. I'm here for you, Vivian. I never had kids of my own. I'll give you a hand anytime you need it. It would be an honor."

"Annie, I can't ask you to do that," Vivian protested.

"Why not? Who says family has to be related by blood?" Annie gestured to Priscilla and Eva and Lillian and all the other Book Biddies seated around the porch. "These ladies are my family. And like it or not, we adopted you a while ago."

They were going to melt her into a giant puddle of tears right here on her porch.

Maya crossed the few feet between them and put her arm around Vivian's shoulders. "Eva's such an amazing fundraiser that I've got a new position open. I need someone to do public outreach at the center, keep us all organized and do some work in the schools, as well. Which means I need someone who is really, really good with kids." She put a finger to her cheek as if she were thinking hard. "Hmm… I wonder if I know anyone who qualifies?"

Everyone started laughing and Vivian looked down the steps at Alex, Amy and Carly. "I guess I like kids okay," she teased. And then her eyes went to Jace. He was watching her carefully from under the brim of his hat, his gaze full of hope and trepidation and warmth.

"Hey," he said quietly, and the entire group went silent. "I've missed you. A lot."

Vivian nodded, not trusting herself to answer. Because if she did, her answer might be to fly down the porch steps and throw herself into his arms, and that wouldn't be fair. Not when she'd told him they were over. So she responded to Maya instead.

"Maya, the job sounds great. But what if I get sick? What if I let you down?"

"How is that letting anyone down?" Trisha gave her still-flat belly an absentminded pat. "I'll need time off when I have my baby. And I'm sure this little one will have all those childhood colds and flus and I'll have to miss work. It's part of life. We'll help each other and cover for each other and make it all happen."

"I can help with the educational programs," Priscilla said. "I don't want to go back to a full-time job, but I can always substitute if you're not feeling well."

"See?" Trisha threw an arm around Priscilla and kissed the older woman's cheek. "There are all kinds of solutions, if we look for them."

"Just think about it, please?" Maya asked.

"We'd really love to have you stay on at the wildlife center," Eva added. "Your work so far has exceeded my expectations."

"Oh, wow. I don't know what to say." Vivian glanced at her watch. She'd have to leave now if she was going to make her flight. But she didn't want to go. She'd never wanted to go. She'd just gotten sucked into her mother's depressing predictions and worst-case scenarios.

"What do you want?" Lillian asked softly. "In your heart?"

"My heart hasn't always been the best judge of what's right for me," Vivian confessed, thinking of Colin. "But of course it wants to stay here, in Shelter Creek, with all of you."

"Then let's find a way to make that work." Jace came slowly up the steps, the kids with him. "We love you, Vivian. We want you in our lives, in whatever way works for you."

Vivian glanced at Maya. "Did you tell him about my report? About my recommendations for Long Valley?"

Maya nodded. "I did."

"It wasn't a big surprise," Jace added. "You'd basically been saying all along that I shouldn't graze my cattle there. I just didn't want to hear it. But I'm the one who made the bad real estate investment. I bought myself some elk and salamander habitat by accident. Not an auspicious start to my ranching career, but I'll live and learn."

Vivian stared at him in wonder and sheer relief. "You are very different from the Jace I first met."

He grinned. "Well, it's been an eventful couple of months. I guess I've changed. You might have had a thing or two to do with that. But it's also me, Vivian. I've grown into this role of mine. I feel pretty comfortable with my choices. And I like being a parent to these three hooligans."

"Hey!" Carly elbowed him in the arm.

Jace glanced down to smile at his niece. "What I'm trying to say is that we're doing all right. So if you want space to rest and get better, we can give you that. We'll be okay. But when you're feeling up to it, we'd love to spend some time with you."

Vivian's eyes prickled with tears. He was so understanding, giving her the room she'd asked for. "And you don't hate me, for what I said in the hospital?"

Jace closed the space between them and reached for her hand. "I could never hate you. I'm way too in love with you for that."

His words chased the last of her fear away. She didn't need to live some sterile, safe life in Manhattan. Not when there was so much for her here in Shelter Creek. She stepped close, went on tiptoe and kissed Jace on the cheek. "I love you, too," she murmured.

"Oh, this is getting very romantic," Trisha exclaimed, and all The Biddies burst out laughing.

Vivian held out her arms to Alex and Amy. They rushed in for a delicious hug. Vivian gave herself a moment to relish the joy of holding them again. Then she pulled away so she could look into their eyes, Alex's gray and magnified behind his cute red glasses, Amy's green and arresting. "What about you two? How are you feeling about all of this?"

"We want to do stuff with you again," Amy said. "Right, Alex?"

"We love you, Vivian." Alex's cheeks were pink, his gaze shy but determined.

There was no way to stop the tears from coursing down Vivian's cheeks. "I love you guys back," she sniffed. And then hugged them again.

"Hey, what about me?" Carly scooped Amy up in her arms and gave her a loud kiss on the cheek. "I want some love, too, you little squirts."

Alex pulled away from Vivian and wrapped his arms around his big sister's legs and held tight.

"Carly?" Vivian needed to know that the teen was on board.

A suspicious glint brightened Carly's eyes. "You'll come for Thanksgiving next week, right? It won't be fun without you."

"I'd love to come for Thanksgiving." Vivian glanced around the group on the porch. "I definitely have a lot to be thankful for."

Jace offered Vivian his hand. Just the sensation of his rough palm against hers felt like home. How had she thought she could leave?

"Viv, whatever life brings, I want to live it with you by my side and in my arms and on our ranch and with these cool kids. But I get that you're worried. That you need to make sure you're taking care of yourself and your health. I promise we'll give you the time and space you need to do that. You don't have to hang out with us *every* day. But we want to be here for you, through it all."

Jace opened his arms and she stepped in, leaning against his chest, feeling his heartbeat so solid and steady beneath her ear. She clung to him, almost swamped with relief. She'd thought she'd never be in his arms again.

He brushed his mouth against her ear, making her shiver. "What do you say?" he murmured. "Will you stick around?"

She'd run from Colin. Run from her diagnosis. And then, when things got hard here in Shelter Creek, she'd almost run back to New York. She wasn't going to run away anymore. "Yeah, I think I will."

"Oh, good." His broad smile carved dimples into his cheeks and she reached up and traced one with her fingertip.

It was hard to believe that this was really happening. Just a few minutes ago she was forcing herself to say goodbye to Shelter Creek forever. Now Jace and The Biddies were offering everything she needed, and all that she wanted. An easier, more flexible job. Friendship, family and people to lean on. And Jace's love. These kids. This life.

Vivian met Jace's gaze and for a heartbeat it didn't seem possible. That life could give so much that was hard and so much that was wonderful, all in the same few months. But now it was here, her future with Jace and the kids, if she was just brave enough to reach for it.

"I'm so glad you love me."

"I plan to love you forever." His blue gaze locked on hers, his heart laid bare for her to see. He loved her. He wanted her so much that he hadn't let her push him away.

She held him close with one arm and opened the other to the kids. They rushed in, Alex and Amy hugging her waist, Carly cuddled under Vivian's arm. And all the scattered pieces of Vivian's heart clicked into place. Somehow, they were going to be together. A family. Forever. No matter what.

EPILOGUE

MRS. SHERMAN STOOD on Jace's rebuilt front porch and admired the blue and white trim that he and the kids had painted last week. "It looks good, Jace. Very nice." She'd toured the house and walked around the barn, as well. She'd seen his cattle grazing in his pastures. She'd even checked out the chicken coop he'd built. Carly was planning on selling eggs at the farmers market for some spending money.

"So what do you think?" Jace asked. He'd waited for this day a long time. And made sure Mrs. Sherman visited while the kids were at school, so they could have this important conversation.

"Well, the house is in much better shape and you've got yourself a working ranch. I'm also glad you've diversified your income by leasing that land by the road. And I'm impressed to hear you'll be coaching the high school rodeo team."

Jace let out the breath he'd been holding. "I'm glad you feel that way."

"And the kids' teachers all say they're doing much better in school. And you're still seeing that nice scientist, Vivian?"

"I am." It had been a few months since Vivian had become so ill and almost left Shelter Creek. But things had been easier since then. Her health had improved. She still lived in her cottage in town, but they spent a few evenings a week together and usually a day on the weekends. She took the time she needed to rest and look after herself. They were in love, and they were in balance.

"And are you two getting serious?"

Jace had a ring picked out and wanted so badly to ask Vivian to marry him. But he was taking it slow. Vivian had a lot on her plate and he didn't want to pressure her. "We're taking our time. But things are moving along." He grinned at Mrs. Sherman. "If I can get up the nerve to ask her to marry me, she just might say yes."

She smiled. "I hope she does. I know I had my reservations, at first, but I could tell, the day we carved pumpkins, that she was good for you. And for the kids. She seems to truly care for them."

High praise, coming from Mrs. Sherman.

He figured now was as good a time as any to ask the question that mattered the most. "So, do you think I can make this all legal? Can I adopt the kids?"

"It's a long process, Jace. But yes, we'll start the paperwork."

He was grinning like he'd just won the lottery, and maybe he had. "Thank you, Mrs. Sherman. For everything. You've pushed me to become a better parent. And a better man."

She winked. *Winked!* "I knew you had it in you, Jace. You just needed a shove in the right direction. Now, I'd better get back to the office. I'll be in touch about the next steps."

Jace walked her to her car and waved as she drove off. But right where the driveway turned the corner, she stopped and backed up. Weird. Was it tule elk? They hadn't been around as much lately. It was early spring, and with more water sources available from the winter runoff, they'd spread out in small bands all around Shelter Creek.

And then he heard it. The sound of footsteps. Many footsteps. Mrs. Sherman got out

of her car and leaned on the door. Jace jogged
down the driveway to see what was going on.
And there, marching up his driveway, were
Bunny Chadwick and the Habitat Heroes.

A surreal sense of déjà vu permeated Jace's
senses as he walked down to meet them. But
it wasn't just the Habitat Heroes. There were
Maya's grandmother and all of her friends
wearing their Cougars for Cougars shirts.
There were Maya and Caleb and Trisha, who
was looking very pregnant now, and Vivian,
too.

"What's going on?" He glanced nervously
back at Mrs. Sherman, his heart sinking as
she made her way down the driveway toward
the crowd.

"Jace Hendricks," Bunny called from a few
yards away. "We have a proposition for you."

Jace looked at Vivian in confusion, and she
jogged up the drive to stand beside him, slip-
ping her small, soft hand in his.

"Don't worry," she murmured. "It's a good
thing."

"Explain to me," he murmured back, "how
Bunny being in my driveway can be good."

"Shush," she giggled. "Just listen."

Bunny and the crowd were closer now.

"Jace, all of these people you see here have been fundraising for a while now. We've been working with a local nonprofit group that buys land and sets it aside for open space. And between all of us, and this nonprofit, we have enough money to buy Long Valley from you at fair market value. We'd like to preserve it as habitat forever."

Jace stared at the crowd, stunned and speechless.

"The wildlife center will manage it," Maya said. "We'll build a boardwalk, so people can walk in without damaging the ponds. We'll make it a nature trail, so they can learn about the tule elk and the salamanders. If you'll sell it to us, that is."

Had he heard her correctly? It was hard to believe. Jace glanced at Vivian.

"You'll get your money back," she said. "You can use it to buy grazing land somewhere else around here. You can expand your ranch."

Their generosity was beyond anything Jace had ever imagined. Emotions filled his chest, too many of them to put into words. So he turned to humor, instead. "How will I know that whatever land I buy isn't home to some endangered animal? I don't exactly have a great record when it comes to real estate deals."

"Don't worry." Vivian kissed him softly on the cheek. "You've got me now. I'll check the land over for you. *Before* you buy."

Jace wrapped his arms around Vivian and looked out at the crowd. "Okay," he told them. "You've got yourself a deal. And thank you. Thank you so much."

Jace held Vivian tight and watched as the Habitat Heroes high fived and the Cougars for Cougars gave each other hugs. The last time Mrs. Sherman had been stuck in his driveway, he'd been a different man. Worried, lost, mourning the end of his winning streak and unable to imagine his life after the rodeo. He'd had no idea that his winning streak was just beginning. And that the prize was all this love and family and friendship and a life so much richer than what he'd had before. He'd been down on his luck back then, but now he knew for sure that he, Jace Hendricks, was a very lucky man.

* * * * *

Get 4 FREE REWARDS!

We'll send you 2 FREE Books plus 2 FREE Mystery Gifts.

His Wyoming Baby Blessing
Jill Kemerer

Her Twins' Cowboy Dad
Patricia Johns

Love Inspired® books feature contemporary inspirational romances with Christian characters facing the challenges of life and love.

FREE
Value Over
$20

Get 4 FREE REWARDS!

We'll send you 2 FREE Books plus 2 FREE Mystery Gifts.

RUNNING TARGET

ELIZABETH GODDARD

LONE STAR STANDOFF

MARGARET DALE

Love Inspired® Suspense books feature Christian characters facing challenges to their faith... and lives.

YES! Please send me 2 FREE Love Inspired® Suspense novels and my 2 FREE mystery gifts (gifts are worth about $10 retail). After receiving them, if I don't wish to receive any more books, I can return the shipping statement marked "cancel." If I don't cancel, I will receive 6 brand-new novels every month and be billed just $5.24 each for the regular-print edition or $5.99 each for the larger-print edition in the U.S., or $5.74 each for the regular-print edition or $6.24 each for the larger-print edition in Canada. That's a savings of at least 13% off the cover price. It's quite a bargain! Shipping and handling is just 50¢ per book in the U.S. and $1.25 per book in Canada.* I understand that accepting the 2 free books and gifts places me under no obligation to buy anything. I can always return a shipment and cancel at any time. The free books and gifts are mine to keep no matter what I decide.

Choose one: ☐ **Love Inspired® Suspense**
Regular-Print
(153/353 IDN GNWN)

☐ **Love Inspired® Suspense**
Larger-Print
(107/307 IDN GNWN)

Name (please print)

Address   Apt. #

City   State/Province   Zip/Postal Code

Mail to the **Reader Service:**
IN U.S.A.: P.O. Box 1341, Buffalo, NY 14240-8531
IN CANADA: P.O. Box 603, Fort Erie, Ontario L2A 5X3

Want to try 2 free books from another series? Call 1-800-873-8635 or visit www.ReaderService.com.

THE FORTUNES OF TEXAS COLLECTION!

18 FREE BOOKS in all!

Treat yourself to the rich legacy of the Fortune and Mendoza clans in this remarkable 50-book collection. This collection is packed with cowboys, tycoons and Texas-sized romances!

YES! Please send me **The Fortunes of Texas Collection** in Larger Print. This collection begins with 3 FREE books and 2 FREE gifts in the first shipment. Along with my 3 free books, I'll also get the next 4 books from The Fortunes of Texas Collection, in LARGER PRINT, which I may either return and owe nothing, or keep for the low price of $5.24 U.S./$5.89 CDN each plus $2.99 for shipping and handling per shipment*. If I decide to continue, about once a month for 8 months I will get 6 or 7 more books but will only need to pay for 4. That means 2 or 3 books in every shipment will be FREE! If I decide to keep the entire collection, I'll have paid for only 32 books because 18 books are FREE! I understand that accepting the 3 free books and gifts places me under no obligation to buy anything. I can always return a shipment and cancel at any time. My free books and gifts are mine to keep no matter what I decide.

☐ 269 HCN 4622   ☐ 469 HCN 4622

Name (please print)

Address   Apt. #

City   State/Province   Zip/Postal Code

Mail to the **Reader Service:**
IN U.S.A.: P.O Box 1341, Buffalo, N.Y. 14240-8531
IN CANADA: P.O. Box 603, Fort Erie, Ontario L2A 5X3

*Terms and prices subject to change without notice. Prices do not include sales taxes, which will be charged (if applicable) based on your state or country of residence. Canadian residents will be charged applicable taxes. Offer not valid in Quebec. All orders subject to approval. Credit or debit balances in a customer's account(s) may be offset by any other outstanding balance owed by or to the customer. Please allow three to four weeks for delivery. Offer available while quantities last. © 2018 Harlequin Enterprises Limited. ® and ™ are trademarks owned and used by the trademark owner and/or its licensee.

Your Privacy—The Reader Service is committed to protecting your privacy. Our Privacy Policy is available online at www.ReaderService.com or upon request from the Reader Service. We make a portion of our mailing list available to reputable third parties that offer products we believe may interest you. If you prefer that we not exchange your name with third parties, or if you wish to clarify or modify your communication preferences, please visit us at www.ReaderService.com/consumerschoice or write to us at Reader Service Preference Service, P.O. Box 9049, Buffalo, NY 14269-9049. Include your name and address.

50BFT19R

Get 4 FREE REWARDS!

We'll send you 2 FREE Books plus 2 FREE Mystery Gifts.

FREE
Value Over
$20

Both the **Romance** and **Suspense** collections feature compelling novels
written by many of today's best-selling authors.

YES! Please send me 2 FREE novels from the Essential Romance or
Essential Suspense Collection and my 2 FREE gifts (gifts are worth about
$10 retail). After receiving them, if I don't wish to receive any more books,
I can return the shipping statement marked "cancel." If I don't cancel, I will
receive 4 brand-new novels every month and be billed just $6.99 each in the
U.S. or $7.24 each in Canada. That's a savings of at least 13% off the cover
price. It's quite a bargain! Shipping and handling is just 50¢ per book in the
U.S. and $1.25 per book in Canada.* I understand that accepting the 2 free
books and gifts places me under no obligation to buy anything. I can always
return a shipment and cancel at any time. The free books and gifts are mine
to keep no matter what I decide.

Choose one: ☐ **Essential Romance**   ☐ **Essential Suspense**
(194/394 MDN GNNP)   (191/391 MDN GNNP)

Name (please print)

Address   Apt. #

City   State/Province   Zip/Postal Code

Mail to the **Reader Service:**
IN U.S.A.: P.O. Box 1341, Buffalo, NY 14240-8531
IN CANADA: P.O. Box 603, Fort Erie, Ontario L2A 5X3

Want to try 2 free books from another series? Call 1-800-873-8635 or visit www.ReaderService.com.

COMING NEXT MONTH FROM

HARLEQUIN®

HEARTWARMING™

Available October 8, 2019

#299 RESCUED BY THE PERFECT COWBOY
The Mountain Monroes • by Melinda Curtis
Hiring down-to-earth Zeke Roosevelt as nanny for her twin boys seems a no-brainer to Sophie Monroe. Zeke figures the "easy" job will tide him over until he realizes he can't keep his eyes off Sophie!

#300 A RANCH BETWEEN THEM
Sweet Home, Montana • by Jeannie Watt
When Brady O'Neil accepts a job caretaking a ranch, he never dreams he'd have to share the place with his best friend's sister, Katie Callahan! Or that he'd have to guard his heart all over again...

#301 KEEPING HER CLOSE
A Pacific Cove Romance • by Carol Ross
Harper Jansen likes her quiet life and doesn't appreciate former navy SEAL Kyle Frasier turning up on her doorstep insisting he's been hired to protect her. She tries to avoid him, but has to admit maybe she doesn't really want to...

#302 AFTER THE RODEO
Heroes of Shelter Creek
by Claire McEwen
Former bull rider Jace Hendricks needs biologist Vivian Reed off his ranch, fast— or he risks losing custody of his nieces and nephew. So why is Vivian's optimism winning over the kids...and Jace?

YOU CAN FIND MORE INFORMATION ON UPCOMING
HARLEQUIN® TITLES, FREE EXCERPTS AND MORE AT
WWW.HARLEQUIN.COM.

HWCNM0919